Other w

Poppy Darke

Poppy Darke and the

BlindFire

NearDeath

Doofus

Lonelytree publishing
27 Derry Grove
Thurnscoe
Rotherham
South Yorkshire
S63 0TT
colinwraight@hotmail.co.uk

First published in Great Britain
In 2023 by Lonelytree Publishing
ISBN: 9798857244425

The DeadBeats

Rock and Roll was never this deadly

Colin Wraight

Chapter 1

Flickering across the darkness of the stormy New York night, the faulty red neon sign cast its intermittent glow onto a shimmering, and wet side-walk. Somewhere high above the towering skyline, fierce sheet lightening fleetingly recorded its passing in puddles and streams of water, as it raced into the drains.

Along the sidewalk and in the street, Yellow cab drivers vied in a deadly competition, a maddening vortex of vehicles and drenched club-goers danced to a cacophony of horns, distant shouts, and excited chatter.

Colonel Harker waited for his men to move into position. Ignoring the crackle of the radio he patiently watched the red-tinged rainwater as it raced a frenetic path down the Humvee windscreen.

A sudden distant beat of drums and bursts of guitar signalled that it was time to move. "Ok, Sergeant are your men in position?"

The DeadBeats

"Yes Sir!"

"You know the drill; nobody moves until I say so!" Pulling up the collar on his rain mac Colonel Harker opened the door and stepped out of the vehicle. Raising his eyes skyward he savoured the refreshing droplets of near-freezing rainwater as they splashed onto his cheeks before trickling down his face and dripping from his chiselled jaw. "Goddam New York!" He growled. Suddenly feeling overly conspicuous in his uniform, he quickly removed his peaked cap before entering the club. Two plain-clothed naval police officers, somehow appearing almost alien in their neat suits and rigid and erect demeanour; awaited his approach before one of them spoke.

"We've got this place sewn up tight sir, there's no way out…"

"I seem to remember you said that last time," He shot the two men a derisory glance. "You two wait here, I'll go and speak to him," The Colonel said and smiled sardonically. "With any luck, he'll come quietly."

Slowly moving through the swirling crowd of dancers and drinkers, some doing both, he made his way to the bar and sat on the only vacant stool. Somewhere beyond the human melee, half-naked bodies and smoke the band was deep into the second chorus of Billy

Jean. "Whiskey… Make it straight!" He cried to the bartender and threw ten bucks onto the counter. "Keep the change… Hey, is Mitch in tonight? Mitch Calvert?"

The barman frowned, snatched up the ten bucks and nodded toward the stage. "Sure, the dude's on-stage man!"

Swivelling on his stool Harker turned to face the mostly obscured stage. Billy Jean had finished and now the first beats of Rio by Duran Duran exploded over the heads of the expectant dancers. Harker shot a questioning look at the barman who was now serving someone else.

"Eighties night… Every Wednesday!" He shouted over the din and sighed with the glumness of a millennial who had been made to endure many eighties nights.

"I guess you're not a fan," Harker grinned. "How long's the set?"

"Too long… Far too long, Mitch should be down after this song!" He replied and forced a fake smile. "Next up we got a transvestite Whitney Euston tribute act, complete with a Kevin Costner look-alike bodyguard… it's all good man! It's all real good!"

"Well, maybe I'll just give that one a miss."

The DeadBeats

As the song ended Harker began gently shouldering and side-stepping his way toward the stage. The dance floor had a stickiness to its surface and was packed with writhing and barely dressed young women and men whose idea of fashion seemed to rely heavily on cheap Hawaiian shirts and chino slacks. Just as Whitney began belting out that she wanted to dance with somebody Harker Spotted the stage door and barged his way forward slipping through into a thankfully quieter, cooler and darker corridor.

Drifting slowly through the void from a point beyond several stacked crates, a Technics keyboard and a set of drums the smell of cannabis reached his nose. Following the trail of pungent smoke to its source, Harker almost tripped over the drunken forms of a barely conscious roady and his half-naked and weed-smoking girlfriend.

Uncomfortable with public displays of debauchery the career military man replaced his peeked cap and gingerly stepped over them. Then he turned. "Err...! I'm looking for Mitch. I don't suppose either of you two know where I can find him?" Suddenly, as he looked at her face for the first time, he realized that she was far younger than he had anticipated and was closer to being a girl than a woman; and more than that she was completely stoned out of her face. "Err, well I guess you don't!" Fake Whitney had somehow morphed her voice into a Fake Madonna and now a painful rendition of 'like a virgin' began to reverberate through the walls, the irony of it was not lost on Harker.

As the corridor turned right through ninety degrees, he saw three doors, the first of which was slightly ajar and lit up from within. Removing his Sig from its holster he chambered a round and moved to a position beside the door.

He knocked twice and then grimaced as he thought better of it, but it was too late now. "Mitch Calvert, you in there?" Only silence met his question, stealing himself he steadied his breathing, pushed the door open and stepped inside.

Pleasantly surprised that his bottle of bud was still where he had left it Mitch snatched it up and downed the remaining liquid in one gulp. His thirst still unquenched he headed over to the bar. "Hey, Tony!" He cried. "Can I get a Bud over here?"

The DeadBeats

The bartender grinned, nodded and took a bottle from a glass-fronted refrigerator. "Hey, cool set Mitch!" He said as he handed over the bottle. "And that's on the house... Oh, I almost forgot there was some old stiff here asking after you about ten minutes ago!"

"Really? Where'd he go?"

Tony shrugged. "Dunno man, I didn't see, maybe he just shot through."

Taking his beer, Mitch retraced his steps, collected his guitar from the stage side and pushed through the various musicians and their equipment as he headed into the backstage area. After two high fives, a low five and one fist bump Mitch finally found himself alone.

Tired, hungry and very aware of his own body odour and damp, sweat-filled clothes he just wanted to take a shower, get changed and go and get paid so that he could blow New York and catch the red eye to California.

Stepping over the unconscious and weed-addled bodies of the drummer and lead singer from fake Transvision Vamp; Mitch rounded the corner, and with a beer in one hand and guitar in the other entered his makeshift changing room.

An explosion of electrifying pain suddenly shot through his body, paralysing every muscle, cramping every sinew and scrambling his brain. Falling stiffly to the floor his body continued to buzz with electricity as the Taser gun clicked in unison.

"You know, I was planning on just coming in here and talking to you man to man," Harker said and stepped out from behind the door. "But after what you did to those guys in Washington, I figured this might be safer... for me, that is!"

Kneeling beside the stricken man Harker handcuffed him and fitted ankle shackles. "Ok I'm going to tell you how this is going down- if you give me any trouble, and I MEAN any trouble I will press this fob in my pocket and those cuffs will deliver a shock similar to the one you just experienced, and believe me I know how much that hurt. You should thank me it was a choice between the Taser and my nine millimetre!"

"Screw you... Asshole!" Mitch spat through the pain and gritted teeth.

"I also extend the word 'trouble' to include insults and bad language!"

The DeadBeats

"Who are you? What do you want?"

"You can call me either Sir or Colonel Harker, I really don't mind either... and I came here for you!" He said softly and sat on the chair in front of the dressing table. "And you are Captain Mitchell Calvert, Navy Seal, commended for bravery; hell, you even got the congressional medal of honour. Three tours of Afghanistan and one in Iraq, you had a great career ahead of you, and you went and threw it all away beating your Commanding officer half to death for a god dammed rag head that would have killed you the first chance he got!" The Colonel paused as if trying to remember something important. "Oh, and I almost forgot... You're under arrest! You'll be returned to the brig where you will serve out the remainder of your sentence and they asked me to tell you they added a little extra for escaping, five years... bummer hey."

"He deserved everything he got!"

"Well maybe he did and maybe he didn't! But as things stand, you're going to serve your sentence at a maximum-security civilian prison, so there won't be any more escapes!" Taking a cell phone from his pocket he keyed in a number and put the phone to his ear. "I got him all hog-tied! You boys can come and get him now!" Returning the phone to his pocket he turned back to his captive. "They'll be here in a short while and your life for the foreseeable future is over! I'm going to make you a one-time offer either you go with them or, and this depends entirely on how you behave, you serve your sentence working for me!"

"Doing what?"

"Well, I'm what they refer to as a Colonel in the United States Navy and you son are still a serving Officer and a Navy SEAL! So, you can probably guess where I'm going with this!"

Mitch sighed heavily. "Looks like I don't have a choice!"

"Getting up the Colonel moved over to Mitch and knelt. "Son, I'm going to remove the chains on your legs, but the cuffs remain for now; if you try to escape or for that matter even fart in my direction so help me god, I will not hesitate to shoot you in the face!"

Pulling Mitch to his feet he handed him his guitar. "I got a feeling you're going need this?"

Mitch shook his head and frowned, "Why? Where are you taking me?"

"You're going home, son! You're going home!"

The DeadBeats

The sound of rushed footsteps suddenly echoed along the corridor and soon the two naval police officers stepped into the doorway.

"Everything is ok guys you can stand down, turns out I won't be needing your assistance after all; Captain Calvert here has decided to re-enlist…" Harker grinned with relief. "Let's get the hell out of this shit hole!"

And somewhere in the background, a fake Rossi from a fake Status quo belted out 'We're in the Army now'.

Mitch rested his head against the cool glass of the lead vehicle's passenger window and watched the civilian world slip away. As the motorcade of three Humvees and two black Sedans headed across Manhattan Bridge and on into Brooklyn, he wondered what hell he had let himself in for. "Where are we going?" He asked, in his mind a little voice was telling him that he hadn't

made any promises to anyone and escape was still possible.

"We got a chopper waiting at Floyd Bennet field airstrip and a thirty-minute flight to your new home."

"So, are we going to lose the cuffs or what?"

Harker grinned. "Hell no, because we both know you've already planned your escape, and then I'll have no choice but to shoot you, and besides there's something I want to show you first!"

For some reason, Mitch was surprised to find the chopper the Colonel mentioned was a Marine Corps Black hawk, and they were soon air-born, skimming New York's skyscrapers as they headed west.

Glancing at Mitch's guitar, the Colonel suddenly spoke. "You play any other instruments?"

"Keyboards, and I can just about get by on the drums!" Mitch said and sighed heavily, then turned his head to look out of the window, he wasn't about to make small talk with the guy who had just ruined his life.

"You ever been in a band- or do you just do the old solo thing?"

Mitch sighed once more, seems there was no avoiding conversation with this man. "Yeh, I was in a band, back in high school!"

"I heard you sing back there! You were good, really good!"

"Thanks!"

"So, do you only do the eighties stuff?"

"No, I sing anything that brings the bucks in… And that reminds me, I didn't get paid tonight!"

The Colonel grinned. "Oh, I don't think you're gonna need to worry about money where you're going!"

Eying the officer Mitch wondered just where that would be, but thought it smart to play along for now. "So, are you going to tell me any more about my mission?" He said and then added. "…Sir!"

"No, not yet!"

The rest of the flight passed in silence and at some point, Mitch must have fallen asleep, because now he suddenly found himself being rudely woken.

"Wake up soldier, your home!"

Stepping out of the helicopter onto a manicured lawn, Mitch found himself staring up at the house, more a small castle than a house. A huge stone-built structure with one large defensive tower and castellations stretching across to a smaller redoubt. Each window on the second and third floors was beset with balconies all of which were illuminated against the darkness by floodlights. The gardens manicured and perfect stretched off into the night, somehow both antiquated and modern in its beauty and setting.

"What the...?" He said. "Where the hell are we?"

The Colonel began walking to a broad set of steps which led up to a huge oak door, guarded by a pair of stone lions. "Welcome to what was once a Scottish castle, our forebears bought it, stripped it down brick by brick and shipped it over here where they rebuilt it exactly as it was!"

"Jeez...!" He cried as he spun around trying to take everything in. "The Marine Corps has certainly come on since I left."

"Something else isn't it!"

Suddenly the doors opened and out stepped the largest human being Mitch had ever seen. Obviously a marine but now dressed casually in jeans and a sweater, unshaven with several days' stubble and his hair was slightly longer than it should have been. "Sir!" He barked in a military manner befitting a Marine Corp gunnery sergeant. "Welcome back sir, our guest room is ready and the evening meal will be served in one hour!"

"This is Gunny Carter; he's in charge of your training. Thank you, Sergeant, carry on!"

13

The DeadBeats

The sergeant turned to Mitch. "Sir would you like me to take your guitar to your room."

Being called Sir jarred somewhat and overwhelmed by events he dumbly handed over his prize possession. "Thanks!" He added almost as an afterthought, and then he stopped in his tracks. "What the hell is going on here Sir?"

"You'll see... Once we're inside!"

Relenting, he slowly stepped through the threshold into the brightness of the interior and allowed his eyes to adjust and absorb what appeared before him. The walls were crammed with photographs and posters; drawn to their content he moved closer to get a better look.

"I... I don't understand!" He said looking at a portrait photograph of the Glen Miller band.

"They were the first, and since those early days there have been many, many good men take their place in these hallowed corridors." The Colonel removed his coat. "You see, many years ago someone, somewhere in the military had this fantastic idea- You take highly trained specialised men and women, you form them into a band, or a dance troop or..." He paused and looked up at the Elvis Poster. "God dam it a circus, and those people can travel the world, they perform concerts, sign autographs; they appear on TV and in films. But all the while they're taking care of Uncle Sam's business!"

"What are we talking about here? Reconnaissance, rescues and assassinations...?" Mitch followed the trail of posters, photographs and framed golden records. "Buddy Holly and the Crickets… I don't believe it!" he whispered incredulously. "The Beach Boys, oh my god tell me you didn't have the Rolling Stones here?"

"Well, they became more or a hindrance than a help..! But yeah, them and many more beside…"

Suddenly rushing up to the third step Mitch stopped in his tracks. "Elvis… You have got to be kidding me. My Pop loved Elvis he always said he would never forget where he was when he died!"

"Well, I got news for you kid, Elvis didn't die he just got old and out of shape so we retired him to Alaska!"

"No… No way...!"

"Sure, spends his days shooting and fishing!" Harker said. "Out of all of them, I thought he was the most obvious, he spent time in the military, and he loved guns, fast cars and Karate! My predecessor

Colonel Parker, you probably heard of him, well many consider them the best of the best!"

"But...! Elvis, really...?" Mitch suddenly spotted a face he recognised. "What about this guy over here? I know for a fact he and his band died in a plane crash!"

"No, he along with two of his band were killed on a mission to recover stolen plutonium, the plane crash was just a story we put out."

"Wait...! Just wait one goddam minute here! Did you bring me here for this? You want me to join your... I don't know. Whatever you call this shit!"

The Colonel smiled. "You already did! All we have to do now is find you a band! Don't worry kid this is going to be one hell of an adventure! Now let's see about getting those cuffs removed!"

Atop towering grey mountains, deep in the chaos of a maddening sky; tiny white flakes, born of freezing air and water popped into existence and began their downward spiral. Teased by the relentless pull of gravity, they flutter, plunge and swirl in a blizzard swept along by bluster and draught, the flakes swarm in a blinding cloud of freezing white noise.

Caught on a gust, a single snowflake breaks free of the crowd and tumbles headlong toward the grey stone of a castle rampart; only to be carried high at the last moment by a wayward up draught. Floating through a barred window the snowflake drifts across the dimly lit room, before finally settling gently on the pert nose of an unconscious woman and instantly melting.

Half-awake and feeling very groggy Brianne Moore- Masterson stared mindlessly at the back of her closed eyelids. As her senses began to stir from their enforced slumber, she became aware of her dry mouth and the bitterly cold draught on her cheeks and nose.

Groaning weakly, she opened her eyes and squinted, focusing on the grey stone ceiling, all the while desperately trying to remember where she was. Summoning all the strength she could muster she raised her head and looked around the room, a look of bemused puzzlement slowly spread across her face, this certainly wasn't the Paris Hilton or anywhere else she had ever stayed. "Hello...!" She cried weakly. "Is anyone here?"

Instinctively her hands patted the bed and then the pockets on her clothes looking for her cell phone. Horrified, she realised that not only was her phone missing but someone had stripped her and dressed her in a red canvas shirt and cargo pants. "What the...? Hey, what the hell is going on around here?"

Pushing herself up into the sitting position she turned her body and placed her feet on the stone floor. Surveying the Spartan room, her gaze drifted slowly up the stone walls and halted at the window. Tendrils of snow carried along on an icy tempest seemed to cut through what was little more than a hole in the wall, stretching and reaching out to her and stroking her face with the touch of deathly cold fingers.

A freezing shiver suddenly shot up her spine causing the hairs on the back of her neck to stand on end. Jumping up she folded her arms and stamped her feet trying in vain to generate some warmth.

"Hello," She cried through now chattering teeth. "Is there anyone here...? Anyone...? I'm cold; I'm very, very cold...!" Charging across the floor she flung herself at the door only to her horror, discover it was locked.

Suddenly a light above her head illuminated bathing the room in a red glow. "Good morning Brianne!" A voice erupted from a hidden speaker. "And welcome to the Fame Game, we are so excited that you have chosen to join us." Applause from an unseen audience cascaded around the room.

Subconsciously noting the heavy but somehow very familiar German voice she first frowned and then spoke. "I know you! Do I know you? Where… Where am I?"

"Brianne, You are the latest lucky contestant on the Fame Game and you are now streaming live to the world. Why don't you tell the audience how that makes you feel Brianne?"

Teeth still chattering she frowned. "I… I don't know, I want to go home, let me out of here; you can't keep me here!"

More deafening applause followed her words.

"Well guys and gals that was Brianne Moore-Masterson and we'll see more of her later; after the break two of the contestants will compete in a head-to-head to stay in the game; and the loser, well we all know what happens to the loser- and that's all coming live, streaming straight into your homes."

More applause.

"Let me out!" Brianne shrieked as she hammered on the wooden door. "LET ME OUT!! I'll have my lawyers on you! Do you know who I am?" She hammered, kicked, spat and shrieked until finally exhausted she sank to her knees. "I'm Brianne Moore Masterson… I'm famous!"

Chapter 2

After waking early and showering, Mitch dressed in the same grubby clothes which he had arrived in the night before. Checking his wristwatch, he realised that he'd only had two hours sleep, but he was hungry and desperately needed coffee. Opening the door to his room he half expected to see a guard posted in the corridor but there was no one there.

Wandering down the stairs he couldn't help but stop and look at some of the photographs he'd missed earlier, especially the MOBO award sitting proudly on a walnut stand.

Mitch shook his head in bewilderment and laughed. "Him...! No way...!"

"He was the last!"

The DeadBeats

The voice spun him around and he came face to face with the huge man he'd been introduced to when he had arrived. "Good morning, Gunny."

"Ah, I see you're looking at the MOBO sir! I liked him, he was a great singer and rapper, but more than that he was a great operator."

"What happened? Why'd he leave? He ain't dead, is he?"

"No Sir, last mission he met a young lady, they fell in love and he suddenly began valuing his own life a little more than was healthy considering his profession! He decided to go live happily ever after!" Then he remembered himself and braced up. "Sir...!"

"Do me a favour, cut out that 'sir' crap, my name is Mitch!"

"Sir... I mean Mitch!"

"That's better!"

"The Colonel tells me you're a flight risk!"

"Does he indeed?"

"This building and the people that have walked these halls have a rich history of service to their country. Those that have made the ultimate sacrifice did so knowing that the world would never know of their heroism. There are men and women in these photographs who the world thinks died of a drug overdose, or they hung themselves or they were in some crazy plane crash! But we know the truth and we honour their memory by maintaining the standards with which they lived their lives!"

"I don't think anyone would ever believe the truth!"

"Sir… I mean Mitch, come with me, and let me show you something." Walking down the stairs Sergeant Carter led Mitch through the back of the building, past the kitchen and outside onto the veranda. "Not far now, it's just down here!" Continuing on he headed toward the boathouse beside a small lake. "This is our unofficial memorial to those we have lost." He said as he entered the old wooden building.

Mitch's mind was still on toast and coffee until he stepped inside. "Wow...!" He said softly. "So many...!" Stepping closer he ran his fingers over the many crudely carved names, some of which he recognised. "There's real history here isn't there?"

"Some of these people are virtually unknown and unremembered except by their loved ones and us, they were riggers, roadies, dancers or backing singers; After they died, they were sent home to their respective families with bogus stories of how they lost their lives, there was no honour and no respect. They are buried in cemeteries the length and breadth of this country and no one but us know they died in the service of their country! The only honour and respect are contained in these carved names."

"I'm quite speechless right now!"

"Mitch, we've been looking for a new team for a long time now, the truth is if we don't come up with something soon, they're going to shut us down. Men with your skills and talent do not come along every day, we need you… The Colonel needs you!"

"You know something...? I need a coffee!"

Sergeant Carter stood to attention. "Breakfast will be served in the dining room!"

"Can you please cut that military shit out?"

The Sergeant took a menacing step toward Mitch. "If you choose to stay, I will be in charge of your training!" He growled. "I'm the one who has been given the job of turning you and the rest of your goddam deadbeat team into a well-oiled military force- and it's going to hurt! It's going to hurt more than anything you've ever experienced in your life." The Sergeant turned to leave. "Sir, I come from an old military family and I am a proud Marine to my core; I find your relaxed and decidedly un-military bearing most annoying, oh and one last thing Sir, I won't be cutting out any of the military shit!" Then after glaring at Mitch for longer than Mitch felt comfortable the Sergeant left the boathouse.

"Ok, I'm in!" Mitch said as he framed the dining room doorway. "You can send me on all the dangerous operations you like, and you can try and get me killed as often as you want but the music is mine! That's the deal you can take it or leave it!"

Colonel Harker carefully cut the rind from his bacon before discarding it beside the last remnants of his scrambled egg, which for some reason he had chosen not to eat, and then he placed the remainder in his mouth. Without acknowledging Mitch's presence, he slowly and deliberately chewed, savouring the smoky flavour he swallowed and then placed his knife and fork back onto the plate.

"Breakfast...!" He suddenly said as he dabbed his lips with a napkin. "It's the most important meal of the day." Then he took a large sip of fresh orange juice. "Captain Calvert you were always in! You were never out! But seeing as we know nothing about music, I'll agree to your terms… Join us, please take a seat, you must be starving!"

Mitch sat on the opposite side of the table. "So, Colonel tell me, how is all this going to work?"

"OK congratulations Mitch, so you're now the lead singer in a rock band. As you travel the world performing concerts and the such-like, Uncle Sam will occasionally call on you to carry out what are as of this moment unspecified missions. The rest of your band will consist of a strike force and your Roadies with be weapon and tech support- I will personally play the role of your manager and the Gunny here is in charge of training, security and discipline… Any questions…?"

"Where's the rest of my band?"

"Now that's a very good question! The tech and support guys we already have but the powers that be have given you six months, that's just twenty-four weeks to source musicians, gel as a band and for Gunny Carter here to turn you all into an effective fighting unit."

"Finding good musicians is going to be hard enough, but to come together as a convincing rock band and train for military operations in such a short time is going to be verging on the impossible!"

The Colonel took another sip of his fresh orange juice. "You just leave the impossible to me." Then he pushed a wad of A4 pieces of paper across the table. "These thirty or so men have already been identified as potentials, they are all Navy seals, Delta force, rangers and a few green berets and I'm giving you just three weeks to audition them and choose your band before your training starts!" Then he suddenly jumped to his feet. "You haven't even seen the best bit, have you? Come with me!"

Mitch followed him through the door and into the hallway where he suddenly turned and headed down another smaller staircase. "You're going to love this!" He cried over his shoulder. "All modern, state of the art; this is brand spanking new, they only finished putting it in just last week!"

The stone staircase was tight and dark, turning three times before they reached a solid wooden door. The Colonel turned and winked mischievously before opening the door and switching the lights on. Stepping inside Mitch found himself once more speechless.

The DeadBeats

"Uncle Sam just spent two and a half million dollars of tax payer's hard-earned cash to give you the best sound and recording studio this side of Memphis!"

Mitch stood in awe. "It's... It's just beautiful!" He said as he stepped up to the computers and control panel.

The Colonel flicked a switch on the wall and lit up a second room beyond a giant pane of glass. "I took the liberty of putting your guitar in the recording suit, the drums and keyboards looked kinda lost without it!"

"This is amazing; I don't know what to say!"

"Needless to say, we have our own producer; she knows what all these buttons and switches do!"

"What happens if the band is no good? What if our music is garbage?"

"Ah that's fine; don't worry about it, we also own our own record label!"

"You got it all figured don't ya'?"

"We've been doing this a long time and we know what we're doing; never forget you're walking in the well-trodden footsteps of legends!" The Colonel turned and placed a hand on Mitch's shoulder. "I chose you to lead this band because I think you're a real good operator but more than that I've seen you perform on stage and I think you're special; you can play that guitar like Jimi Hendrix and you sing as good as anyone I ever heard!"

Stroked by the compliments and dazzled by the promise of a recording studio Mitch stood in silence.

"We're auditioning the first ten at Camp Pendleton, so go get yourself cleaned up and I'll see you on the chopper in thirty minutes!"

"One thing sir...!"

"Yes...! What is it?"

"I want final say on who is in this band, on content and musical direction; I don't want to be singing Sinatra or carrying some halfwit because his old pop is a five-star General!"

"I guess we can talk about all that kind of stuff later!"

"No, we talk about it now!" Mitch said and held out his hands. "Or you might as well put the cuffs back on right now!"

"Ok, ok I agree to your terms. But let me tell you this, there is nothing wrong with a little bit of ol' blue eyes!"

29

Camp Pendleton was four hours and two refuelling stops to the west situated in San Diego County, California and the scene of much of Mitch's own training. Strangely, he was looking forward to seeing the old place and found himself lost in memories as he gazed out of the open chopper door.

"We're almost there!" He cried above the wind rush.

"How do you know?"

"I can smell the bullshit!"

The Colonel laughed, he knew all about Marines and their bullshit.

The Black Hawk hovered a thousand feet above their designated landing area; the pilot waited patiently as six troop carrying Chinooks took off in formation, seemingly heading out to sea.

Hanging his head out of the door Mitch watched them disappear over the horizon and then began looking for familiar buildings and quickly located his old accommodation block. "Seeing this place brings back some horrible, horrible memories!" He cried. "This place almost ended me!"

No one was listening.

The Chopper began its descent and landed beside a small green

hanger where a Humvee awaited them.

"I almost forgot; I took the liberty of obtaining a uniform for you!"

The Colonel handed Mitch a kitbag. "You might need to introduce it

to a hot iron!" Then he grinned with satisfaction. "We can't have an

Officer of the Corps walking around Pendleton in ripped jeans, can

we now?"

"Jeez colonel do I have to...?"

"What did you expect? A sequinned jumpsuit?... If so, we do have

some! We have a great seamstress she can work wonders..!"

"No, it's fine let's not go down the sequin route! It's been done

already!" Grudgingly taking the bag Mitch followed the Colonel out

of the helicopter and climbed into the back seat of the Humvee,

where he quickly changed.

"So where are we going?" He asked.

"The guys at the MCCS have kindly organised the use of one of

their buildings for us, but we have got to be out by 1700 hours!"

31

The DeadBeats

The journey was short, no sooner had they entered the Humvee than they seemed to be getting out. The base was awash with Marines, some marching in squads, others doubling to their next lecture or period of instruction and others off duty and carrying out personal admin.

"I hate to say it!" Mitch said. "But it's kinda good to be back here!"

"Well don't get comfortable Captain, I want to be out of here inside three hours."

Making their way inside the building they were met by a young marine dressed in fatigues who stood to attention and saluted when he saw them coming. "Sir, everything you asked for is ready...!"

"Thank you, Lieutenant Morales, if you would care to lead the way we'll get this show on the road!"

The lieutenant led them to a table contained within a large hall, which faced a stage containing a keyboard, a guitar and a set of drums. Then he pulled the chairs out for the two men to sit. "Refreshments will arrive shortly sir!"

"What about the men? Are they ready and do they know what's expected of them?"

"Yes sir, I believe they are and they do."

"Send the first one in!"

As the lieutenant disappeared through a door at the side of the stage, Colonel Harker removed several files from his briefcase and made himself comfortable. "Of course, these guys have no idea why they're here, they think we're putting together some kind of entertainment troop for our military serving overseas… The men you're about to see have all been invited to attend based on their military record and their ability to play a musical instrument."

Without warning the first performer walked on stage and nervously shuffled into position behind the mic, before standing to attention.

"Name...!" The colonel cried.

"Sir, Cruz SIR...!"

Opening the file with the name Cruz on the front, the colonel read several paragraphs before speaking quietly to Mitch. "This one is a Navy Seal, sniper and demolitions expert; three tours of Afghanistan and one in Iraq!"

"He's kinda stiff isn't he, looks like Uncle Sam's trying to ram him from behind!" Mitch sniggered.

"Ok, Cruz tell me something interesting about yourself!"

The DeadBeats

"I'm a Marine sir and I love America!"

"I see what you mean!" The Colonel whispered behind a clenched fist, and then louder to Cruz. "That's not what I meant soldier! But let's continue, what are you going to perform for us today?"

"I'm going to perform the star-spangled banner on the keyboard sir!"

Mitch raised his hand. "Err no I don't think so! You know any Guns N Roses?"

"No sir! But I guess I could do something by Elton John!"

"Jesus Christ!" The Colonel sighed. "Well, I guess the star-spangled banner it is!"

Cruz steadied his breathing as he sat down and then took his time to stretch his fingers and just as he was about to begin Mitch once more raised his hand.

"I want you to do Great Balls of Fire by Jerry Lee Lewis; can you do that?"

Fidgeting uncomfortably on the stool Cruz slowly began to shake his head. "Why no sir, I… I don't think I can!"

"Have you ever heard the song?"

"Yes, sir I have but… But I can't play it!"

"That's all Cruz, thank you for coming; can you send the next one out when you get backstage?"

"What the hell was that all about?" The Colonel asked. "You didn't give the poor guy a chance!"

"I know what this band needs and it wasn't him. We need…!"

Raised voices at the door behind them stopped the conversation in its tracks.

"What the hell's going on back there, Morales?" The Colonel yelled angrily and stood up.

Physically trying and failing to hold back a large black marine in dress blues, Morales looked flustered and red-faced. "Sir I'll have him in the brig right away!"

"No, let him through." Mitch said. "From what we've seen so far it can't hurt any. What can we do for you, Marine?"

The Marine approached the two officers and stood to attention. "I'm Marine 1st class, Leroy Scott. I'm sorry to intrude sir but I heard a rumour about what you're doing here today and well I'd like to try out sir."

"Try out…?" The colonel cried. "This ain't no football team!"

35

The DeadBeats

"I know that sir, I'm a singer… A rap singer sir, I'm a real good one too!"

The Colonel physically winced. "Rap...!" He bellowed. "You call that singing- Get the hell out of here!"

"But sir...!"

"Sorry son, we have no vacancies for a rap singer. Unless you can play one of those instruments up on the stage there, I suggest you get the hell out of here before the Lieutenant throws you in the brig."

The Marine sighed with disappointment and looked to Mitch for a second opinion. "Sir I can play all of those instruments and more besides! I sing in the mess and the guys love it, they really do!"

"Sorry...!" Mitch said. "But it's like the Colonel said… We don't need any more vocalists!"

Reaching into his pocket the Marine pulled out several pieces of paper folded neatly into quarters and then thrust them into Mitch's hand. "Take a look, sir, please just take a look!"

Morales placed a hand on the marine's chest. "If you're not out of this building within the next ten seconds you'll be spending the foreseeable in the brig! Now get...!"

As Marine Leroy Scott sloped off Harker and Mitch re-took their seats at the table. "Ok, Morales let's see the next one, what is he?"

"She's a drummer sir!"

"A female woman...?"

"They usually are sir!"

"Ok let's have it!"

"This is Corporal Holly Lightfoot, she's twenty-two years old and as I said she plays the drums!"

Suddenly a small, slightly framed figure dashed past the desk. "Sorry guys!" A rushed female voice cried. "So, let's make this quick, my platoon's got assault course training in ten minutes and I don't want to miss it! What do you guys want to hear?"

The Colonel smiled. "What can you do?"

Suddenly noticing his rank, she jumped to attention. "Sorry sir, I didn't know…"

"It's fine Marine, as you were… Now tell me what you can do!"

"I can fight as good as any man and I play the drums better than any man sir"

"Well let's hear it!"

The DeadBeats

Sitting behind the drums the room suddenly exploded with ear-splitting beats, which continued shaking the room for the next three minutes. Then she dropped the drumsticks, stood up and jumped off the stage. "That's all I got time for sir. You know where to find me if you think I'm good enough!" and with a quick salute, she was gone.

"What the hell was that?"

"That sir...!" Mitch cried. "Was a whirlwind and one hell of a drummer! What's her trade?"

"She's part of Recon platoon, wants to go Navy seal!"

"I like her...! I think we should consider her!"

Raising an eyebrow, the Colonel blew out hard. "A female… I don't know! Let's see what else we got. "

"What have we got next Morales?" Mitch said and suddenly felt a little more positive about the mountain they wanted him to climb; maybe the Marine Corps did have a band hiding somewhere in the ranks.

"Err we have one keyboard player sir; the remainder were all drummers and well they heard Lightfoot and walked out!"

"OK send him out."

Tripping on wires the Marine stumbled onto the stage, steadied himself and then pushed his thick black-rimmed glasses back up the bridge of his nose. "Good afternoon Sirs! My name is Sergeant Luke Massy, I'm twenty-three years of age and I hail from Pennsylvania!"

"Ok calm down Marine this isn't X factor and I'm no Simon Cowell!" He said and proud of his joke, flicked a smirk and a sideways glance at Mitch. "What are you going to play for us?"

"Sir I going to play Tchaikovsky's symphony no.6 in B minor, also known as the Pathetique Symphony…"

"Wow…! Wait…!" The Colonel cried. "Can you do Great balls of fire…?"

Settling into the Humvee rear seat Mitch got comfortable as it pulled away on its short journey to the helipad. "Well, I guess it wasn't all that bad! We found a drummer!"

"God dam Tchaikovsky! What the hell is wrong with young people today, I'd rather have listened to that other guy who wanted to rap!"

The DeadBeats

Suddenly remembering Marine Leroy Scott, Mitch reached into his pocket and pulled out the now-crumpled pieces of paper. "I thought he was kinda brave bursting in there the way he did."

"He lacked discipline! He's supposed to be a goddam Marine! You just can't go bursting into places you haven't been invited!"

Mitch laughed at the Colonel's words as he unfolded the sheets of paper. "Hell, Colonel us Marines burst into countries uninvited all the time!"

"I guess we do!"

"Stop the vehicle!" Mitch said and then louder. "Stop the goddam vehicle!"

"What the hell are you doing now?"

"Look at this!" Mitch said and thrust the pieces of paper into the Colonels' hand. "I want this Marine in my band!"

"But RAP!" The Colonel shook his head in disbelief. "Look at the words the guy is a lyricist and he's good, he's really good!"

"Well, if you insist!"

"Let's go find him! I want him on that chopper today! And while we're at it I want that girl too!"

colin wraight

"A goddam rapper and a goddam female... I don't know which one

I hate the most! God dam deadbeats!"

Chapter 3

"Just look at it!"

"It's amazing!"

"Unbelievable!"

"Ok, guys...! Enough now! I know it's amazing, unbelievable bla bla bla!" The Colonel said and placed his hat on the table beside the old grandfather clock. "We gave you the brief in the chopper; the big question is are you in or are you out?"

"I'm in, I am so in...!" Private 1st class Holly Lightfoot shrieked with barely containable excitement. "Sorry, I'm just so pumped right now...! This is just so incredible! Look at all of this history! That guy there…" She pointed to an old 1950's promotional poster. "He's one of the greatest drummers of all time!"

Leroy Scott scowled. "I was a huge fan of this guy, he got a MOBO man; He made out like he was from the hood, from the street, like he was some kind of gangster and all the time he worked for the man?"

"You in or out...?"

"You couldn't drag me out of here with a Humvee; I'm definitely in!"

The Colonel turned to Mitch and grinned. "Would you like to show these two deadbeats what's in the cellar, I'm going to turn in for the night!"

Dropping her heavy kitbag Holly scanned the hallway for a cellar door. "So, what's in the cellar?"

"You might want to get an early night yourself; you and I are flying to Jacksonville, North Carolina first thing in the morning...!"

"Lejeune...?"

"That would be the Marine Corps Base Camp Lejeune to you Captain! There's some guy in the Marine Raider Regiment I want you to see, who plays bass guitar and can sing some too." With that, the Colonel turned and slowly began trudging his way up the staircase, and then he stopped beside a large photograph of Buddy

43

Holly and the Crickets. "Lightfoot, Scott I need you to know this is going to be no walk in the park; it's going to be hard, dangerous and dirty! You get captured on foreign soil and we will deny your existence! People tend to lose their lives doing the kind of work we do… You bite the bullet in training or on a mission, all that will happen is you will get your name carved into the boathouse! No medals, no fanfare and no one will ever know what you did for your country!"

"Boathouse…? What boathouse?" Leroy Said, and then realised he'd said it out loud. "Oh sorry… You carry on sir…!"

"No, you're right Marine, I was rambling." He said wearily. "I'm sure Mitch here will show you the boathouse… Goodnight everyone…!"

"Cowboy…!" The young woman shrieked and snatching a night robe from the floor beside the bed covered her bare breast. "Cowboy wake up he's here!"

A male form stirred under the white silk bed sheets. "What...? Who's here?"

"It's John, my husband; he's just pulled up." Quickly sliding into her panties, she hurriedly dressed in jeans and a t-shirt. "Cowboy, he'll kill you, for god's sake get up, grab your stuff and get the hell out!"

As consciousness reared its ugly head and the thin veil of alcohol-induced drunkenness began to clear Sam Willis AKA Cowboy opened his eyes. "Your husband is here?"

"Get out...!" She screeched and kicked the bed. "Will you get the hell out?"

Cowboy shook his head clearing his thoughts. "Your husband is here? Jesus Christ that's my Commanding Officer!"

"Please, just go!"

Both stumbling and falling out of bed Cowboy grabbed his shirt and jeans and dashed for the window. "He catches me in here I'm finished!" Opening it he checked the street was deserted and then threw all of his clothes onto the grass below. Blowing the girl a kiss he quickly followed, climbing naked down a drain pipe.

The DeadBeats

Dropping the last few feet onto the neatly cut lawn, he winced with pain as he caught his toe on an abandoned child's tricycle. Still cursing the child's toy Cowboy gathered up his clothes and then realised to his horror that his boots and Stetson were nowhere to be seen.

"If you would like to follow me Colonel Harker, the Brigadier General will see you now!"

Leaving his cap and overcoat on the chair beside Mitch, he stood up. "I don't know what's going on, but it looks like we're about to find out! You wait here!"

"Sir, they probably just don't want to lose a good marine!"

"Nothing they can do about it!" Following the young Marine along the dimly lit corridor, he was led to a door with a large and imposing brass nameplate. Colonel Harker smiled; it was a name he knew well. "It's alright marine I'll take it from here."

"But...!"

"Off you go Marine...!"

Tapping twice on the door Harker waited to be invited in.

"Harker...!" A voice boomed from somewhere inside the room. "Get in here you old goat!"

Pushing the door open Harker grasped the hand waiting on the other side and shook it warmly. "Been a long time Ben!"

"Too long Harker, I believe the last time I saw you was in Iraq about... well it must be almost ten years by now!" The Brigadier released his grip and returned to the seat behind his desk. "Sit down! So, tell me what on earth are you up to these days?"

"You know how it is! They got me doing a little bit of this and a little bit of that!"

"Really...! I understand you're here to see one of my men!"

"That's right...!"

"What exactly do you want him for- because let me tell you he's a real asshole!"

Loath to lie to his old friend Harker shifted uneasily in his seat. "I'm putting together a special operations team and he's made our short list, other than that I'm not at liberty to say!"

"He's made a goddam shortlist! Did you just not hear me? The guy is a first-class dick!"

Harker shrugged. "He's got skills!"

"Well, I'm afraid you're out of luck, right now he's in the brig and if his CO gets his way it's where he will stay for the foreseeable!"

"So, what did he do? What's he guilty of?"

"He's guilty of being an asshole! Two nights ago, he gets busted in bed with an officer's wife, that officer was his Commanding officer. He grabs his clothes and jumps out the window. He then has the goddam temerity to knock on the front door and ask for his boots and Stetson!"

"Jesus...!"

"Jesus indeed, he was naked at the time! A fight broke out; they were still going at it when the police arrived! He beat two policemen half to death with a child's tricycle! If they hadn't tazered him god only knows what would have happened!"

"Can I see him?"

"Sure, you can see him but I'm not sure what good it will do! He's waiting to be transferred to NAVCONBRIG at Miramar! The law is the law and that boy is going to jail- I'll contact the brig and let them know you're on your way down there!"

"Thank you, Brigadier, it was good to see you again!"

"Next time you're in the area you should come for dinner, I'm sure the wife would love to see you again!"

"I'd sure like that sir." Harker stood, and before leaving the room shook hands with the Brigadier. "Let's go Captain Calvert, we got a man to bust out of the brig!"

Mitch got up quickly and fell in beside the Colonel, leaving the Headquarters it was only a short walk to the holding cells. Different camps always have a different feel to them. Pendleton always seemed like home to Mitch but Lejeune had a different feel about it, it was just too regimented; heartless with an almost soulless character. He didn't like the place and couldn't wait to leave.

The sergeant major, looking smart in his dress blues was already awaiting their arrival. Standing smartly to attention as they approached, he saluted. "Sir we have the prisoner restrained and awaiting your further instruction sir!" He barked without pausing for breath.

"Do you have an interview room here Gunny?"

"Sir, yes sir!"

"Ok let's have him moved in there!"

49

"Sir, if you would care to follow me, I'll show you to the interview room!" Completing a full about turn the Sergeant marched into the building, timing his walk to arrive at the doors just as the automatic sensors opened them.

Inside the corridor was cool but brightly lit; the only noise bar the sound of their boots on the marble floor was the quiet buzz of the air conditioning units.

"How many prisoners are you holding here Gunny?" Mitch asked.

"There's twenty-three Sir!"

"Kinda quiet in here, isn't it?"

"Here at Lejeune we run a tight ship sir, we keep them quiet as mice, it gives them time to think about their actions!" The Sergeant suddenly stopped and opened a door. "If you gentlemen would care to wait inside the prisoner will be along shortly."

Colonel Harker quickly took a chair on one side of the grey desk which was situated in the middle of the room. Noticing there was only one chair remaining Mitch remained standing, and leaned against the wall.

"Before he gets here there's something you need to know!"

"What's that...?" Mitch said.

"This guy is really good, I'd like him on board, and Well... Back in New York if you had turned down my, how shall I put this...? Invitation...! There's a good chance he'd be standing where you are right now if you catch my drift!"

"I see, so apart from the fact he clearly likes the ladies, single or otherwise and has no problem assaulting senior officers what does he offer?"

"He's been a Sergeant three times...!"

"Three times...?"

"Ok so he's a real bad boy, struggles with authority but, and this is the 'but' I'd like you to listen to. He's part of the Marine Raider regiment and has been on the front line of the war on terror for the last five years- His experience and professional capability are next to none. The boy is also a top-notch base guitarist and can sing some too! If he accepts my proposal, you are the man that will have to control his slightly wilder tendencies!"

The sudden heavy tap on the door stopped their conversation in its tracks.

"Enter...!" The Colonel cried.

The DeadBeats

As the door opened two burly-looking Marines carrying long white truncheons entered the room. Behind them appeared a Marine, his wrists and ankles bound by chains, his otherwise handsome face a mass of bruising, swelling and congealing blood, his demeanour and painful limp suggested other concealed injuries to his torso and legs.

To his rear, the imposing Sergeant Major stood holding a clipboard. "Prisoner delivered as ordered sir!"

"It's alright Gunny you and your men are relieved!"

"Sir it is my duty to report that this prisoner is dangerous and prone to violent outbursts sir!"

"It's fine Gunny, we can take care of ourselves- Now if you would care to close the door on your way out, I would be very much appreciative!"

As the last Marine left the room and the door closed Harker finally looked up at the prisoner. "You look like you just went twelve rounds with Mike Tyson!"

"Mike Tyson would only have lasted six Sir!" The prisoner snarled belligerently.

The Colonel laughed. "I think I believe you, take a seat, Marine!"

The chains rattled noisily as he manoeuvred his pained body into the chair. "Are you two Officers my lawyers, because if you are, you're wasting all of our time, I'm as guilty as hell!"

"No, actually we are here on another more pressing matter. I'll get straight to the point we're putting together a sort of special operations unit..."

The prisoner sighed heavily. "Why me...?"

"This may sound kinda stupid, hell it sure sounds stupid to me, but our special operations unit is looking for someone with your particular skill set!"

"Demolitions...?"

"No.!"

"Assault team commander...?"

"Well yes and no; we already have our assault team commander in Captain Calvert here!"

"What is it then...?"

"I understand you play a mean base guitar...?"

The prisoner stared and then slowly frowned. "Sorry, I think I must have misheard you because...!"

Mitch suddenly spoke up. "After you escaped the wrath of the husband, why did you go back and knock on the door; you didn't even bother to dress?"

"I'd left my boots and my Stetson inside, they once belonged to my daddy, he gave them to me on his death bed and I wasn't about to lose them!"

Mitch nodded. "I see...! You then proceeded to beat two policemen half to death with some kid's tricycle!"

"Hell, maybe that one's on me! But one of them pulled a gun, the training kicked in and the next thing I know... The next thing I remember is seeing the bike; it was the only weapon available to me... I guess none of this was the kids' fault, I'll buy him a new one when I get out of here!"

"By then he's going to need a much bigger bike!"

The Colonel raised an eyebrow. "You just described a toddler's tricycle as a weapon! Personally, I would have described it as small or blue... or fun!"

"Everything and anything can be a weapon, Sir!" The Prisoner said and stroked the unusually long fringe out of his eyes. "They told me five to seven years… All that asshole had to do was hand me my hat and boots and all of this unnecessary could have been avoided."

"Maybe you shouldn't have screwed your commanding Officers wife…!"

The prisoner grinned at the memory. "Well yes Sir! I guess there is always that!"

Mitch turned to the Colonel. "I kinda like this one; I think we'll take him!"

"Marine, if you want adventure, if you're willing to die for your country and if you're willing to play your guitar in my rock band, we'll have you out of here within thirty minutes!" The colonel said and returned the prisoner's file back inside his briefcase. "If not, we'll bid you a good day and an enjoyable incarceration!"

"I'll play my guitar, on one condition…!"

"What's that…?"

"Those ass holes outside give me my boots and hat back!"

"Anything else…?"

"Yes… My friends call me Cowboy!"

The Colonel stopped and momentarily stared at the prisoner. "Know this ass hole...! I'm not your friend, I'll call you anything I goddam like because I'm a Colonel and YOU WILL address me as Sir or Colonel!"

"I'm afraid you may have misunderstood me, Sir! I said my friends call me Cowboy!"

After a brief staring contest in which Cowboy lost, Harker turned to Mitch. "Captain Calvert, are you sure that you want this man on the team!" He growled.

"Oh yeah, sure I'm sure!"

Chapter 4

"So, you want us to call you what?" Holly sneered and shot a sideways glace at Mitch.

"Cowboy, you guys can call me Cowboy!"

"Is that like your name or something you just gave yourself?" Scott scoffed.

"No, it's a nickname," Cowboy said clearly irked at the questions and fondled his Stetson with barely contained anger. "My folks owned a ranch and once the guys in my Platoon found out the name stuck... And I like it! OK!"

"That's enough Holly, Scott," Mitch said. "Cowboy they're just messing with you man, chill out."

Holly smiled. "Come on Cowboy let's show you around this dump!"

"Yeh man my stage name is Devil Dawg," Scott said. "I'm a rap artist!"

"Rap...! Hell, no one told me we're doing rap! I thought maybe light rock and a touch of country."

"Scott or Devil Dawg is here for his ability to write great lyrics!" Mitch insisted. "No one has even mentioned us doing rap!"

"I think it would be cool." Holly interrupted loudly, as she tried to support her newfound friend. "Done properly, it might be good!"

"Well, we're not talking about this right now, Cowboy needs to get unpacked and get settled and the Colonel and I still have to find a keyboard player."

Skipping up several steps of the great staircase Holly stopped and turned around. "You need to see all of these pictures, the photographs and all of this history; it will truly blow your mind."

Cowboy threw a derisory glance at the countless multitudes of images on the rogue's gallery. "You know that looks all nice and everything, but I'm kinda tired, I'd just like to hit the bunk right now; well, that and maybe get a burger… Does this place have a bar?"

"Sure, we got a bar but you don't get to use it until you earn it." The Colonel cried from afar and then suddenly appeared framing a doorway which would prove to be his office. "Guys, could you keep the noise down, some of us still have work to do; and Mitch I'd like to speak to you first thing in the morning about this keyboard player problem we have."

Bidding everyone a goodnight, Mitch finally made it to his room on the first floor, intending to get a shower, instead, he collapsed exhausted onto his bed. No sooner had he closed his eyes than there came a light knock on the door.

"Jesus Christ." He whispered, and then louder. "Come in!"

Opening the door just wide enough, Cowboy took a step inside the room and stood with one hand on the door handle and an unopened beer bottle in his other. "Sorry to disturb you Sir, but I just got to thinking; I used to know this guy in Delta, his name was Chow...! Tony Chow; well, he was a hell of a keyboard player. Last I heard he was out and living in Miami, just thought I'd let you know before I have too many of these." He said and held the beer bottle up. "But yeh, he was really good, probably the best I ever saw."

Mitch sat up. "Thanks, Cowboy, I'll speak to the Colonel. You know, I was going to take a shower and get my head down." He said wearily. "But right now, I think you should show me where you got that bottle from!"

Cowboy grinned.

"Ok, guys settle down and listen up." The Colonel said and took one last sip of his morning coffee. "As you all know we're struggling to find a keyboard player, the Cap and I auditioned a couple but they weren't quite up to it. Our latest recruit, Cowboy here, assures me he knows where we might be able to find one! Consequently, I want all of you to take a road trip, get to know each other and bring me back a musician."

"Road trip Sir?" Mitch said and frowned. "What...? So, we're hiring a car?"

"Hell, no Marines! The band's tour bus is in the garage. It's got a full tank and the keys are in the glove compartment. While you're having your first little adventure together, I'll be in Washington DC sorting out a few loose ends... Goodbye, and good luck." Then he got up to leave. "Oh, you might have to give it a bit of a scrub; the last guy was kind of a slob."

Holly's face lit up. "A tour bus!" She cried. "We've got a tour bus? Oh, My God! Where is it?"

The Colonel pointed. "The garage is that way."

"Come on guys!" She said as she rushed out of the room and disappeared into the corridor.

"Well, I guess we'd better take a look." Mitch said and eagerly followed as the remainder of the band trailed behind.

"I'm in here guys!"

The tone of her voice told Mitch it wasn't going to be good news. Filing into the garage they fell in beside her and stood staring in silence at the site before them.

"Like I said…" The Colonel poked his head inside the garage. "She needs a bit of a clean!"

"You said it was a tour bus!" Holly whined, her face a picture of disappointment.

"You said it just needed a bit of a clean!" Mitch added glumly.

Kicking the rust-covered driver's side wing Scott shook his head in disgust. "Man...! This ain't no tour bus, it's a goddam Winnebago!"

"No, it's not just any Winnebago!" Cowboy said. "It's a piece of shit Winnebago! Hell, even a junkyard dog wouldn't sleep inside this!"

The DeadBeats

Colonel Harker smiled sarcastically and spoke with a mischievous glint in his eye. "This vehicle is a solid piece of American engineering and is mechanically sound; sure, she's seen better days but fortunately for her, she's got you, and you have got all night to tart her up."

"That would take more than one night sir!"

"It is what it is Cowboy!"

"It's a god-dammed abomination, sir!"

"As I said, it is what it is!"

Far beyond the towering tree tops, above the distant horizon, the sun began its rise, hidden behind grey and cloud-filled skies. Birds, oblivious to the rain and impending storm filled the air with chitter chatter and the music of their morning chorus.

After only two hours of sleep, Mitch was exhausted as he trudged into the garage. "We all set then?" He said wearily and tossed his rucksack through the open door of the RV.

Cowboy grunted, took a sip from his coffee and offered the mug to Mitch, which he refused. "The others are on their way down." He said.

"I'll drive, you want to get the doors open and we'll get this piece of shit outside." Climbing into the driver's seat he patiently waited while Cowboy located the open button for the electric roller shutter doors. As the doors opened cold air and daylight rushed in, suddenly feeling wide awake Mitch gunned the engines, engaged drive and chased by billowing black smoke from the exhaust, pulled out of the garage onto the tarmac drive and then stopped and turned the engine off.

"Jeez, man it looks much worse in daylight," Scott said as he climbed into the back and sat in the chair behind the driver. "Dude, we sure are living the rock and roll dream!"

"Where's Holly?"

"I'm here...! I'm here!" She cried as her kitbag hurtled through the door and slammed into the small fridge. Climbing in and kicking the bag to the back of the vehicle, she sat down. "Ok, people!" She said brightly. "Who's up for a wild road trip?"

The DeadBeats

"Guess I'm riding shotgun," Cowboy said as he slid into the passenger seat. "Does anyone know the way?"

"There's a map behind the sun visor, so are we all set then?" Mitch said and turned the ignition key, the engine growled three times before it burst into life, sending huge billowing clouds of black smoke from the exhaust. As he engaged first gear and pressed the gas pedal the engine backfired with an ear deafening boom. Roosting birds' content in their morning song suddenly exploded on mass into the sky wheeling and turning in great flocks. "Think we better hit the road!"

"Miami here we come! Do you think we'll get some beach time in?" Holly said.

"Shit man! I didn't bring my shorts!" Cowboy added.

"Guys we got a fifteen-hour drive ahead of us, if you need the john, I suggest you speak up right now because I ain't stopping until we need gas which I guess will be somewhere near Tupelo."

Reaching up, Cowboy grabbed the map and unfolded it across his lap. "Drive on my good man, you're going to take a right, eastbound onto route twenty-two. Wake me up when we get to Birmingham and we'll switch seats," Leaning back as the RV pulled away Cowboy tilted his Stetson over his eyes. "If anyone needs me, you'll find me right here, fast asleep... So, if you kids could keep the noise down, I'd much appreciate it."

"Hell, no man, we need tunes! I can't go fourteen hours without some beats," Scott cried. "Has this wreck got a radio?"

Turning the radio on, Mitch tuned into the only station without crackly interference. "Sorry guys all we got is some news channel, might as well switch it off!"

"Wait...!" Holly interrupted. "What did he just say? Mitch, turn that thing up."

He laughed. "That's as loud as it goes- But I think he said some celebrity or other has gone missing!"

"Sure, she has!" Cowboy sneered from beneath his Stetson. "She'll turn up, just after a little of that good old publicity!"

"Didn't another one vanish on a photo shoot a couple of weeks ago?" Holly said. "What the hell was her name?"

Cowboy tilted his Stetson back, and with a huge smile on his face looked over at Holly. "That was the incredibly beautiful Vanessa Tilson, daughter of George Tilson III, and owner of Tilson shipping

65

consolidated; the family are seriously rich. I remember back in training I had her naked body plastered all over my wall. Boy, she was the star of many a…"

"You're disgusting!!"

"Why, Holly you have one filthy mind! I was going to say dream! But hell, we can go with what you're thinking too!" Cowboy laughed and retreated under his Stetson.

"Asshole...!"

Eating up the tarmac at a piston straining fifty miles per hour the RV rattled, creaked and swayed eastward, leaving nothing but a trail of black smoke and the occasional startled wildlife. Minutes seemed endless, and hours a lifetime as the clock ticked the day away with a monotonous sweep of the second hand, and by the time Mitch turned off the highway to refuel he was exhausted and thankful that he wouldn't have to drive again.

"Guy's wakeup we're just outside Birmingham Alabama!" Mitch gave a sigh of relief and switched the engine off. "If you need the john or food, I suggest you go now; you've got until this heap has drunk its fill."

Stirring groggily Scott yawned and stretched. "Are we there yet?" He said and then pushed his huge frame up into a sitting position.

"We're at the gas stop," Holly said and rubbed her eyes, then looking at Scott she grimaced. "How the hell did you manage to sleep all this way on the floor?"

"The Devil Dawg can sleep any time any place; when you've been a marine as long as I have you learn to sleep every chance you get..."

"Because a marine never knows when the next chance will come!" Cowboy finished the sentence and then adjusted his Stetson.

Holly leaned into the front of the RV. "Tell me Cowboy do you ever take that thing off your head?"

"Why, sure I do sweet cheeks..."

Rolling her eyes, she fell back into her seat. "Let me guess! You take it off only when you're having sex?"

"I'll have you know I've never had sex in my whole life, but I sure have made love many, many times!" Cowboy laughed.

"You're a pig!"

"I'm a pig?" He cried in disgust and turned to face her. "I ain't no little old pig! Sweet cheeks, you just don't know me yet."

"You two either get a room or knock it off!" Mitch ordered. "This place has a diner; I suggest we all go inside and get something to eat."

"Did someone mention food?" Scott said and jumped to his feet, causing the RV to sway on its springs. Ducking his head to avoid the skylight he began threading himself through the interior. Stepping over discarded kit bags, rucksacks and guitars he made for the door. "Man, we need a bigger vehicle, how is the Devil Dawg meant to fit inside this thing?" He whined. Squeezing his huge frame through the door he stepped down onto the concrete forecourt and stretched. "I could eat a lame horse!"

"You move kinda quickly for such a big man," Cowboy commented as he too exited the RV. After straightening his denim shirt and adjusting his Stetson he shined the toe of his left boot on his right calf. Still dissatisfied with his appearance he reached into his top pocket and pulled out his Ray-bans. "My public awaits!" He said, winked at Holly and donned the sunglasses.

The log cabin effect diner looked old and still had a water trough and hitch to tie up horses out front. Climbing the steps, they paused on the veranda and Holly peered through the small window beside the door. "Looks like you're going to feel right at home here Cowboy."

"You trying to say this is a real classy joint?"

"No, it's cheap and full of dick heads!"

"Aw sweet cheeks, and I was beginning to think you liked me."

The roar of approaching motorcycles caused them to cease their bickering, and as they turned to watch, a half dozen leather-clad hells angels thundered off the freeway and pull up in front of the diner, parking in a neat line.

The Old Knuckleheads, low riders and more modern Harley-Davidsons looked in much better condition than their riders. These dishevelled and dust-covered men with their old leather and ripped denim fetish seemed at odds with their pristine bikes. Mitch had them weighed up immediately as what he termed Sunday morning bikers, men who longed for the freedom and the lifestyle but in reality, worked in offices and on construction sites. But on a closer look one

69

of the men was wearing high-leg combat boots and another clearly had a Marine Corps tattoo on his right forearm. Also, they were all clean-shaven and their hair was all wrong, too short and only a comb away from being smart. Mitch had been around Marines his entire adult life and he had also entertained real hard case bikers in some of the shittiest bars in America. These men were fakes, but they had a feeling of menace about them, there was something hostile about them and suddenly Mitch felt threatened.

"Eyes on...!" He said quietly.

"Already on it boss," Cowboy replied.

By now the first of the bikers had dismounted and was casually strolling towards the diner entrance, he was big and muscular and walked with the self-assured confidence of a leader. Slowing as he reached the steps, he fixed his gaze on Holly and then slowly looked her up and down, pausing just a second too long at her breast.

"See something you like?" She snapped.

The biker smiled and then spat some gum onto the veranda beside Mitch.

Scott took a step to his left coming face to face with the stranger and blocking the biker's gaze. "The lady asked you a question ass hole!"

The biker sneered in defiance and glared up at the huge man standing before him. Sensing unwavering fearlessness, the biker broke first and in a momentary show of weakness glanced over his shoulder to ensure the remainder of his gang were right behind him.

"Hey man I didn't mean anything by it, call off your dog!" The biker said as he stared at Mitch. "I was just being friendly."

Standing aside Scott allowed the man and then his friends to pass by, not once taking his eyes off them. The last of them, was a small athletic-looking guy, with a large scar which began on his chin and cut through his lips before terminating at his nose fixed his eyes on Mitch and shouldered Scott as he walked by. Once they had disappeared inside, he relaxed. "I guess that's what you would call a real nice Alabama welcome!"

"Stay alert...!" Mitch said. "I don't think these guys are what they seem. Let's grab some food and get the hell out of here."

The DeadBeats

Taking his shades and placing them in his shirt pocket and then removing his Stetson Cowboy was the first to enter the building, and subconsciously chose a table so he could observe both the bikers and the only exit. "I don't like those guys I say we take them outside and kick their teeth down their throats!"

"No, we can't afford to be arrested. Let's just stay cool and eat!" As he spoke, he spotted something hurtling through the air towards Scott's face, snatching his hand up he captured the projectile barely before it reached its target and then casually placed it on the table.

"Hey, man!" Scott snapped angrily. "Who threw that?"

"They're really starting to piss me off!" Cowboy growled through gritted teeth and visibly tensed up in his seat. "If this goes down, I want that big guy… I'll take the dickhead with the scar too; I didn't appreciate the way they looked at Holly!"

Holly blushed under the twinkle she suddenly noticed in his blue eyes and then laughed nervously as she tried to compose herself. "What the hell Cowboy! You ass hole, that's exactly the way you look at me!" She shook her head in mock disbelief and then looked over her shoulder at the bikers. "Guys you're messing with the wrong people! Just cut out the shit!"

"It was only a screwed-up menu guys." Mitch said picked up the offending item and tossed it in a nearby bin. "They ain't worth it."

Sensing trouble, the waitress dithered nervously in her decision as to which table to approach, one look at Cowboy's face sent her scurrying to the bikers. Slipping a notebook and pen from her apron she smiled as brightly as she dare without cracking her pasted-on makeup. "If you boys are ready, I'll take your order now."

Scarface immediately reached out, placed his arm around her waist and then let it drift lower than was polite. Jumping out of his way with the nimbleness of past experience, she was both a yard short and too slow on this occasion and he forcibly yanked her back and forced her onto his knees.

"I bet you're kinda pretty under all this makeup!" He said and sniffed her cheeks.

"Let go of me!" She demanded without fear, a veteran of many male incursions this was not the first man to grab her. "Or I'll have to ask you to leave."

The first idea that Scarface had of someone quickly approaching was the flicker in the eyes of the waitress, the second was his head

73

being ripped back and all four prongs of a fork being placed precisely against his left eyeball; he froze.

"I bet you're kinda pretty under all this dirt!" Holly growled and eased pressure onto the fork. "Now let her go or I'm going to kick the living shit out of you right here in front of your friends, and then when I'm through doing that I'm having your eyeball battered and deep-fried with my fries!"

"Wow!" Cowboy whispered under his breath. "What a woman!"

"I'd do as the lady asked if I were you, she doesn't take kindly to assholes!" Mitch sighed as he suddenly realised, he wasn't going to get to eat after all. "Come on guys let's go, I'm not so hungry now."

Licking his dry lips nervously Scarface released his grip allowing the waitress to wriggle free and scamper behind the till. "I want you out of here, all of you; now get!" She cried. "Or so help me god I'm calling the Sherriff!"

As Holly eased pressure on the fork Scarface pushed her away and defiantly jumped to his feet. "What do you say we take this outside you little bitch?"

"Sit down!" The voice was deep and southern and came from the mouth of the large biker. "That little girl just took you out with a kitchen fork, what do you think she's going to do to you outside? Sit the hell down."

Seething with anger and with violence coursing through his veins Scarface grudgingly did as he was told and slowly sank back into his chair. "I'll be sure to see you real soon!" He spat in Holly's direction.

Moving forward Scott loomed menacingly over the bikers table and glared at the one who seemed to be the leader of the gang. "I'll be outside if any of you girls want to join me, I'll be more than happy to wait while you decide which one of you goes to the hospital first."

Chapter 5

With the Stetson and sunglasses returned to their rightful place, Cowboy settled into the driver's seat. Glancing into the wing mirror at the neat row of Harley's he smiled mischievously. "Is anyone else thinking what I'm thinking?"

"Leave it, man!" Mitch pleaded. "We don't want any more trouble on this trip; let's just get the hell out of here."

"Ok is everyone on board and is everyone happy?"

"No!" Scott said sullenly, mimicking a petulant teenager. "I'm hungry! Like I'm really, really hungry!"

Gunning the engines Cowboy spun the back wheels sending up a cloud of dust and blasting stones over the bikes. "Oops sorry boss, my bad!"

"Screw 'em!" Mitch said and grinned.

Arriving in Miami shortly after midnight and driving the last hundred and fifty miles, Scott pulled the RV over on some wasteland just outside town. "Boss we're here."

Mitch stirred in one of the back seats, stretching his back he yawned. "What time is it?"

"It's midnight."

"You should get your head down; it's too late to do anything else today."

Balancing the tray of cups with one hand and carrying several paper bags in the other, Cowboy turned the handle and as the door opened, he forced his boot into the gap. "You guys wake up, I got breakfast!"

Scott's face appeared instantly at the driver's window. "Food man, I smell food! Did someone mention breakfast?"

"Here," Cowboy said and passed him a paper bag and a plastic cup from the tray. "It's kinda greasy crap but it's better than nothing."

"You're my hero, you funny little cowboy hat-wearing freak!"

The DeadBeats

"Good morning everyone, I trust you all slept as well as I did," Mitch said groggily, taking his breakfast bag he placed it on the floor preferring to sip his coffee first. "You know, I'm not so sure this camping thing is for me."

"I'm with you on that!" Scott said.

"So, Mitch, what's the plan for today?" Holly said.

"This guy, this Tony Chow was last known working at a marina. So, I guess we get down there, find him and make our pitch." Mitch said wearily as he rubbed his eyes and then ran his fingers through his hair. "Man, I feel like shit! Anyhow, I guess Cowboy here knows what he looks like so he's with me and you two rest up, you'll be doing the first driving stint on the way back."

After a brief farewell, Mitch and Cowboy moved out onto the highway and hailed a passing taxi. Soon they were downtown Miami and heading for the seafront and a horizon that seemed full of masts.

"Kinda pretty ain't it!" Cowboy said and spotting two barely dressed ladies on the sidewalk he stuck his head out of the window to get a better look. "This sure does look like my kinda town."

Mitch smiled and was about to speak when the cab suddenly pulled over.

"The Marina you're after is just over there." The driver said and indicated towards an entrance barrier and gatehouse across the road. "That'll be twenty bucks!"

Cowboy was already on the sidewalk straightening his Stetson when Mitch was handing over the cash. Opening the door, he got out and threw Cowboy a sideways glance. "It's ok man I'll pay for the cab!"

"Hell Mitch, put it on the expense account!" Cowboy laughed. "Ain't Uncle Sam sponsoring this little adventure?"

"Let's go!" Mitch said and strode out for the Marina.

The gate attendant squinted at the blurry outline of two strangers; he could barely make them out as they crossed the road and walked straight toward him. As they came closer, he was better able to focus through his cataracts and scrutinized them with the engrained suspicion of a long-term security guard

"Hey, old timer...!" The one wearing the Stetson said.

Bracing at the suggestion that he was somehow an old man and past his prime, the security guard surveyed the strangers with contempt. "What can I do for you boys?" He said gruffly.

Mitch immediately recognised the military bearing in the old man.

"We're Marines Sir and we're looking for one of our old buddies."

"Marines huh...! Me too, three tours of Vietnam although you'd never know it the way I'm treated around here."

"We're looking for Tony Chow!" Cowboy said. "Last I heard he worked here!"

"Yeah, I know him, though he doesn't work here no more. He was fired about three maybe four weeks ago."

"Why was he fired?"

"He turned up for work drunk more times than he turned up sober, hell some days his hands shook worse than mine and I got Parkinson's. Anyway, I heard he got into a fight with one of the patrons and they had to fire him. There's only so much help you can give to a man who doesn't want to help himself."

"What do you mean?"

"I tried to take him under my wing but the man's troubled, just like all the young'uns he wouldn't listen! The problem is there's too much soldier in him and he doesn't know how to be a civilian. He never said anything, but I think he's seen and done things no man should; Life is only going to go one of two ways for Tony Chow, he'll either kill himself or he'll kill someone else." The security guard paused.

"… Shame though, hell of a musician."

"Do you know where we can find him?"

Flashing Cowboy a withering look, the security guard turned and headed back into his small gatehouse. "Sure, I got an address and I'll give it to you, but not your friend in the hat, I don't like him too much!"

Cowboy stifled a laugh. "What do you mean 'you don't like me'? What the hell have I done wrong?"

Returning with a small piece of paper in his hand he pointed a slightly shaky finger at Cowboy "You look like a real asshole! When I was in my prime, I'd have kicked your ass all the way down this street! In Vietnam, we knew how to deal with assholes! Marine my ass, I bet you never even saw combat…"

"Sir, I'll have you know I was a Navy SEAL and I've seen plenty of combat…" Cowboy baulked.

The security guard looked him up and down and then winked at Mitch. "Really…? You still look like an asshole to me! What's with the dumb hat and the mirror shades? Who do think you are? John Denver?"

"They sure don't make Marines like they did in your day, Sir!" Mitch said and held out his hand.

"I guess they don't" As he handed over the address, he turned his attention back to Cowboy. "I'm just messing with you kid, Semper fi and all that!"

"You're a real funny guy!"

"I know!" The old timer laughed as he shuffled back into his guard box.

Unfolding the slip of paper Mitch frowned. "Hey old man, what the hell is this?"

"That's the Heartbreak Hotel guys, and it really is down at the end of lonely street!"

"What the hell?" Cowboy said.

Mitch shook his head and screwed the piece of paper up in his hand. "He's in the veteran's hostel; five bucks gets you a bed, bath and one meal a day!"

"Jesus H Christ, I heard about those places!"

The black vinyl-covered seat was hot and uncomfortable to say the least, but that in itself was the least of Holly's problems. Scott had fallen fast asleep not long after the other two had left and was now snoring with the relentless din of a freight train.

"Scott...!" She snapped angrily and prodded him on the shoulder, but the slumbering giant failed to respond. "For Christ's sake Scott, will you pipe down already? Asshole!" Consumed by frustration she switched the radio on and began turning the old tuning dial, skimming quickly past the white noise and only pausing on a station long enough to decide if she liked the music on offer. Settling on a local station she slumped back in her seat and tried to calm down.

Holly tapped along to the beat as Dolly Parton tried to persuade some harlot called Jolene not to take her man, and as she followed the words, she began to wonder just exactly how good looking was this Jolene? After all the young Dolly was stunning and she had the figure to match. Holly shook the thoughts from her head but her lips couldn't resist a comment. "Dolly he ain't worth it and that Jolene, well that woman is just bad news … You should have kicked her ass

down the sidewalk." The song soon finished and at the top of the

hour, it was time for the news bulletin.

About to look for another station she suddenly stopped to listen…

"And we have yet more woe for the troubled celebrity star maker

TV series, now a second contestant from last year's scandal-hit show

has gone missing under mysterious circumstances. Shortly after

being the first to be evicted the much-maligned Lena disappeared and

police are still searching for the fitness influencer…"

Holly turned the dial to retune as static interference drowned the

news readers' voice out.

"The starlet Brianne Moore-Masterson; Stepdaughter of the author

Robin Masterson, and the celebrity who went on to win the most

popular reality show of last year has not been seen since attending

the film premiere of The Voodoo Child in Zurich at the weekend…

More to follow on this and other stories"

"Probably off her head on drugs somewhere… She'll turn up!" Scott

said groggily.

"Oh, you're awake then?" Holly snapped and turned the radio off.

"Have you any idea how loud you snore?"

"Yeah, about that...! I talk in my sleep too; did I say anything?"

"I don't know you asshole; I couldn't hear anything for all the snoring!"

"Oh, you're really pissed?"

"Forget it! Just don't ever fall asleep anywhere near me ever again!"

Scott laughed. "You know I'm sure I read somewhere last week that some German supermodel went missing in Berlin. They say she had a hugely public spat with some paparazzi, got into a cab and no one has seen her since..."

"Just another attention whore...!"

"What?"

"Well just look at them, fame for the sake of fame; vacuous, plastic, talentless attention-seeking bitches, and that's just the men; the women are ten times worse!"

"I take it you don't approve of the whole celebrity culture thing!"

"It's all about the fake tan, the make-up and whose laying on top of them today, and yes I'm still talking about the men!"

"But we're in a band, aren't we all about the fame thing?"

The DeadBeats

Holly slowly shook her head and glared at Scott in disbelief. "Are you serious? I mean are you frigging serious I spent my whole life learning to play the drums! Please don't compare me to those people!"

"Look, hanging around here isn't doing either of us any good, let's take a time out!"

"What are you talking about?" Holly said glumly.

"On the way here, I noticed a karaoke bar across the road!"

"You're kidding right?"

"No! I say we go over there right now and rock that place! Come on it'll be fun!"

"Ok, but we're not drinking! I am not getting drunk!"

"Absolutely...! There's nothing like a little alcohol-free humiliation!"

The freshness of the early morning breeze was just a pleasant memory now as the sun burned fiercely high in an azure blue sky. Sea bird's dove, swooped and hovered in hope of a morsel or titbit and cried out in disappointment as the two men finished off their burgers. Mitch checked his watch and frowned. "Times getting on man, we need to find this guy and get on the road!"

Gaggling tourists and their excited offspring in town for a day or a week, hoping for sand, sea and excitement headed for the seafront; a stark contrast to the beautifully rich promenading in their designer clothes and obscenely expensive jewellery, the sidewalks were now alive with the hustle and bustle of midday in Miami. Amongst the throng a street vendor wearing a top hat and a sparkling multi-coloured jacket vied for space to sell sunglasses and another dressed as a bear sold buckets and spades. Nearby a golden living statue stood as still as possible and hoped for enough money for dinner. On the street corner sitting on an old carpet a rag-tag busker, belted out a Rod Stewart classic. Beside a tatty rucksack a sign on a piece of cardboard read 'US Marine Veteran, thank you'. Admiring music lovers danced and crowded around; one little girl placed ten bucks into a hat, smiled and thanked him for his service as his battered old acoustic guitar gave their memories a theme tune.

The DeadBeats

"Chill dude!" Cowboy grinned and took a long sip of his coffee. "This is nice just sitting here all alfresco, eating a burger, drinking coffee and watching the world go by!"

"We need to get going, Google maps says the hostel is just around the corner! Holly and Scott will be wondering where the hell we got to."

"Yeh about that...! Forget the hostel, he ain't there."

"How do you know that?"

Finishing his coffee Cowboy stood. "Because my friend we've been listening to him for the last twenty minutes."

Jumping up Mitch spun around to get a better view of the busker. "What? But that guy can sure as hell sing and he's a non-too-shoddy guitarist either!"

"Sure, he is but he's a whole lot better when he tickles the old ivories, if you catch my drift!"

Drawn to the melodic chords like moths to a light, they pushed through the dispersing crowd and arrived just as the busker finished a song. Carefully placing his guitar on the ground, he retrieved his upturned baseball cap, and noticing the large amount of money it contained he thanked his audience.

"Well, if it ain't my old friend Tony Chow?" Cowboy cried. "Long time no see dude!"

Tony squinted up and tried to remember the stranger before him. "Do I know you, gentlemen? Look if you've come from Big Ricky, you tell him he'll get his god dammed money! And if you're cops don't worry, I'm moving on, I'm going right now!"

Cowboy removed his hat. "It's me, Cowboy! You remember me?"

A dawn of realisation spread across Tony's face. "Cowboy...? Cowboy...? Is that really you?"

"Sure is Chow man!"

"Well, I'll be dammed! What the hell are you doing here?" He cried and held out his hand which Cowboy shook eagerly.

"Why, we came all the way down here just to find you! My friend here, his name is Mitch and he's got an offer you might want to consider."

"Well, guys I tend to listen better when I got a drink inside of me... And food, food also works." He said nervously scanning the street and the faces of the people milling about on the sidewalk. "Why don't we go somewhere a little less public?"

The DeadBeats

Shuffling across the blanket he had been sitting on Tony retrieved a wheelchair and proceeded to unfold it. "You guys wanna grab my stuff and we'll get out of here."

Throwing Mitch a look of shock Cowboy scooped up the guitar. "What's with the chair dude?"

"IED strike in Afghanistan...! They took both legs just below the knee!" Easily sliding into the chair, he avoided the stares of both of his visitors which he knew must surely be there. "Died twice in the chopper and once on the operating table in Bastion, But I'm still here so I don't want anyone feeling sorry for me... Especially you Cowboy because even in this chair I can still out-drink and outshoot you!"

Turning away Mitch grimaced.

Cowboy grinned. "Well, I don't know about that, maybe we'll get a chance for you to put your money where your mouth is."

The bar Tony had taken them to was a seedy and dimly lit basement room, down a backstreet and not the sort of place the tourists visited or even knew about. A huge flat-screen TV above the bar was showing American football as an ageing Juke box blasting out a Bon

Jovi track drowned out any hope of hearing the commentary.

Ordering drinks they moved to a table and sat down, all three of

them subconsciously opting for a position where they could see all of

the exits and protect their rear.

"OK, guys so what's going on? Why are you here?"

Mitch took a long sip of his Bud, and then he took a deep breath and

prepared himself. "I'm so sorry Tony, we came here to recruit you for

a Special Forces unit we're putting together. I need elite operators

and the best musicians...! I didn't know about your legs man... I know

it's shitty us showing up here like this!"

Tony laughed. "You came here without looking at my records...!"

"It's my fault!" Cowboy said apologetically. "I recommended you;

this is all on me man."

"Hey guys, it's ok; look on the bright side I made thirty-seven bucks

today. Yesterday it was only twenty-two, so you know things are

looking up!"

The DeadBeats

As three men entered the bar Tony slowly braced up. "Shit...!" He spat. "It was nice to see you again Cowboy, but you better take your friend and get out of here."

Following Tony's fleeting glances and scenting the sudden change in atmosphere Cowboy stood up, taking his empty bottle of Bud with him. He then removed his Stetson before carefully placing it on the table beside his sunglasses. "So, who are these clowns?"

"Hoods, they work for a guy called big Ricky... Just leave it Cowboy, this isn't your problem!"

"What is it? You owe him money?" Mitch said, sighed heavily and also stood up.

"No, these guys are here because he thinks I sort of slept with his daughter."

"And did you?"

"Kinda!"

"Kinda?"

"OK, so I slept with her... once or twice! It's no big deal- She's an adult for god's sake, he should just chill the hell out!"

As the three men approached the table Cowboy stepped between them and Tony. "Ok guy's, that's close enough!" He slurred feigning drunkenness and smiled. "Look! We know why you're here and we all know Tony can be a real asshole with the ladies but…!"

"I'm an asshole? Gee Cowboy I'm sure glad you're on my side!"

"That's right Tony is an ASSHOLE and he apologises for any upset he may have caused to you nice gentlemen and what's his name?"

"It's Ricky…!" Tony said. "His name is Big Ricky."

The three men stood menacing, motionless and silent.

Realising the situation wasn't going to end well Cowboy resigned himself to impending violence. "That's right my good friend here apologises to… Big Dicky…!" Cowboy laughed and still feigning drunkenness swayed unsteadily on his feet. "Big Dicky…! You guys see what I did there? Come on let's just sit down, have a drink and talk about it!"

"Get out of the way assholes!" One of the strangers growled and opening his jacket showed Cowboy and Mitch he was carrying a pistol. "This piece of shit ain't worth dying for, one way or another he's coming with us!"

The DeadBeats

"Gee Mitch I'm scared! He's got a gun, what should I do!" Cowboy cried and then burst out into laughter. "Sorry, I was just thinking about Big Dick… Too funny…!"

"Can you just stop playing around and hit the big guy."

Flipping the empty bottle in his hand so that he was holding it by the neck Cowboy jabbed the base into the face of the guy in the middle who stumbled backwards as blood exploded from his nose. Using his momentum, he then smashed it over the head of the hood to his right. Stunned by the speed of the attack the third man fumbled for his pistol but was floored by a single punch to the temple and unconscious before he hit the ground.

"It's ok Mitch I'm fine I didn't need any help! You just stand there and watch!" Cowboy said sarcastically. "I'll take care of everything!"

Mitch grinned and then turned to Tony. "The way I see it we need a keyboard player and you need to get the hell out of Dodge- Are you in?"

"Hell, yeah I'm in! But, dude I ain't got no legs!"

"I got a feeling you're gonna fit right in! Cowboy here ain't got no brain!"

Hiding under her wide-brimmed straw hat and oversized shades Roxana Luca opened her door and peered up and down the quiet Budapest cul-de-sac, looking for anyone loitering with a camera or notebook. Wearing a flowing yellow polka dot summer dress, white high heels and carrying a Versace clasp Roxy (as the press called her) was already late, with only a garbage truck doing its rounds and no sign of the usual paparazzi she stepped out onto the gravel drive and rushed to the safety of her sky-blue Porsche Carrera.

Roxana, a world-famous supermodel, would-be actress, pop star and advocate for animal rights and veganism breathed a sigh of relief as she slammed the door shut and gunned the car's powerful engines to life. Glancing at the screen on her iPhone several messages all told her the same thing, she wasn't just late she was only minutes away from missing the audition of her life.

Throwing the car into reverse she checked her mirrors and was aghast to see the refuge truck blocking her path.

The DeadBeats

"No..!" she cried and wound the window down for a better look. There was no gap and no way around. "Hello!" She cried out to the nearest refuge collector, a swarthy-looking man in orange overhauls. "Can you move the truck please; I'm late I need to get past."

Barely even bothering to look at her the man shrugged nonchalantly and then turned his back completely.

"Excuse me!" She cried angrily and with no reply, she jumped out of the car and strode over to the man prodding him on the shoulder. "I said excuse me...!"

Turning to face her. "Yes!" he replied simply.

"You're blocking me, I need to get out!"

"You will just have to wait five minutes! There is nothing else to do!"

"I can't wait!" She snapped angrily and removed her sunglasses so the man could see her face. "Do you know who I am?"

The man shrugged. "You wait!"

As she spun on her heels to return to her car the man suddenly reached out covering her mouth with a white cloth, momentarily confused she could offer little fight as the chemical took hold and soon passed out. Catching her before she hit the ground the man hoisted her up and easily tossed her into the back of the refuge truck. Then climbing onto the footplate of the truck he banged on the cab, a signal that they had their quarry.

Pushing his head through the open door of the RV Mitch looked inside. "Scott, Holly are you here?"

"Deserted man...! Where the hell have they gotten to?" Cowboy said.

"Jesus Christ...! This is all we need; I told them to stay the hell here!"

"Hold on a second!" Cowboy said and cocked his head. "I can hear singing and it's headed this way!"

Holding each other up and giggling at their inebriation Holly and Scott made their way toward the RV. It was raining men in a drunken staccato rhythm with a Scott-sized ad hoc rap attached wherever he could get a word in.

"You're drunk!" Mitch growled angrily.

The DeadBeats

Holly stood to attention and saluted. "Sir...! Hollybops and MC Scott reporting for duty sir!" She cried and stifled a barely concealed giggle. "Sir it is my duty to report that Hollybops and MC Scott having left their post did frequent a local bar and take part in a karaoke competition Sir! It is also my duty to report that said individuals having entered said competition did indeed win two hundred dollars with the song 'It's raining men! Sir...!'" Collapsing in a fit of giggles she withdrew the wad of notes from her pocket and waved them at Mitch and Cowboy.

"Get in the goddam RV, I'll speak to you when you're sober."

"Sir, yes Sir!"

"Hold on a minute," Scott said and doubled over. "I think I'm gonna puke!"

Chapter 6

Throwing the file clear across the table Colonel Harker glared at Mitch, struck dumb with anger, he forced out one single word. One that would open the door to a tirade of abuse. "Deadbeats...!" He spat through clenched teeth. "God dammed dead beats!"

"Sir, I couldn't just leave him there."

"Jesus H Christ Mitch! This ain't the Salvation Army!" Harker shook his head and then consciously tried to calm himself down. "Mitch, I can see you did this with good intentions but we are not the VA, I'm trying to put together a team of operators, and what have I got? I'll tell you what I've got, I got a rapper that I don't need, I got a woman with questionable special forces training and now to top it off you give me a man with all the skills but no legs!"

"Sir, give these guys a chance and I swear you won't be sorry!"

The DeadBeats

"Oh, I'm sure with a little rehearsal you deadbeats could entertain the troops, and sure maybe we can train Holly up to some standard but how in the hell are you planning to go into battle with a guy with no legs?"

"Well Sir, I've given this a lot of thought and I think maybe I have a plan!"

"This place is amazing," Tony said as he lifted himself clear of his wheelchair to get a closer look at the photograph of Glen Miller and his band. "Just look at these guys! And they were the first?" He said. "Amazing...!"

"I still haven't grown tired of all these old photographs," Holly said and pointed. "This is my favourite Elvis Presley standing right where I am now! The rest of the world thought he was in Germany and all the time he was right here."

Slumping into his chair Tony sighed heavily. "They're not going to let me stay, are they? How could they? I have no fucking legs! I should never have come here!"

"Mitch has been in with the Colonel for the last two hours, don't worry I'm sure he's doing all he can to keep you. You're one of us now!"

Cowboy, who up until now had been sat quietly on the third step of the staircase, suddenly spoke. "I gave them your name, it was me who got you here, if you go then so do I!"

"Me too...!" Scott added.

"We're a team!" Holly said. "One out, all out!"

"Guys I don't want you to do that... Please, I'll be fine!" Tony said. "I'll be just fine!"

Tony had barely finished speaking when Colonel Harker's office door suddenly opened and the two Officers strode out into the hallway.

"Ok, assholes." Harker barked. "Listen in; training begins tomorrow morning at zero six hundred hours. You have ten weeks to prove you have what it takes, I want no excuses, no dramas and certainly no womanising and drunkenness, and yes Cowboy I'm looking at you. Sergeant Chow welcome back into the military, if you don't know what 'blades" are I suggest you type the words Oscar and Pistorius

into YouTube and watch the videos because tomorrow you're getting
measured for them.

"What, really… Oh my god, I don't believe it!" Tony cried and
punched the air. "Yes...! Yes Sir...!"

"I wouldn't get too excited if I were you! You got more work to do
than the rest put together. Ok, you bunch of deadbeats I suggest you
get some food inside of you and turn in for the night." With that, he
returned to his office and slammed the door behind him.

Sidling up to Mitch Cowboy whispered in his ear. "How the hell did
you swing us keeping the Chow man...? You threatened to resign
your ass, didn't you?"

Ignoring the question Mitch simply smiled, turned on his heels and
headed for the kitchen and food. "Man, I could eat a horse between
two bread wagons, and I hear tell there's a refrigerator containing
some Macaroni cheese with my name written all over it!"

The call came late, just after midnight and just as Sherriff Manfredo
Ortega had thought Friday was done. Having spent most of the day

chasing illegal immigrants along the border, he was dusty, tired and stinking of dried sweat; not to mention hungry, man he was hungry.

"Control...!" He said wearily into the mic, causing the radio to crackle and beep.

"Control...!"

"You got any more on the incident?"

"That's a negative Sherriff, there's a truck driver at the scene awaiting your arrival."

"Copy that control, I'll be on location presently!"

Rounding the bend, the first thing he saw was the amber hazard warning lights of the truck, the second was a body lying in the road and the truck driver standing beside his parked trailer. "Oh, Shit man...!" He growled, pissed at the knowledge that this was going to be a long night. "God darn it!"

Pulling over, he opened the door and stepped out. "Sir...! What happened here?" He cried as the trucker walked toward him. "Did you hit him?"

"No Sir, he was already on the road when I got here- There's more back there, maybe you should take a look."

The DeadBeats

Kneeling beside the body he noted the shoulder rig and absent weapon, he also noted the single gunshot wound to the forehead. "Sir you might want to return to your cab this man has been shot!"

"Sherriff that's not all, like I said there's more back there!" The trucker said fearfully and indicated to an area beyond his trailer.

Following the trucker's ashen gaze, the Sherriff rose to his feet and unclipped his pistol. "What the hell happened here?" He said to himself, and moving to the front of the truck, he paused momentarily using the huge vehicle as cover while he surveyed the scene. Now with a weapon in one hand and flashlight in the other, he stepped out into the open; covering his arcs he began slowly moving forward. A second bullet-riddled and lifeless body pointed the way to a large vehicle partially hidden and embedded in the scrub.

Pushing his way through the undergrowth, he soon found himself looking up at the open door of a coach and the slumped form of the driver. Treading carefully on the broken glass he began to climb the steps and on moving inside he realised the coach wasn't a coach, but some kind of luxury high-end RV.

Using his flashlight, he made his way through the full length of the interior and searched the vehicle for signs of life or clues as to what

happened. Suddenly aware that he was treading on spilled paper h\
bent down and retrieved one of the crumpled sheets and turned it
over. Staring at the familiar image of four girls performing on a stage
in front of thousands of adoring fans, the Sherriff suddenly realised
where he'd seen it before; a larger version of the same picture
adorned his daughter's bedroom wall. "Strawberry Island..!" He said
as the picture tumbled from his hand.

Reaching for the mic clipped to his right shirt pocket, he pressed the
button. "Control, we have a situation here…!"

With a glass of milk and a huge bag of Doritos in one hand and a
triple-stacked plate of steaming ribs in the other Scott stepped into
the studio, and then stopped in his tracks. Beyond the control room,
he could just about make out the form of someone with a guitar. As
his eyes adjusted to the dimness, he realised the person sitting on the
piano stool in the middle of the darkened sound studio was Mitch.

He seemed to be intermittently playing chords and writing
something down in a book that was placed on top of the piano.

The DeadBeats

Slowly moving closer Scott Strained to hear but heard nothing as the room's soundproofing did its job a little too well. Finding himself at the control panel he placed his supper to one side and turned up the volume slide.

The movement caught Mitch's eye and he waved. "Hi Scot, couldn't you sleep too?"

"Oh, I can sleep man! I was just hungry. "

"I can't hear you! You need to press the speak button, why don't you get in here and tell me what you think…? I got a melody and a couple of verses but I'm kinda stuck now!"

Squeezing his huge frame through the door Scott offered Mitch the plate of ribs which was waved off. After placing the plate on top of the piano Scott sat at the drums. "Why don't you play, show me what you got."

"Ok, but it's kind of a work in progress. I'm ok with the music but the lyrics kinda suck!" Placing the guitar in its stand Mitch began to play the piano, his fingers deftly moving smoothly over the keys.

Suddenly holding up his hand to stop Mitch playing Scott grinned. "I like the melody but why don't we give it some beat? Let's go again!" He said and picked up the drumsticks.

Eying his friend quizzically Mitch placed his fingers back on the keyboard, after four notes Scott began to match the melody with a drum beat. "There you go!"

"I like it!" Mitch grinned. "I didn't know you played."

"You never asked… But FYI I can play just about any instrument to a certain level; I'm just not what you might call stage worthy!"

Shadows and movement in the control room signalled the arrival of Cowboy. Who, without a word walked into the studio, picked up a guitar and began laying his base against the beat.

Eyes closed and lost in rhythm Scott was oblivious to Holly's appearance and obvious irritation at someone else playing what she considered to be her drum kit. "What the hell...? You think they brought me here to make the tea!" She cried as she prodded him fiercely on his shoulder. "Get the hell off my stool, Scott!"

Grinning mischievously, he handed her the drumsticks and quickly moved out of the way allowing her to take up position. "Don't mind me; I'll just be over here looking for a tambourine or maybe a triangle!"

"Let's not get too far ahead of ourselves cupcake, you should probably just stand in the corner and hum for now!" Cowboy said and laughed.

"Just do it quietly!"

"Very funny Hollybobs...! If anyone wants me, I'll be playing with all the shiny buttons in the control booth!"

"Try not to break anything!"

"This is bullying man!" Scott said sullenly, and then he grabbed his milk, Doritos and ribs. "These are mine; don't nobody be asking now cos' you ain't getting none; Get your own!"

Sealing himself in the control room, Scott sat down and pressed the speak button. "Ok guys let's do that again from the top."

Chapter 7

Carrying her open laptop, Holly rushed into the studio and placed it on the desk. "Have you seen this?" She cried breathlessly.

Mitch and Cowboy ceased their strumming and looked up; loath to leave their muse they both unplugged their guitars and joined Holly in the control booth.

"So, what's a cooking' Hollybops?" Cowboy said grinning.

"Look!" She said. "Two of those girls that went missing have turned up; they're streaming live right now!"

"So!" Mitch said. "Doesn't that kinda mean they weren't missing to start with?"

"Yes! But according to the commentary they're about to fight to the death, in something called the Fame Game!"

"I told you they'd show up eventually!"

The DeadBeats

"Fight to the death! Come on!" Cowboy laughed. "You don't think it's real, do you?"

"I think I do! I've seen the news interviews with the families of these girls, and honestly, I think they were kidnapped!"

"Get the hell out 'a here Holly!" Mitch laughed. "It's just a stunt on one of those dumb reality shows! Hell, it's even got a name; it's called the Fame Game."

Turning up the volume she turned to Mitch. "Just shut the hell up and watch!"

"Ladies and Gentlemen welcome to the world's greatest Game! The Fame Game...!" Said a computer-disguised but clearly German-accented voice as video footage of each missing girl showed them sitting in their cells. "As you can see, we have selected only the most beautiful, talented girls for your entertainment and delight. Ten contestants are about to begin a journey that

only one can survive! That's right boys and girls only one gets to live to be famous forever and the best part? Well, the best part is it's entirely your decision, you get to vote who lives and who... dies!"

Suddenly the laptop screen flickered and the images of the girls disappeared to be replaced with a large golden star.

"Is this guy serious?" Cowboy said. "I mean, really...?"

Mitch shrugged. "It's just a lame publicity stunt, those girls; well, those girls will turn up soon enough!" Using his index finger, he closed Holly's laptop. "I suggest we all turn in; I hear the boss is getting up at dumb o'clock to meet his training team."

"Wait, what? Why the hell do we need a training team?"

"Cowboy, your guess is as good as mine!"

"And now it's time, ladies and gentlemen; boys and girls. You're watching the Fame Game and your votes have been counted, they have been weighed and they have been verified. Tonight, streaming live for your delight Brianne Moore-Masterson will take on Amelie Caron in the Fame Games Top Trumps." Fake applause rattled around the room bouncing off the stone walls and cardboard cut-out audience.

Peering into the monitor Brianne shuddered at the state of her reflection, and hardly recognising the mascara-stained mess staring back at her began to sob. "I just want to go home!" She said tearfully and nervously looking at the woman sitting beside her added. "Why

won't they let me go home?"

The woman, her face bruised and bloodied, he hands trembling with

fear, swallowed hard and moistened her dry lips with a small darting

tongue. "We are taken!" She uttered in a thick French accent. "I fear

we are in great peril; I think maybe they want to kill us!"

"My name is Brianne!" She whispered.

"I know who you are! We will not be friends only one of us will

survive this night. That person is me!" Amelie said, her voice was

cold, hard and monotone.

"You will answer five questions each, the winner will go through to

the next round; the loser... Will not!" More wild applause filled the

makeshift studio. "And so we begin; Amelie you will go first! In July

this year who received the most likes on Instagram you or Brianne?"

Nervously looking into the camera Amelie frowned as she tried to

cast her mind back to that month. "Err... Brianne...! No wait! I don't

know, maybe it was me... I'm going to say I did!"

"Amelie, you received five thousand two hundred and fifty-three,

mostly down to your incessant and quite frankly sickening social

media coverage of your grandmother's death and your subsequent inheritance." The voice paused while fake hisses and boos filled the room. "Brianne, I can tell you now that you received a grand total of four hundred and twenty-two. Both a paltry and pathetic amount, but hardly surprising as at that time your father had checked you into rehab for your little cocaine addiction, and you thought we didn't know about that. Amelie wins the question."

More wild applause.

"Brianne your question is this! Which of you has the most failed celebrity relationships?"

Brianne smiled wryly, her father often accused her of spending all of her time on social media, which of course was true. Fortunately, on this occasion, Instagram and Facebook had ensured that she already knew the answer. Glancing over at her competitor she began to believe she could survive this particular game. "She did!" She said as confidently as she could. "Three cancelled weddings, one cancelled engagement and an affair with a married man!"

Wild cheers and applause rang out.

"And so contestants, we stand at one all, and now to the next round! This year Brianne drunkenly crashed her boyfriend's car on purpose to publicly punish him for kissing another woman, Amelie what was the make and colour of said vehicle?"

Her eyebrows furrowed as she stared at the woman beside her. "It… it was definitely blue, no wait, it was red; I'm going to say it was a red car. Maybe it was a Porsche Or an Aston Martin! I, I don't know!"

"I need an answer!"

"It… it was a red Porsche!"

"Brianne, why don't you give her the bad news!"

"I'm so sorry." She said as she bit her lip. "It… It was an orange Mustang!"

With the realisation that she was now behind, tears of terror began to well in Amelie's eyes before barrelling down her cheeks, and as the recognition of her fate began to dawn, she grabbed Brianne's hand and held it tightly.

"So, the scores stand at two to one in favour of Brianne; If she answers this next question correctly she wins!" The voice paused for what seemed like an age to the two girls. "Brianne, last year Amelie's seventeen-year-old sister was photographed in a compromising position with a much older movie action hero; To win through to the next round I want you to tell me and all of the people at home the names of his poor wife and three children?"

Her lips dry and trembling, Brianne opened her mouth to speak and paused while she glanced helplessly at her competitor; before bursting into tears. "I won't do it!" She blubbed. "You... You can't make me; I want to go home; I just want to go home!"

"Answer or forfeit!"

"I can't...!"

"Brianne..! Is that your final answer?"

Chapter 8

Holly stared at the headline plastered across the front page of the newspaper, and let her mind absorb the information it conveyed. "She's dead!" She said the words with surprise and utter disbelief.

Pausing his relentless channel hopping on Sponge Bob square pants, Cowboy tossed the remote control onto the cushion beside him. Boredom and a lack of alcohol forced the question from his lips. "Who's dead?"

"Amelie Caron's body has been found in a Paris hotel room… My god, he's killing them; that dumb game is actually killing them!"

"Ain't that Brianne chick half American or some such?"

"Yeah, on her mother's side."

"Well, I guess Uncle Sam's gonna have to poke his big old nose into things now!"

"Someone mention Uncle Sam?" Colonel Harker asked as he popped his head around the door frame. "You guys... If you would care to join everyone else outside, it would be very much appreciated."

"What's going on?" Holly said.

"Snap to it, Marines! Cowboy, that means you too! Outside now!"

Holly sighed. "Oh geez, I sure don't like the sound of this."

Following the Colonel into the coolness of the twilight air, they joined Mitch and Scott who were already waiting.

"So, what's happing Mitch?" Cowboy said and sat down on the top step.

"I don't know, but it can't be good!"

"Ok guys, settle down; I got you out here for a little meet and greet." The Colonel smiled mischievously. "We have very little time and much to do, and to that end, the Marine Corps has kindly donated their very finest to act as your training team!"

Cowboy let out an audible groan, and the others turned and stared at him. "You were right, Mitch this ain't good!" He said. "Ain't good at all!"

The DeadBeats

The roar of motorcycles suddenly filled the air and only got louder as they came into view.

"I got a bad feeling about this!" Holly said as the bikes stopped in a line and the riders turned their engines off.

"Boys and girls, I give you SEAL team 4!"

"Hey, Holly!" Scott said. "Look at the guy on the end, isn't that the dude you threatened to scoop his eyeball out with a spoon?"

"No, it was a fork!"

"You in trouble girl, big trouble!"

The bikers dismounted and kicked their stands out before strolling over to Colonel Harker. In the blink of an eye, their demeanour went from west coast biker to full-on Marine.

"Sir, Seal team 4 reporting for duty Sir!" Their leader said and sprung to attention."

"Thanks, Gunny, but I don't want to see any more of that military bullshit while you're here; no ranks, no drill and certainly no uniforms. I take it you've had time to peruse the training package Gunnery Sergeant Carter emailed you yesterday.

The Gunny nodded and flicked a sideways glance at Mitch.

"You and your boys have just six weeks to turn my team into a cohesive and effective fighting unit. OK, they're all yours!" And with that Colonel Harker turned and strode back up the steps and into the house.

Gunny waited for Harker to leave before speaking. "Ladies, I'm guessing you remember us from the diner!"

Cowboy sneered and glared at Scarface.

"Well, me and my boys ain't all bad! We engineered that meeting to find out what kind of people you are and the good news is you're my kind of people."

"That sure is a dangerous game you were playing!" Scott said and looked over at Scarface. "Someone could have got real hurt!"

Scarface laughed. "Relax big guy; that waitress you guys rescued was my wife! Hell, she doesn't even work there, she's an actress!"

"So, you were only pretending to be an asshole!" Holly said.

"Oh no, I really am an asshole! I just don't go around touching up waitresses! Nice move with the fork by the way!"

Gunny held up his hand to silence his man. "My men and I are not your friends; we will never be your friends. We are here to do a job, which we intend to do well. It will be tough and I don't expect all of you to be here at the end. What I do expect is determination and teamwork! Do not let yourselves down, do not let your team down. Over the next twenty-four to thirty-six hours, I intend to assess you as individuals and as a team. What happens after that depends on how well you do- and I suggest people, you do well!"

Scarface piped up. "Your physical assessment begins at 0400 hours; I want you in sweats and running shoes! Ladies, my advice is that you get some food inside you and turn in for the night. I'll see you on the helipad."

"Jeez, Mitch!" Cowboy groaned. "I didn't sign me up for no boot camp!"

"Me either!" Scott added.

"Guys, we've all done this shit before; a little running never hurt anyone!" Holly said as she watched the motorbikes disappear down the drive. "I say we show these assholes what we can do."

"I tell you now, they'll make us run a few miles, maybe do a few press-ups; a few sit-ups and just generally make us sweat; don't worry about it!"

"Well, guys it's way past my bedtime so I'll be seeing you all in hell!" Cowboy said and then added. "0400? Why so goddam early?"

"Yeah, I was just thinking the very same thing!" Mitch said and headed inside. "Goodnight, see you all in the morning!"

Opening his eyes Mitch wondered if he was dreaming, yawning lazily he rubbed his eyes and felt that it was surely only moments since he fell asleep; but the clock on his bedside table told him it was shortly after midnight.

The noise was quite real and from the din emanating from the ground floor, it sounded like a riot was taking place. "Goddam Cowboy, you better not be drunk again!" Mitch grumbled and sat up on the edge of the bed.

No sooner had he tied the laces on his old running shoes than his room door suddenly burst open and several masked men dressed in black rushed in and wrestled him to the floor. Hooding him, they tie wrapped his hands behind his back and pinned him to the floor.

The DeadBeats

Gasping for breath, he fought against the ties that bound him but soon gave up when he realised there was no hope of escape. "Who are you? What's happening?" He cried, but deep down he knew exactly who they were and what they were doing.

Soon they dragged him to his feet and frog-marched him outside, where he was roughly loaded onto a Humvee. "Where are you taking me?"

"Shut your mouth! Don't speak unless asked a question!" A voice growled in his ear. "The big guy has hospitalised two of my men; tell him to stop struggling or we'll taser him!"

Mitch grinned. "Scott!" He shouted. "Scott, it's alright; Put the nice men down and do as they say!"

The sounds of violence and cries of pain immediately ceased, only to be replaced by the sound of the Humvees engine as the vehicle charged down the road.

"You'll soon be loaded onto a chopper!" The voice said. "When we drop you off the physical assessment begins; It comprises a half-mile swim, a one-hundred-meter free climb and a thirty-mile hike over rough terrain- Once you hit the beach, you are to locate a rucksack; the rucksack contains suitable clothing, boots, a map and a compass.

If you drowned you fail, if you fall you fail, If you are captured by my men you fail and if you do not reach the house within eight hours you fail- Do you understand?"

Mitch nodded.

The vehicle slowed to a halt and two men dragged Mitch out of the door and threw him to the ground, landing heavily he grimaced. "Hey, assholes watch what you're doing!" He growled, only to suddenly feel the impact of a boot on his ribcage. The pain exploded across his torso knocking the air from his lungs, gasping for oxygen he raged and fought the ties that bound him. "When this is over me and you are going to be having words!"

"I told you to keep your mouth shut tough guy!"

"Untie me, we'll see how tough you are!"

The man laughed. "Load him into the chopper."

Hauled to his feet and still gasping to regain his composure, the two men dragged him across the helipad and then pushed him onto the floor of a Black hawk.

"I swear to god, if you touch me one more time, I'll rip your arms off!" Scott growled through clenched teeth, it was all he could do to not snap the tie wraps binding his wrist and beat the pair of them to death.

Dwarfing his kidnappers, they barely stood level with his chest and sensing his barely contained rage they threw each other a look of caution; even though he was hooded and bound, roughing this one up wouldn't end well for them.

"Point me in the direction of the dammed chopper!"

Climbing aboard, a voice ordered him to sit on the floor which he duly obeyed.

"Hey, who's that? Is that you, Scott?"

"Shut the hell up!"

"Yeh, You ok?"

"Yeh I'm ok- It would take more than these pussies…!" The sudden arrival of another vehicle beside the chopper abruptly ended the conversation.

"Take your hands off me, you prick!" Holly shrieked furiously as she was shoved violently out of the back of the Humvee and then physically picked up. Headbutting her assailant, he dropped her and stumbled back. Instantly two more pair of hands grabbed her, dragging her kicking and screaming to the helicopter.

"Pipe down people! We're about to go airborne and I would hate for any of you pussies to accidentally fall out of the door!" Gunny said and smiled at his own joke.

"Screw you!" Holly barked.

As the rotors wound up and the chopper began to lift, their hoods were finally removed. "This is not a team effort; you are to complete this test as an individual!" The Gunny said. "The lake is five miles long, and you will be dropped at intervals of approximately one mile apart- Do you all understand what is expected of you?" He said and glared at each one of them until he received a nod. "The first man goes in five minutes."

"Don't you think you should untie us first?" Mitch said.

The Gunny grinned. "What? And spoil all the fun! Hell, I'm just messing with you! Cut them loose boys!"

Ignoring the signal to turn around to give the Marine access to the tie wrap, Scott simply tore his wrists apart snapping the plastic straps with ease. "I'll go first!" He said grumpily. "If I have to spend one more minute inside this whirlybird, someone is going to have their

asses kicked."

As the Chopper came to a halt and hovered some thirty feet above

the lake the Gunny threw open the door and tossed out the fast rope.

"Don't forget you got just eight hours."

"Yeh, yeh..!" And with that, the big man disappeared out the door,

and into the night.

"Holly, you wanna go next!"

"No, not really, but I guess I got no choice!" She said and made her

way to the open door.

"Have you got fast rope experience?"

"No...! I'll take the express route!" She said and jumped into the

night.

"That one sure has got balls of steel!" The Gunny cried above the

roar of the rotors. "Not sure I would have jumped!"

"Can you see her? Is she swimming?"

"This is a test, there are no backsies! Ok, Cowboy, you're up!"

Peering out of the door Cowboy shuddered. "Hell Mitch, it sure

does look cold down there!" Then he turned to Gunny. "I'll be seeing

you guys later... Stay frosty people!" Expertly descending the thick rope to within feet of the water, he allowed himself to drop into the lake. Surfacing with cold shock, he gasped for air and knowing he had to exit the freezing water as soon as possible he struck out for the distant shoreline.

Maintaining a steady rhythm and controlling her breathing, Holly forced the searing pain of the sub-zero temperatures from her mind. Concerned about the onset of hyperthermia, she knew that her priority was to exit the water and get dry as quickly as possible.

After what seemed like an age she finally touched the lake bed, stood up and waded ashore; and with a stroke of luck, she spotted her rucksack just fifty yards off to her left placed on a rock.

Breathlessly jogging over to it, she tore open the drawstring and pulled out the contents which included a full set of fatigues, socks and boots; quickly stripping naked she donned the dry clothes and then sat down to put the socks and boots on. Warming quickly the shivers soon ceased allowing her to look at the map and take stock of where she was.

Once she was satisfied with her bearing and direction of travel, she folded the map and placed it in her pocket with the compass; then hitting the cliff hard she began climbing.

Not built for climbing, Scott struggled and cursed his way up the cliff face; in a matter of minutes, he had gone from angry, wet and cold to angrier, sweating and exhausted. Taking an opportunity to regain his breath, he rested his rapidly tiring body on a narrow ledge. Gulping in mouthfuls of air he strained his eyes through the darkness of the night trying to see how his comrades were faring, but saw nothing and no one.

Knowing time was against him he sighed heavily and began climbing again. "Man...!" He said breathlessly. "I just wanted to make music... Goddam it!" after twenty more minutes of grunting and scrambling the vertical climb became less steep and the going easier. Soon enough the granite gave way to vegetation and Scott finally collapsed on the summit. As he lay there for a while he stared up at the starry sky and allowed his breathing to calm and heart rate to normalise. "I don't deserve this..!" He growled. "Not one little bit!"

Judging that he still had approximately seven hours left to cover the thirty miles, his spirits were raised by the simple mathematics of his situation. As long as he kept to a decent pace, he knew that he could speed march the distance comfortably, and as long as there were no complications or navigational issues he could avoid having to run, and boy did he want to avoid running.

Taking the map and compass from his pocket he took a magnetic bearing on a distant mast blinking in the darkness; and once satisfied of his direction of travel set off.

Gaining height easily Mitch reached the top of the cliff in quick time, kneeling he listened to the noises of the night, acclimatising his senses to the world around him; to the crickets and the birds, he listened to the sway of the grass and creaking of the trees. Knowing the training team would be keen to target him he was loath to take a direct route, which they would probably be expecting. After a quick look at his map, he figured a dog-leg around to an old logging track in the north may add five miles to his route but he had more chance of avoiding his pursuers.

The DeadBeats

Assuming SEAL team 4 had staked out the top of the cliff Mitch moved stealthily through the undergrowth. Slowly traversing away from the lake, he stayed in the shadows and allowed the North Star to guide him. As the ground opened up and he was forced out into the open he had no choice but to begin his run for home.

Thankfully, the heavily worn game trails eventually gave way to the old logging tracks which he had noticed earlier on the map. Now warming to the task and almost enjoying the solitude, he could open up his stride and begin to eat into the many miles ahead of him.

A short, shrill scream suddenly cut through the night, erupting out of the darkness, Mitch immediately skidded to a halt and then very slowly sank to his knees. His first thought was has Holly been caught, but he knew she wouldn't scream like that. This was guttural and full of terror; was it an animal, a bird or was the sheer eeriness of the night playing tricks on his mind? Remaining motionless he listened. Something, somewhere in his gut told him this was no Coyote or wild cat. Scanning his arcs of fire, he suddenly felt naked without his sidearm.

Somewhere in the far distance, beyond the impenetrable veil of dense vegetation and towering trees, the sounds of a man shouting angrily could be heard intermixed with the faint almost imperceptible noise of a woman sobbing.

Glancing in the direction he should be travelling Mitch cursed under his breath, whatever the noises he was hearing were; he simply couldn't ignore them. Somewhere out there in the night, someone was in a lot of trouble.

Silently moving off, he headed through the brush allowing the angry man to guide his direction. As the voices grew louder so did the unmistakable scent of death, of rotting flesh and spilled blood, which Mitch knew only too well.

Hidden just inside the treeline, he crouched down in a small dip behind a clump of grass and observed the small dilapidated log cabin some fifty meters away. Now closer to the building, it was clear multiple women were sobbing and begging not to be harmed.

With the darkness on his side, he broke cover and dashed over to a battered old Toyota pickup parked beside the cabin. Noticing the keys had been left in the ignition, he quickly and silently pocketed them. The stench of death was now heavy in the air and as he rounded the cabin he saw why; several dead hogs were strung up in a

tree, their guts spilled and still steaming in the dirt.

Quietly making his way to a window he dared to peek inside, a

split-second glance was all he needed. Two men armed with

crossbows and hunting knives stood menacingly over three

somewhat battered, bruised and bloodied girls. Their half-naked

prisoners huddled in terror; eyes averted not daring to look at the

snarling monsters before them.

"Blondie's mine!" One of them growled. "I sure gotta have me a

piece of that! She gonna be my wife! She gonna love me and cook

me some hog!"

"You hurt'em, Ray!" Said the other one, his voice whiny and full of

fear. "They told us not to hurt them!"

"Shut up… I ain't handing these pieces of ass over to anyone! I'm

keeping 'em! No one knows we're here; we can have some fun. Hell,

we can do what we like all the ways out here in the middle of

nowhere! These here girls are my bitches now!"

Mitch had heard more than enough; moving to the door he placed a

hand on the latch and taking a deep breath he steadied himself. This

was no action film, this was real life and there would be no outrageous rescue plan; what this situation required was rapid, direct and extreme violence.

Like the fuse on a grenade, Mitch gave himself a countdown and then exploded through the door. Paralysed with shock the two men failed to react in time; the first step inside brought him instantly within range of the smaller of the two men who Mitch felled with a single, vicious punch to the throat.

By now the second man's brain was attempting to compute the attack and he was bringing his crossbow to bear. He was too slow, Mitch took a half step to his right and grabbed a full handful of the man's groin, twisting violently with every ounce of strength he could muster. The big man froze, abject unconscionable pain fried every brain cell in his head, unable to move or scream or even think he just stood mouth agape and stared at the man before him.

"Hi, Ray... I'm Mitch!" He said and smiled. "How do you feel about being my little bitch!!"

Unable to reply, Ray stared mindlessly back.

"No..! Are you not up for that? Well, I gotta say Ray, I'm real disappointed!" Tipping his head back slightly to give himself more

133

leverage Mitch smashed his forehead into Ray's nose and released his grip on the man's groin."

Ray stood motionless, his mindless eyes staring into space; as his hands slowly released the crossbow, his knees began to buckle and he toppled over, smashing his head on the corner of a table as he slumped to the ground.

"Girls, you can stop with the whole crying thing now, you're safe, I'm going to get you all out of here." Walking over to one of the hunters' beds he snatched up three horse blankets and tossed them to the girls. "Get yourselves warm and covered up and get yourselves in the pick up outside. While you're doing that, I'll be tying up the Chuckle brothers here! Snap to it people, I'm on the clock so some urgency please!"

"Who are you? What you did was amazing!" Said the red-haired girl and the only one who wasn't still crying.

"Oh, I'm Mitch! Who are you girls? How did you end up here?"

"We're Strawberry Island!"

Mitch paused and stared at the girl. "Strawberry Island?" He asked, "What's a Strawberry Island?"

Unaccustomed to this dose of pop ignorance she frowned. "Well..!

We're the group!" She said, but noticing the look of puzzlement on

his face she suddenly felt the need to add context. "We're the group

Strawberry Island, we're singers... Have you never heard of us?

We're quite well known you know! We were kidnapped by those two

pervs!"

Suddenly the penny dropped. "Oh, right... Yeah sure, sure I've

heard of you!"

"So, who are you? Are you like, the police or something..?"

Mitch smiled as he tried to bide time for his brain to work out a

believable excuse for his presence, but he couldn't come up with

anything that would sound even barely credible. "err..! No, actually

I'm like you; I'm a singer in a band- Time for introductions later,

right now I think we should just get the hell out of here!"

Chapter 9

The Sherriff's jeep slowly crawled up the drive, and then came to a halt before the questioning, frowning gazes of several Navy seals and one Colonel. Opening the door, Mitch stepped out into the morning sun and gave Cowboy and Scott a nod before turning to Colonel Harker.

"What the..?" Harker scowled. "You better not be about to tell me you got arrested?"

Sighing wearily, Mitch shook his head. "You're not gonna believe this, but I sort of ran into a little trouble along the way..."

"Join your men, I'll speak to you later; we're just waiting for Holly looks like she failed the test too."

"Holly's not here?" He turned to Scott and Cowboy. "You guys not seen her?"

Both men shook their heads and Cowboy added. "Maybe we should go look for her."

"It's ok, I'm here; don't move, I'll be right down."

Everyone's heads followed the sound of her voice and quickly settled on the second-floor open window and Holly's beaming face.

"Sorry guys, I kinda got tired of waiting, so I came up to my room and took a quick shower; I hope you don't mind sir."

Harker grinned, he couldn't help it. "It's fine Marine, as you were! Get dressed and get your butt down here!"

Ducking back inside Holly panicked and removed the bath gown to reveal a huge stinking lie, she also revealed wet and muddied fatigues. Stripping naked she dashed into the bathroom and showered at breakneck speed, and then dressed in a clean tracksuit without drying herself. Slipping her trainers on as she rushed from her room, she sprinted down the main staircase and only slowed to an amble as she emerged into the morning sun.

"Hi, guys." She said casually and threw Cowboy a look. "What kept you? I've been waiting here over an hour?"

"Sure, you have!" He said with a smirk on his lips and eyed her with suspicion. "What's up? Did you lose your towel?"

"Ok pipe down!" Colonel Harker barked. "If I find out any of you cheated, you will do the test again tonight, and mark my words this time I'll double the distance! Now get yourselves cleaned up, get some food inside of you and meet me out here in two hours; I managed to get the shooting range booked for you today, the training team will be sharpening your weapon handling and hostage situation skills. Mitch I'd like to see you in my office right away!"

Following the Colonel up the steps he wondered how on earth he could ever make his story believable; he hardly believed it himself.

"So, let's have it Captain Calvert, tell me in words of one syllable how in god's name you ended up being dropped off by the local sheriff… And please don't tell me you got yourself arrested!"

"Well, Sir it's like this; you remember that big-time girl group that went missing last week…?"

The Colonel frowned. "Kinda!"

"Well, Sir… I kinda found them!"

Cowboy levelled his Glock at the target and fired off a double tap to the chest and then a single shot to the forehead. "You cheated, I know you cheated; you didn't complete the swim quicker than me, you certainly didn't scale that cliff quicker than me and the run... Please, no frigging way! You cheated!"

"It kills you to think that a woman can beat you at something! Doesn't it?" Holly said and kicked a door in before firing at an effigy of a terrorist holding a bomb. "Maybe you're just not as good as you think you are!"

"Cupcake, you cheated, I know you cheated and nothing will ever change my mind!" Cowboy quickly reloaded and allowed the working parts of his pistol to ease forward. "I just want to know how you did it- I'm kinda guessing you took a cab or hitch-hiked!"

"Or, you massive asshole, maybe I just swam, climbed and ran quicker than you did, and you can't accept the fact that I'm better than you!"

"You cheated!"

Dissing loudly, she shook her head in mock disappointment. "Well, I guess you will never know!"

The DeadBeats

"Ok, we're done, looks like all the bad dudes are dead, let's get the hell out of here!"

"You two, either cut the chitter chatter or get a room! You're like an old married couple!" The range master barked.

Holly scoffed at the mere thought and Cowboy pulled a face of horror.

"Good score, excellent skills now get out of here and send the next pair in."

Making their way back to the start, they removed the magazines from their weapons and made them safe. "The shooting and all is kinda good but I sure am looking forward to getting back into the studio; gotta get myself some serious guitar time!"

Replacing her range glasses with sunglasses, Holly nodded. "Roger that!"

"Mitch, Scott you're up; Only way you're gonna beat our score is if you cheat!" Cowboy said sarcastically as he looked at Holly.

"Dear god Cowboy can't you just shut your big fat mouth!"

"You wanna know how I know you cheated?"

"Sure, you're going to tell me anyway!"

"I know... Because I sure as hell cheated, and you were here well before me!"

"You are such an asshole," Holly said and then laughed. "I won't even ask; I guess it involved a cell phone hidden about your person and a call to some adoring young woman who just happened to be in the area in err I'm guessing, a little red pick-up!"

"Wait a goddam minute... How do you know it was red?"

"While you were busy smooching in the front I was slipping under the tarp!"

"No way!" He laughed. "I guess Scott is the only one who actually completed the test- Who's gonna be the one to tell him?"

"Don't look at me, I ain't telling him shit! I say we keep our mouths firmly shut!"

Brianne hugged her knees tight to her chest, her only defence against the freezing chill as it cut deep to her bones causing her to shiver uncontrollably. Gently feathering her dry and cracked lips with her tongue, she suddenly realised she had neither lipstick to cover the unsightliness nor Chapstick with which to ease her suffering. The cold was one thing but being without a mirror and make-up was unbearable, she imagined what she must look like and tears began to well in her eyes and for the first time since she was a child she didn't have to worry about smearing her mascara.

"Brianne!"

The now familiar voice made her jump. "Get lost!" She said and wiped her eyes.

"Brianne, you are now streaming live to the world... Why don't you give your fans a wave? They're all rooting for you!"

"Fuck you!"

"Congratulations you're still alive, which means you made it to the next round. Through your social media, the whole world has witnessed your dedication to physical training. From Pilates to Yoga and from weights to the rowing machine your endless pursuit of physical perfection is there for all to see.

"Leave me alone!"

"Brianne today you have been selected for the game entitled 'Run for freedom'! While you slept we took the opportunity to place a running machine in your room..."

Wiping her mouth, she glanced around the room until her eyes fell on the machine, it was no little coincidence that it was the same machine as the one she had at home. "Dick head!" she mumbled.

"I can see what you're thinking and yes you are right this is your very own running machine taken two days ago from your villa!" He paused to chuckle at his own genius. "Brianne, in front of me I have every time from every run you ever posted on social media; today you must run not for your life but for Zack's...!"

She frowned. "What...? I don't understand!"

"Oh dear, this will upset him, I'm talking about Zack, your first boyfriend, your first love and the boy you dumped to go backpacking around Australia!"

"What's happening? What have you done?"

"He's here Brianne, he's come all this way just for you! So, for viewers at home this is what is going to happen. Brianne's personal time for ten kilometres is forty-two minutes, all she has to do to save her ex-boyfriend's life is beat her record!"

"Fuck you! He's not here, you don't have him!"

The DeadBeats

"You have five minutes beginning now, to start running; if you fail to run he dies, if you fail to beat your best time he dies. What the hell I might just kill him anyway!"

"You don't have him...! You can't!" She suddenly doubted her own words. "Prove it! Let me speak to him!"

"NO! You now have four minutes and thirty-three seconds!"

"I don't believe you!"

"I don't care what you believe, but I strongly suggest you climb aboard that running machine Brianne- If you fail this, mark my words, he will die! You now have three minutes to start the run!"

Climbing off the bed she eyed the running machine with terror, she felt weak and exhausted and seriously doubted she could complete this task. "I can't do it- Please don't kill him!"

"This is insane!" Holly said, unable to take her eyes from the computer screen, she waved the others to come and watch. "You gotta see this!"

"Jeez Hols, What the hell!" Cowboy said pained at having to watch yet more internet computer crap. "You know we all got better things to be doing."

"If Brianne doesn't run ten kilometres in under forty-two minutes they're going to kill her ex-boyfriend!"

"Has she started running yet?" Mitch said as he looked up from some sheet music.

"She just climbed on the machine… There she goes, she's started!" Completely engrossed in the spectacle, Holly fell silent.

"She's panicking, running too fast; that girl is going blow out before she's halfway!" Suddenly interested, Cowboy muscled in beside Holly to get a better view.

"Come on Brianne!" Holly said. "Slow down, pace yourself and control your breathing! You can do this!"

"You do know that she can't hear you!"

Holly frowned. "Shut up knuckled head… I know that!"

"Five bucks says the ex-boyfriend's a stiff by midnight!"

"You're on dipshit!"

Starting the run, Brianne tried to steady her breathing and fell into a tired and lethargic pace; with every step, her confidence and speed fell. Stumbling to her knees the machine spat her out onto the floor, where she collapsed sobbing. "I can't...! I can't do it!" She cried.

"Then he dies right now! Or Brianne, you can use some of that self-determination and belief that you like to preach to us lesser mortals on social media!"

"Screw you!"

"Come on girl!" Cowboy spat. "Get on your feet, get on your feet and run!"

Holly turned and frowned. "I thought you didn't care; dead by midnight and all that!"

"I don't like bullies and that asshole is the grade-A kind! I just hope someone gets the chance to put a bullet in his face!"

"They gotta find him first," Mitch said as he popped his head over Holly's shoulder to take a look at the laptop screen. "Look out of the window above the running machine..."

"I see a snowy mountain peak."

"That's right Cowboy, a snowy mountain peak and I'm sure the boys at Intel are trying to ID it as we speak!"

"If he's made one mistake..." Holly said. "He'll sure as hell make more!"

"Look at the window itself; small, barred and see the walls... I've seen walls like those when I was stationed in Germany; It's a castle, he's holed up in a castle in some European mountain range..." Mitch smiled. "There can't be that many of them!"

"So that means he's rich," Holly added. "Dirty filthy stinking rich!"

"What's that by the wall, it's glowing?" Cowboy said. "It appeared out of nowhere."

"Some kind of light... I don't know, it wasn't there a moment ago, I think it's moving towards her!"

The feeling was brief and fleeting, like the warmth from a distant candle, the unmistakable feeling of someone else standing beside her.

Brianne wiped the tears from her eyes and dared to look up. "Who's there? Doofus is that you?" She whispered.

"Who the hell is she talking to?" Cowboy said. "I don't see no one else."

"She's getting up, I don't believe it she's getting back on the machine!" Holly said in disbelief. "Come on Brianne you can do this!"

"She can't hear you!"

"Shut up!"

The presence gave her strength and no longer feeling the loneliness of recent days Brianne began to run. "I know you're here Doofus!" She whispered. "I can feel you! I can hear you!"

Chapter 10

"Operators welcome to Fort Benning and Jump school; my name is Sergeant Alex Johnson, and I'll be your chief instructor whilst you're here at 1st Battalion of the 507th; I understand you are all Jump trained, so today as a refresher we will be doing a HALO jump. If all goes well we'll move on to the rigid wing."

"Rigid wing?" Holly said and then tapped Cowboy on the shoulder. "What exactly is a rigid wing?"

"It's exactly what the man says, it's a wing that's kinda... Well, it's kinda rigid!"

Holly frowned. "I'm not sure I like the sound of this! And Sergeant, I haven't actually done a HALO jump yet!"

"Well, young lady sure seems like today is your lucky day, we'll be exiting a C130 at thirty-five thousand feet, and after reaching terminal velocity you will deploy your chute at three thousand; keep an eye on your altimeter and don't panic if anything goes wrong remember you got your reserve."

Holly swallowed hard and tried to cover her fear with a smile.

"It's ok to be scared, cupcake!" Cowboy said and grinned. "You'll enjoy the ride! It's kinda better than sex."

"Shut your face, Cowboy! Anything would be better than sex with you!"

"We'll now be moving into pre-jump where we will all be going through the drills and then you'll be breathing pure oxygen for approximately thirty minutes before boarding... Any questions?" He paused briefly. "Ok people, gear up."

Following a cork-screw trajectory, the C130 climbed into the blue sky, and the near-vertical aircraft gained altitude with ease. Sitting across from the rest of the team Mitch looked at each one of them in turn. Cowboy, fearless as usual looked like he was on nothing more than a Sunday school outing, Scott was clearly praying to the god of parachuting but was doing his best to hide it; Holly's face on the other hand was quite green, her eyes were shut tight and she was trembling.

"Holly!" Mitch shouted above the din of the engine. "You ok?"

She nodded.

She seemed more than scared and Mitch suddenly had a feeling that he knew why, leaving his seat he moved across the fuselage and knelt by her side. "You haven't done this before, have you?"

Holly vigorously shook her head.

"Jesus!" He sighed and shot a concerned glance at Cowboy. "How the hell…"

"I was sick in the med bay that whole week, they never got around to recycling me onto the course!"

"Well, I can see you're scared but you're going to have to jump anyway! If you refuse, they'll kick you off the team."

She nodded.

"It's alright Cupcake!" Cowboy said. "We can jump together; I'll take good care of you! It'll be over before you even know it!"

Holly smiled. "And there's me thinking you were an asshole!"

"Oh, I'm still asshole Cupcake, just not today!"

The DeadBeats

As the ramp began to lower a blast of ice-cold air rushed in filling the fuselage. "Stand up!" Sergeant Johnson bellowed and watched as the team moved to the rear of the craft. "Green light, Go. Go. Go!!"

Without giving Holly time to think Mitch and Cowboy Grabbed an arm each, dragging her out of the aircraft with Scott close behind pushing and plunging into freefall. As they plummeted toward the ground they stayed close together, holding onto one another.

Watching Holly's eyes, Mitch waited for the terror to pass and as soon as she gave him a nod he released her and moved away from the others.

Falling at terminal velocity Holly remained in the free fall position and watched her altimeter. Hitting three thousand feet she pulled her rip cord and looked up to check her chute was opening, and then drifted gently toward the ground. Landing on her feet she quickly removed the harness and ran yelping toward Scott, who had landed nearby.

"That was freaking amazing!" She screamed excitedly. "I wanna do it again right now! That was better than sex!"

Scott grinned. "Well in that case you're either doing the sex thing wrong or you're doing it with the wrong person."

colin wraight

"Wow, that was incredible!" She cried breathlessly.

"So, you're still alive Cupcake? I can't tell you how happy that makes me feel!" Cowboy said and laughed as he approached Mitch. "My money was on her making a Holly-shaped crater!"

"I wanna do that again!"

"No problem!" Mitch quipped. "We got a night jump just as soon as the sun goes down!"

"Night jump? You mean jumping in the dark!"

"That's kinda the whole point!" Cowboy said and smirked at the obvious return of Holly's fear. "Don't be scared, you won't even see the ground coming up to bite you!"

Holly nervously licked her lips. "Night jump- That's fine, I… I can do that! Sure, it'll be a blast!"

"Ok, guys the trucks coming to pick us up, get your gear!"

As the truck neared, Scott squinted through the midday sun. "Is that who I think it is in the passenger seat!"

"Jeez!" Mitch spat. "It's Colonel Harker! What the hell is he doing here?"

"Maybe he's come to do the night jump with us?" Cowboy said.

153

The DeadBeats

Opening the door as the truck came to a halt the Colonel jumped out. "How's it going, guys? Are you enjoying yourselves?"

"Have you come to join us on the night jump sir?" Cowboy said mischievously.

"No Cowboy, I haven't! But I do have some rather interesting news for you all! And I thought I'd come out here and tell you myself."

"This can't be anything good!" Cowboy said glumly.

"General McNamara's daughter turns eighteen next week and I kinda volunteered you guys to perform at her birthday party!"

"Tell me you're joking, Sir?"

"Well, you should know by now that I never joke- I just thought it would be good practice."

"Sir!" Mitch said as seriously as he could. "We haven't had any time to practise, we have no performance and no playlist! I can't help thinking that this is a huge mistake!"

"You guys are going operational in a matter of weeks, so you will do this and you will do it well!" He paused to allow his words to hit home. "You got the night jump and then tomorrow Mitch and Cowboy you're doing the hard wing! Then you deadbeats will have the rest of the week to get your act together!"

"It's the Rigid wing,Sir!" Cowboy said correcting the senior officer.

"Cowboy! Rigid wing, Hard wing; What's the difference?"

"Sir!" Holly said. "Why aren't Scott and I doing the Rigid wing?"

"Because I know that was your first jump and by the way I was seriously impressed; I didn't think you'd go out the door!"

"I didn't really get a choice, Sir!"

"You and Scott don't have enough jumps under your belts and you'd probably die!"

"That's fine by me, sir!" Scott said as he smiled with relief.

"After the Night jump, you three head back to the house!"

"Three Sir?"

"Oh yeh, I almost forgot! Someone is waiting in the back of the truck for you!"

Suddenly a familiar face appeared around the side of the canvas at the back of the truck. "Guess who guys!"

"Tony!" Holly shrieked. "You're back!"

"I sure am, and guess what I got!"

"Oh my god!" Holly said and began running toward him. "You got legs, don't you? Show me!"

The DeadBeats

Leaping onto the sand Tony landed upright on his two-carbon fibre prosthetic blades. "Cool hey- They wouldn't let me come back until I could run four hundred meters in under a minute. But you know what the coolest part is?" Launching himself into the air Tony spun and kicked an invisible target above his head before landing. "The Chow man got his mojo back!"

Holly rushed in for a hug just as the rest of the team crowded around. "Good to have you back man," Cowboy said. "And I mean that in every sense of the word."

"Thanks guys, not long ago I was a homeless bum with no hope and no life; but you saved me... I owe you my life!"

"Ok, that's enough of the chit-chat!" Colonel Harker barked. "You deadbeats, climb on the truck and let's get the hell out of here!"

"Good morning gentlemen today you're going to be using the AR53 Rigid wing." The instructor pointed to a table at the side of the classroom, which held a large triangular object. "The Wing is made of a top-secret carbon fibre reinforced composite; Lightweight and highly manoeuvrable when in level flight, speeds of up to two hundred miles per hour can be achieved; the radar cross section makes the piece of equipment the ideal tool for covert delivery of airborne troops… Are there any questions so far?"

Rolling his head to the side Cowboy removed his sunglasses. "How do you steer that thing?

"Well, I'm glad you asked!" The Sergeant said a little too excitedly for Cowboy's liking. "Steering is by way of flaps much in the same way you would steer a jet, but once you get the hang of it, you'll find that you can achieve lateral turns just by moving your body."

Mitch raised his hand like a schoolboy in class. "Sergeant, exactly how many people have died using this equipment?"

"Well, sir… Em! I guess at the last count… Notwithstanding bird strikes!"

"How many sergeant?"

"Four hundred and twelve sir!"

"Are you telling me that four hundred and twelve people have lost their lives using this thing?"

"That's the civilian equivalent! Ours is much better it hasn't killed anyone yet."

"Oh well, I guess that's ok then!" Cowboy said sarcastically.

"How do we land?"

"Well sir, with this particular version, deployment will take place from a black hawk at twenty thousand feet. On your wrist, you will be wearing a sat-nav, and you'll follow a pre-arranged flight path back to this airfield."

"That isn't what I asked!"

"Well sir, once you're over the airfield you need to drop down to two thousand five hundred feet or thereabouts and then go vertical." The Sergeant used his hands to further drive home the procedure. "At three thousand feet you jettison the wing and simply pull your rip cord."

"Sounds like a walk in the park!" Cowboy said and slowly shook his head in disbelief.

"Oh, I almost forgot, once the wing is released it will self-destruct on impact… So, guys please don't land near it!"

"Hell no!" Cowboy snapped and leapt out of his chair. "That thing got a bomb inside it?"

"Err, well Sir, yes it does; that's what makes it self-destruct!"

"Jesus H Christ! Are you people insane or what?"

"Let me just clear something up! The rigid wings you will be using today do not contain bombs; the ones you will fly operationally behind the lines most certainly will."

"This whole thing just gets better and better!"

"Might be fun though!" Mitch said. "I always wanted to be Superman!"

"They're trying to kill us, man; I'm telling you; they want us dead!"

The Sergeant suddenly raised a hand to stop the conversation. "Guys, once you've mastered this equipment, you'll never look back, I promise you there's no other ride like it on the planet. If you have any problems or doubts at any time during the flight, simply jettison the wing, freefall down to two thousand feet and pull your rip cord."

Mitch nodded. "I guess it's time to gear up!"

Chapter 11

"This is dumb, man!" Cowboy whined. "Playing to a bunch of scrawny kids…!"

"Lighten up, it could be fun," Holly said and spun one of her drumsticks in her hand. Then she used the same drumstick to part the stage curtains. "They're kinda close to the stage."

"They look bored, gonna be a tough crowd!"

"Ok, guys let's do this!" Mitch said and headed for the stage. "Take my lead, I'll count you in!" Making his way to the front of the stage, he picked up his guitar and placed the strap over his head. After waiting for the rest of the band to get into their positions, he approached his microphone. "Hi guys we're the Deadbeats and we're going to be singing some songs for you tonight, we hope you enjoy it…" A sudden screech of ear-splitting feedback interrupted his introduction and caused the crowd to cover their ears. "Sorry about that guys, just a technical glitch; Anyhows I'd just like to take this opportunity to wish…!" He suddenly realised that he couldn't remember the birthday girl's name. "… The lucky lady a very happy birthday!" Shooting a glance toward Scott he received a thumbs up from backstage. Hitting the strings of his guitar he launched into a rendition of Johnny be good.

"What the hell is this?" Colonel Harker cried.

"It's Johnny be good Sir!" Scott said and shrugged. "You know, Michael J Fox, Back to the Future and all that… Eighties retro!"

"What the hell was he thinking? These kids weren't even alive then." The Colonel barked and peered out from behind the curtains. "They hate it, we need to do something!"

"Sir, these things take a couple of songs; he's just getting them warmed up!"

"Jeez, I got a band who thinks thirty-year-old songs is the way forward, I got a four-star General who I've got to face first thing in the morning and explain why his daughter's party was the pits and do you know what else I got...?"

"No sir.."

The DeadBeats

"I got a hall full of moody, pre-pubescent spoilt brats staring at their iPhones. Scott, please do something! Anything! just do something!"

"I don't know Sir; we can't just change a set we've been rehearsing all week!" As Holly drummed the intro to Dexys Midnight Runners, Come On Eileen Scott wondered if he dare. "Well, sir maybe there is something, it's a long shot, it's our own music…!"

"Whatever it is do it! can't be any worse than this!"

Reaching into his pocket Scott pulled out a memory stick and plugged it into his control panel. "Mitch is going to kill me!" He said and picked up a spare microphone. As Eileen came to an end Scot burst onto the stage. "Yo..! Yo, Leroy Scott is in the house…!" His deep voice boomed around the hall. "Getting' down with the DeadBeats!"

Spinning on his heels Mitch glared and mouthed. "What the hell are you doing?"

"Guys, we got something real special for you tonight, this is our song and you great people are going to be the first to hear it… Holly Lightfoot give me some beat!"

Holly's face lit up as she assaulted to drum set.

"Chow man hit those keys let's get this show on the road...! Ok...

Ok, let's go!" He boomed. "Getting' down with the Deadbeats, sittin'

on the back seat..."

Seeking out the Colonel at stage side Mitch glared at him, all he

received in return was a shrug. There was nothing else to do but go

along with Scott and finish the song.

"Stand up, let's dance... Get down, getting' down! Ok, Mitch let 'em

have it!"

Mitch grinned, it seemed Leroy Scott could rap after all; Spinning

his guitar onto his back he took hold of the mic and as he began to

sing he noticed a group of girls dancing while others appeared to be

filming the band on their iPhones. Soon the whole audience was

going crazy and by the time Scott began to rap his chorus segment,

they were going wild.

"Ok, guys we'll be back after this short break!" Mitch cried over the

screaming audience and then placed his guitar in its stand; before

jogging off stage with the rest of the band.

"Oh my god!" Holly shrieked. "That was insane! They loved us!

They loved you're song, Mitch!"

Mitch shook his head. "I don't know about that guys! That was all Scott, he was amazing the way he got those girls all riled up!"

"People..!" Cowboy said. "You're right that was amazing and all, but what the hell do we do now? How do we go back out there and top what we just did?"

"Ok..!" Mitch said. "We change the rest of the set; we go with the Red-Hot Chilli Peppers, then the Queen stuff and the Back street boy's material and we finish off with the Foo Fighters and Scott it would be just great if you got any more of that rhyming stuff, you just feel free to adlib."

"You got it, Bro!"

"What the hell is going on out there!" The Colonel said. "Sounds like a riot!"

"No, listen they're just screaming for the DeadBeats to get back on stage!"

"Let's go!" Scott said. "Mitch just leave the chorus to me I got something that I think will fit just fine!"

"Get out there guys, let's do this!" As the Colonel watched them return to the stage he got the strangest feeling that the whole plan of having a low-key band had just gone out of the window.

With one song flowing seamlessly into the next and Scott's rapping whipping the crowd into a frenzy, it seemed like only seconds before they were coming off stage again. The screaming and chanting began immediately. "Down with the DeadBeats, down with the DeadBeats…" The whole building seemed to tremble under the weight of sound.

"They're insane, I ain't never seen anything like this!" Cowboy cried.

"They want an encore!" Holly shouted over the din. "They want your song again!"

"No!" Mitch cried. "I've got something much better." Then he turned and headed back out onto the stage.

"What the hell is he doing now?" Cowboy said.

"Are you having a good time?"

The audience whooped and screamed their delight.

"Well, I got a huge surprise for you and our birthday girl. "Ladies and Gentlemen, I give you…" He paused. "I give you The incredible, the amazing Strawberry Island."

The DeadBeats

Suddenly the girl band appeared from a side room and ran past a goggle-eyed Cowboy. "What the hell, how did you pull that one out of the hat?"

Once more the audience erupted into a deafening roar.

"They owed me a favour," Mitch said with a grin as he returned from the stage. "I kinda saved their lives!"

"You know those girls and you didn't think to mention it?" Cowboy shook his head in disbelief. "Boy, are we going to party tonight?"

"Forget it," Mitch said. "They flew in to do a couple of songs and then they're leaving right after!"

"Jeez man, I can't catch a break!"

"Oh my god, Candy is singing Pink Champagne! My favourite song it's been number one in the charts for the last six weeks!" Holly squealed with barely concealed delight.

"Candy?" Cowboy asked.

"She's the lead singer."

"And my future wife, guys I think I may be in love!"

Saying their farewells Strawberry Island ran off stage. "Listen to them." Candy cried. "It's not us they want… It's you!"

"Thanks for showing up girls!" Mitch said.

The crowd's chanting was deafening but the words were clear.

"Deadbeats, DeadBeats, Deadbeats..."

"Let's not disappoint!" The Colonel herded them back toward the stage. "Get your asses back out there!"

Bursting onto the stage the crowd erupted at the sight of Scott. "Ok, Ok Let's go!" He boomed into the mic. "Gettin' down with DeadBeats, sittin' in the back seat..."

And the crowd screamed...

The stillness and the silence seemed almost surreal after the craziness of the previous night. Was it real? Did it happen? Or was it just an insane dream? Holly lay cosy under her duvet just smiling at a spot on the ceiling, allowing her brain to play the memories across her mind's eye.

Only the beeping of her cell phone brought her out of her daydreaming. Reaching out to her bedside table she fumbled around until her hand fell on the device and then lazily brought it to her to view the screen. First, she frowned, then her eyes widened until she exploded from her bed, rushing headlong out of her room she banged

on doors. "Mitch… Scott… Tony… Cowboy get up, get out here!"

Forgetting the rules, she flung Mitch's door open, ran in jumped on

his bed and began bouncing up and down like a child trying to wake

him up.

"What the hell, are you insane? Woman, what are you doing?"

Zeroing in on the noise the rest of the band suddenly poured

through the door.

"What's wrong with you?" Cowboy said groggily. "Why are you

making noise!"

"Two and a half million!" She cried.

"Two and a half million what?"

"Views!"

"Holly, please stop bouncing, I've got a hangover, I got me a

headache from hell… So, you know, enough with the noise and just

tell us what's going on!"

Jumping off the bed she held up her phone for Cowboy to see the

screen. "Those kids, those beautiful kids last night filmed the

performance of our song, some of them uploaded it to YouTube and

now two and a half million people have watched us."

Cowboy stood speechless for once.

"Guys!" Tony said breathlessly and slumped into a chair. "Guys, do you know what this means!"

Scott nodded. "We're a band!"

Mitch sat up in his bed. "We're a real band!"

"We're gonna be famous!" Cowboy added and then corrected himself. "Hell, we are famous!"

Looking at her cell phone the smile fell from Holly's face. "Oh my..!" she said as calmly as she could. "Guys, we just hit three million and it's still climbing."

Cowboy blew out hard as he tried to compose himself. "Well, you know what this means?"

"What?"

"Someone's gonna have to tell the Colonel!"

Casper Von Swartzstein carefully applied his eyeliner, then blinked several times at his reflection in the mirror; he smiled at the results, his face was perfect, he was perfect. After using a disposable wet wipe to clean his hands he moved from his dressing table to a full-length mirror and surveyed the powder blue suit he had chosen to wear for the day. Turning to observe his posterior he grinned.

"Schon!" He whispered in his native tongue and then in English. "Beautiful! I am truly a handsome man!" Glancing at his gold Rolex watch his face instantly screwed in anger. "Manfred! Where are you?" He shrieked, and then louder. "Manfred..!"

Manfred was late, Manfred was always late; Shuffling along on the stone floor Manfred pushed the master's breakfast trolly as fast as his tired old legs would allow him. Reaching out with his trembling, and bony glove-covered hand he turned the handle and as the door swung open groaning on its ancient hinges, he awaited the inevitable onslaught.

"Where have you been, you stupid old man?" Casper barked. "You are late, I distinctly remember requesting breakfast be served at eight o'clock! You bring me breakfast- It is almost dinnertime; this is not good enough. I am a busy man; this is simply not good enough Manfred; we must get better." Overwhelmed with emotion Casper covered his mouth. "It's just not good enough!"

"I… I am sorry sir!" When he spoke, his voice was hoarse and weak. "It's the cold sir, you know how it plays havoc with my arthritis!"

Casper relented and physically tempered his voice. "I apologise most unreservedly Manfred; I sometimes forget how advanced in years you are! Perhaps when I am less busy I will arrange to get you some help."

"Thank you, sir, but that is quite unnecessary! I proudly served your father until his death and his father before him!"

Casper smiled. "So, how do I look!"

"Quite fabulous indeed sir!" Manfred said but understood the true meaning of the question. "Two hundred million views sir!"

"How are the preparations proceeding for the next contest!"

"The gladiatorial ring has been erected in the great hall and the votes have been counted and verified! The corresponding guests are now dressed appropriately."

"And last night's loser?"

"The body is on its way home as we speak sir!" Manfred turned to the food trolly. "Could I possibly tempt you with a little coffee sir!"

The DeadBeats

"No take it all away, I'm not hungry after all!"

"And this evening's meal sir, do you have a preference?"

"A Happy Meal!"

"Salad or fries sir?"

Casper patted his stomach ruefully. "Alas Manfred, one cannot afford the indulgence of our once most friendly fries."

"A most wise choice sir!

Chapter 12

Pounding his fist on the desk, Colonel Harker glared at Mitch. "How in the hell did this happen?" He spat. "You guys were meant to go under the radar, a low-key band playing small venues..."

"With all due respect Sir, it wasn't me that told Scott to change the song list! And it certainly wasn't me who...!"

"God darn it, Mitch!" The Colonel spat and slumped into his chair.

"I don't see how this changes anything, sir. We can still do this; Maybe it'll be better!"

"Better? You haven't cut the record yet and you're already number one on the download charts!" He closed his eyes and took a deep breath. "I had a telephone call from something called 'Saturday night live' this morning, and they want you guys to perform the song this weekend. Oh, and they weren't the only ones, there's others!"

The DeadBeats

Mitch's mouth fell open and his eyes widened in disbelief.

"Saturday night live? That's huge, that's massive!"

The Colonel frowned as talking to an idiot. "Massive, huge! Are you insane? The band isn't ready for that yet, and besides I already turned them down… This is all moving way too fast. I say we slow this joy ride down, play a couple of gigs…"

"Sir, It's too late for that! The cat is out of the bag!" Mitch said and pushed his hands deep into his Jean pockets. "Somehow between us, Scott and I wrote something great and people like it! I say we do a studio recording today and use some of the footage from the party as a temporary video until we come up with something else."

"OK…OK!" He said and stared out of the window for several seconds before speaking again. "You still had a few weeks of military training to finish, but I'll have to cancel it and tell the brass that the Deadbeats are now operational… Looks like you guys will be doing some on-the-job training! I hope you're up to it."

"And Saturday Night Live?"

"No..! No way, we still have to work on the band's persona and your cover stories… Your hair is still too short and you all stand up straight; darn it, Mitch, you still look like soldiers… For god's sake man, slouch."

"Sir..?"

"Uncle Sam took dumb civilians and made steely-eyed killers out of you; now I've gotta turn you all into greasy rock stars!"

"Greasy..? Sir, Rock stars are really a thing of the past and the Deadbeats will never be greasy!"

"And where the hell did that name come from? I didn't sanction no group name!"

"It was Holly's idea, Sir. She thought it would be a great way to honour all those names in the boat house!"

Realising the decision was out of his hands Harker relented. "Oh ok, well yeah: When you put it like that… I'll have to just kinda like or lump it won't I!"

"Yes, Sir you will!"

"By the way Mitch, it's a great song, but there's a question I have to ask..!"

"What's that?"

"You got any more songs like that one stashed away?"

175

The DeadBeats

Jumping, and squealing with delight Holly burst into the studio carrying a small transistor radio; covering her mouth, she tried to stifle another squeal but it escaped through her fingers anyway. "Guys, guys we're on the radio!" she said excitedly. "They're playing it, they're playing our song!"

Scott's eyes widened. "Oh my god, that's me; On the radio… That's my voice..! Right there! Where's my cell phone?" He cried as he dashed from the room. "I need to call my mom!"

"And there it is listeners!" The DJ said brightly "'Down with the Deadbeats' doing the business on the download charts and we still have no idea what this band even looks like!"

"Maybe they're just really ugly!" Said another voice.

"That's right guys the DeadBeats are either butt ugly or it's one hell of a marketing ploy; My guess is it's the latter!" The DJ laughed at his own joke. "And now it's the top of the hour so it's over to Chloe with the news and weather!"

"Did that guy just call me ugly?"

"Don't take it personally Cowboy, he's only saying what us girls already know!" Holly said and slapped him on the shoulder. "Ya, big dope!"

Straightening his tie, Casper closed his eyes and then whilst massaging his temples took a long deep breath through his nose; after momentarily holding the air in his lungs he very slowly exhaled and opened his eyes. Then he exploded with barely concealed rage. "I do not ask for very much, my needs are small; Am I not a good and fair employer? Manfred..! Manfred once again you have let me down! Are you not ashamed of yourself?"

Staring blankly at the stone floor Manfred waited for the onslaught to abate as it usually did; zoning out the voice he began to think about Casper's father, a gentleman who rarely if ever raised his voice. Times were changing, and not for the better. Suddenly it occurred to the old manservant that being hard of hearing probably wasn't such a bad thing.

The DeadBeats

"Are you even listening to me? You're not even listening are you."

Seething with anger Casper kicked a chair over, and then in a complete about turn his voice softened. "Image Manfred... Image is everything; I cannot afford to be lacking in this area. It does not matter that the viewers cannot see my feet; Everything must be just so!"

Blinking back into the present Manfred realised he'd completely missed most of what his master had said but as a pause had suddenly appeared in his words he felt he ought to speak. "I must apologise most sincerely for my oversight Sir; in future, I shall endeavour to lay out the correct colour socks!" He said the last three words with resignation and only the slightest hint of exasperation.

"Blue suit, blue socks Manfred; it's not difficult. We really must try harder, mustn't we?

"Whatever you say, sir!"

"Yes, that's right 'whatever I say! Now off with you!" As he inspected his face in a mirror Casper suddenly had a thought. "Oh, before you go, I almost forgot to ask; has last night's unlucky loser been returned to her family?"

"Yes sir, the unfortunate young lady was flown out this morning!" He replied and paused for a reaction or comment from his boss but received none. "If there's nothing else I'll prepare your evening meal."

Shuffling in his seat Cowboy tried to get comfortable. "What's this about?" He said to no one in particular. "I'm missing a ball game for this…"

"Shut up Cowboy!" Holly said. "It's just a game- What about me? I'm missing Jersey Shore!"

Colonel Harker and Gunny Carter suddenly entered the room. "Ok, ladies settle down; our visitors are delayed somewhat, once they arrive all will be revealed!" Handing several files to the Gunnery Sergeant he indicated with a wave of his hand that they should be dished out.

The sudden sound of a descending helicopter swooping down onto the helipad caused everyone to look out the window.

The DeadBeats

"Looks like our friends have arrived!" Leaping from his seat Cowboy dashed to get a better view of the aircraft. "Jesus!" He cried. "That's… That's the President's chopper! Don't tell me Cowboy gets to meet the President today?"

"Get outta here!" Scott said grinning and pushed Cowboy out of the way so he could see.

"Sit the hell down people! You are not meeting the boss today!"

"So, who are we meeting?" Mitch said, slightly irked at not getting a heads up.

If I told you, you wouldn't believe me!" The Colonel said and grinned as he left the room. Returning moments later, he ushered their guests into the room. "ok guys, the gentleman in the suit on my left is Agent Ricky Martello of the secret service and this other Gentleman to my right is one Mr Henry clench.

"Oh, No… No," The shuffling elderly gentleman held up a hand. "My friends call me Doofus!" He said somewhat nervously in a slow southern drawl. "Jane asked me to… to come here; she said I might be able to help you nice people." Apprehensively glancing around the room his eyes fell on Cowboy. "I believe we have met sir, although you might not remember me!"

"As in 'Jane' our President?" Cowboy grinned. "And, I remember you too, but that was two years ago and my face was covered in camouflage cream!"

"I remember… Well; I would, I remember everyone!"

"Henry, why don't you go and take a seat while I speak to these people!" Agent Martello said softly.

"I.. I like your song!" Henry said as a parting shot and then went to the back of the room and sat down.

"Guys, as your Colonel has already told you my name is Agent Ricky Martello of the secret service. Myself and Henry over there are here on behalf of the President."

Turning in his seat to look at the strange man at the back of the room Mitch was taken aback to see him take a children's book out of a grubby old plastic bag and begin colouring in a picture with coloured pencils. "What the hell is his deal?" He said.

Martello's voice suddenly took on a new, almost threatening property. "Mr Clench is an asset of the United States of America and no matter what he says or what you may or may not see him doing you will not speak of him outside of this building- You will also treat him with the utmost respect; Do I make myself clear?"

"What's his job?" Holly asked.

Martello paused and smiled in Henry's direction. "Why, Henry here cuts the white house lawn!"

"Once every two weeks on a Sunday, after church; If I got time, I'll cut yours too… I like to mow the lawn!"

"Ok!" Holly said and frowned.

"What the hell is this about?" Mitch said impatiently and shared a sideways glance with Tony, who was seated beside him.

"This people is about one Brianne Moore Masterson!" Martello said. "As you are probably aware some nut job has kidnapped god knows how many celebrities. He's forcing them to compete to the death live online. Miss Masterson is not only a citizen of the USA but her father Robin Masterson is best friends with our boss, the President!"

"So, the boss wants us to rescue her?" Mitch asked.

"No, the boss wants you to rescue all of them, or at least the ones still alive by the time you get there!"

"And where exactly is 'there'?" Mitch said.

"We don't have that information yet…" The Agent said and shot a glance at Henry. "The perpetrator of this crime is very adept at covering his tracks, but have no fear the finest minds in our intelligence services are tracing him as we speak!"

"It's a castle…!" Holly said. "It's obviously some kind of castle."

"That's right," Henry said smiling broadly from the back of the room. "Just like… Like in a big old fairy tale!"

"And it's real cold as well!" She added. "The girl's cheeks always look so flushed!"

"Well, we got a suspected European medieval castle on a mountain and where ever it is, it was snowing on Thursday. We know this much because the camera panned around and momentarily showed us a window. Through said window, we could see snow and the side of a large mountain."

Harker suddenly interrupted. "Given time intel will identify this area and pinpoint the castle. Meanwhile Deadbeats welcome to mission zero, you're task will be to find, infiltrate and rescue these young people. To that end, we will immediately be relocating to Europe and begin by playing a few small gigs in London."

The DeadBeats

Holly shrieked with excitement. "London, you mean London, England?"

"Whatever other kind of London is there?" Harker barked. "I suggest you ladies start packing, and in all this excitement." He glared at Holly, who shrank in her seat under his gaze. "Don't forget your instruments."

Cowboy raised a hand. "Are Agent Martello and the Lawnmower man back there going to be joining us on this little excursion?"

Baulking at Cowboy's words Martello gritted his teeth and then answered. "First of all, we'll be around to hold your hands, don't you worry about that and secondly you will address the gentleman at the back of the room as Mr Clench. When you become friends and believe me you will, he may allow you to call him Henry; and one day years and years from now he might even let you call him Doofus…"

"That's all well and good Agent Martello, But let me tell you that I was there two years ago on the SEAL team that was involved in the rescue of the Presidents boy- And I know all about your man back there! I heard the rumours and I've seen with my own eyes what he can do!"

"Then Cowboy, I suggest you keep that mouth of yours shut and just be thankful he's on Team America!"

"Hi... Hello everyone... Err excuse me!" Henry suddenly said. "Err... Sorry to interrupt and all but I'm kinda hungry... What, what time is dinner served?"

"It's alright Henry, food is on its way!" Martello said changing his tone. "If someone could show us to our rooms, I believe Henry here would like a nap before eating!"

"Gunny Carter will be here shortly!" Harker said. "Meanwhile, I'd like to speak to you in my office."

Martello nodded and smiled, then turned to Henry. "You going to be Ok here Henry!"

The ageless man smiled broadly. "I'll be just fine right here with my newfound friends!"

"He's safe with us!" Holly said. "Go, I'll take good care of him!"

After the two men had left the room Mitch turned to Cowboy and whispered in his ear. "This is weird man!"

"You haven't heard the half of it!" Turning to see Henry happily humming a tune and shading a tree green in his book, Cowboy then shot a glance at the door, and once he was sure Harker and Martello weren't in earshot he spoke. "You remember those Arabs who took the President's kid a couple of years ago?"

Mitch nodded.

"Well, by the time we got out to that shack all the bad guys were toast; There were bodies all over those woods. I found one guy impaled halfway up a tree and another ripped to shreds, they said a bear did it but I dunno man; the whole episode was crazy."

"What's this got to do with the old man?"

"One of the guys on the team has a brother in the local Sheriff's department, and rumour has it they found one of them alive, before he died he was rambling about balls of light and being attacked by a ghost!"

Mitch burst into laughter. "A ghost? Get outta here man, you're shitting me! I still don't see what any of that has to do with old Henry over there?"

"I saw some crazy things; things that I can't explain. I was there at the end; That weird old guy took a bullet to the chest; one minute they're reading him his last rites and the next he's walking out of the hospital with his mother!"

"His Mother?" Mitch said and shook his head in exasperation. "What?"

"I'm telling you there's something very weird about him!" Suddenly realising someone was now standing in front of them he stopped talking.

"My...My Mom says I'm special; she doesn't like it when people call me weird!"

"Mr Clench!" Cowboy said and blushed. "I'm sorry man, I didn't mean anything by it."

Henry simply smiled and held up the picture he had been colouring. "Do you like my picture? I have been doing this since last night." Then he lowered his voice. "Jane doesn't know but I was colouring way after my bedtime."

Mitch frowned. "When you say 'Jane', I take it you mean the President?"

"Yeah, she's my bestest friend in the whole wide world! We've known each other since we were just kids!"

"Mr Clench can I ask you a question?"

"Why of course you can sir!"

The DeadBeats

"Why are you here? What are you bringing to this party?"

Henry opened his mouth and then paused as if something was stopping him from speaking. "Ms Jane said, that I'm not allowed to say, but very soon you will see…" He said and chuckled. "What, what I'm bringing to your party!"

Chapter 13

As the private jet began its bumpy descent into London's Heathrow

airport, Colonel Harker grinned at Mitch.

"Ok, so what's so funny?" He asked and sighed heavily. The flight

had been long and with only the Colonel to look at he'd tried to sleep

for most of it.

"Nothing much, I'm just looking forward to seeing your faces!"

"What are you talking about? What have you done?"

"You'll soon see!"

After touching down the Lear Jet began taxying toward the

terminal. Holly bounced and beamed with excitement. "I wanna see

the palace, oh my god will we get to see William? There's a thing

called Soho; we have got to go there!"

"What's a Soho?" Cowboy asked as he gazed out of the small

window.

The DeadBeats

"It's a street or an avenue or something; it's just rammed with bars and restaurants and..."

"Strippers, does it have strippers?"

Holly shook her head in disgust. "Probably..!"

"Ok, I'm in!"

"You're a pig!"

"That's right cupcake, a pig that now thanks to you knows where to find the strip joints in this god-forsaken crap hole!"

"This is England, it isn't a crap hole... Is it?" Holly said and frowned.

As the jet came to a halt The Colonel climbed out of his seat. "Guys, there's a chance things could get kinda crazy in the next half hour. So, stick together and don't get lost..."

"What are you talking about?" Mitch said, eyeing his superior suspiciously.

"Well, there's a chance someone released the fact that you guys were arriving here today!"

"That's what you were grinning at earlier; it was you; you did that!" Mitch growled as he nervously glanced out of the window. "Why would you do that...? What happened to the covert rescue mission?"

"You're rock stars, people, time for you to start behaving like it; now get your gear and go greet your fans!"

"Guys, it's time to show the dog the bone!" Cowboy said.

"And we all know who the 'bone' is! Oh wait, I know what you're thinking Cowboy; it's written all over your dumb face!" Holly quipped as she retrieved a small holdall from the overhead stowage compartment.

Cowboy grinned mischievously. "I have no idea what you're talking about!"

"Let's see! You're thinking hordes of screaming female fans and your very own hotel room!"

"You got me all wrong cupcakes, I'm not that kinda guy!"

"Course not!"

"Sorry to crash the party but only Holly has her own room, the rest of you guys are sharing!"

"What the hell, sir!"

"Cowboy, I kinda always had you down as the bad boy of the band; the only difference is you will do the bad things when, and how I tell you to!"

The DeadBeats

Distraught and lost in self-pity the musician hugged his guitar for comfort. "All those girls, wanting me, screaming my name and nothing! I can't do nothing? It was the only reason I came on this dumb gig!"

Holly laughed loudly. "Serves you right you dumb ass!"

Leaving the aircraft, the team found themselves on a drizzly and grey London day; making their way across the tarmac to a side entrance they entered the terminal.

"Jeez man, what the hell is wrong with this place?" Tony whined. "If it gets any wetter my legs are going turn to rust!"

"Carbon fibre doesn't rust numb nuts!" Holly said flatly and then more excitedly. "This is where the King lives guys; come on this is going to be amazing!"

"And it's so dammed cold!" Scott added.

"Pipe down! Can you hear that?" The Colonel snapped and then stopped dead in his tracks, allowing the others to hear what he was hearing.

"Sounds like a riot!"

"That's right Scott, a god dammed riot! I only hope you people realise how much your lives are about to change!" The Colonel took a deep breath. "When you get out there just wave, smile and keep walking! The local cops will take care of the crowd; Just try to get to the coach unscathed! Let's go!" Opening a frosted glass door, a wave of noise exploded into a cacophony of deafening screams, cries and clapping.

"My god!" Scott shouted. "This is insane man!" His words went unheard, drowned in a sea of noise.

As The Colonel led them out, a wall of Police officers suddenly surrounded them, both protecting the group and forcing them along through the maelstrom of swaying, crushing sea of screaming fans.

Clinging on to one another as the surging horde buffeted them, clamouring, clawing hands forced their way through the black wall desperate to touch them, only to be forcibly repelled by the increasingly irritated Police contingent.

Struggling to stay upright on his carbon fibre blades Tong grabbed cowboys' shoulder and leaned on him for support. After what seemed like an eternity they were being stuffed inside a coach, and suddenly they could once more breathe.

"What the hell!" Scott barked breathlessly. "Just what in hell man!"

"That was insane!" Holly added and slumped in a seat almost in a state of shock. "Can we never do that again?"

"Why am I in this stupid costume?" Brianne raged angrily, now beyond fear of her captors she was fuming. "I look ridiculous!" She waited for a reply to come through the speaker, and when none came she spoke again. "Just kill me and get it over and done with, why don't you?!" Again, no reply came. "Bastards!"

"Good evening Brianne!"

Not expecting the voice, and startled she spun to face the speaker on the wall. "What's going on? Why am I dressed like this?"

"Brianne you are now streaming live to the entire world! The public has voted for you once more, how popular you must feel! You will take part in tonight's entertainment; Brianne and Simone you will shortly be entering the arena of the gladiators and only one of you will continue on this amazing journey, the other will be leaving the show tonight!"

A sudden knot of fear formed in her stomach. "You mean, you're going to kill one of us?" She said flatly and then realised 'Simone' was a name she hadn't yet encountered. "And who the hell is Simone anyway? You psychopaths can do what you like, I'm not playing your stupid games anymore!"

"Simone, Brianne; The games are about to begin! When your doors open please make your way into the main hall!"

"No!" Brianne barked. "No, I won't! I'm not doing it!"

"I would advise you not to keep your viewers waiting!"

Fatigued, cold and scared Brianne began to sob. "No, no I won't do it! If you want to kill me just do it!"

"The viewers have spoken with their votes and whether you like it or not your participation in this game is, unfortunately, not up for discussion!"

Without warning the door to her room suddenly opened and in stepped the biggest, ugliest and meanest-looking man she had ever seen. She stared in both abject terror and wonderment. "No...! Please no, I don't want to do this!" She sobbed. "I...I just want to go home!"

The stranger growled one word. "Out!"

Beyond frightened and aware that her whole body was trembling, Brianne shuffled nervously past the giant and out into the corridor.

The DeadBeats

Barely able to walk and feeling like a condemned woman, the thought that death, any death would be better than this living nightmare settled in her mind.

 Feeble and fatigued with lack of nourishment she hobbled along, only now coming to realise just how bad of a condition she was. The corridor was short and gloomy, and soon the man placed a hand on her shoulder forcing her to turn left into a small, dark doorway and a steep descent down the narrowest of spiral staircases. The steps were uneven, and the stone smooth from hundreds of years of wear; maybe she stumbled or maybe she leapt into the void on purpose, before Brianne knew what had happened she was tumbling head over foot into the welcoming arms of the dark abyss.

 Throwing the door open Harker surveyed all before him, a look of disappointment spread across his face. "Guys…!" He said, frustration edging his voice; then he closed the door behind him and stood watching them with his arms firmly placed on his hips. "Guys! You're meant to be a rock band! Just look at you! Cowboy, what are you doing?"

"Why sir? I'm reading this magazine! Is there something you want me to do?"

"Mitch..!"

Mitch opened his eyes. "I wasn't asleep sir; I was just resting my eyes!"

"Holly, Tony, Scott what's going on over there? What are you doing?"

"We're streaming the latest Fame Game, sir!" Holly said.

"Guys, come on; you're meant to be a rock band! I'm not expecting sex, drugs and rock and roll but I thought...!"

"Would you like me to get drunk sir?" Cowboy offered. "Or I could always go and seduce the girl down on reception! I'm really up for doing both especially if it's an order!"

"Oh, I'm sure you would like that wouldn't you?" Holly spat.

"Hell cupcake, I don't mind sharing the workload! I'll get drunk, you go seduce the receptionist!"

"Get lost you pig!"

"Pipe down you two!" Harker barked angrily and then suddenly marched over to the television and yanked it off the wall. "Well, if you don't know how to be rock stars I guess I'll have to do it for you!"

"What the hell are you doing sir?" Holly shrieked and jumped out of her chair.

"What you deadbeats should be doing!" He growled and then proceeded to march over to the window and toss the tv outside, watching as it plummeted several stories to the ground where it exploded into a thousand pieces on impact. Then he turned. "Management will more than likely call the police; before they arrive I'd like you to empty the mini bar and make this room look like it's been gang raped!"

"What the…!" Mitch objected.

"People, if you don't make the front page of every god dammed newspaper in this country I will be sorely upset! Cowboy I suggest you go do your thing with that pretty little receptionist!"

"Sir, you may have just lost your tiny mind but that's one order I'll be more than happy to oblige!" Climbing out of his seat Cowboy placed his Stetson firmly on his head and then adjusted its position. "See ya' later losers!" he said and headed out.

"Sir..!" Mitch barked. "What the hell are you doing? You just released Cowboy on the local populous! Hell, I wouldn't be surprised if he wasn't brought back by a baying mob on the end of a pitchfork!"

"I'll tell you what I'm doing! I'm turning the Deadbeats into rock stars! Dirty, greasy, party-loving rock stars!" He barked and then paused. "Stop worrying, Cowboy will be just fine, a little old pitchfork never hurt anybody!"

"I sure hope you know what you're doing!"

Tony suddenly let out a small laugh.

"What's with you?" Holly said. "What's the joke?"

"I was just thinking…!"

"Thinking what?"

"Well, if I know Cowboy like I think I know Cowboy, nine months from now there could be dozens of little cowboys wandering around London wearing teeny weeny little Stetsons!"

Blushing at the thought, Holly pursed her lips as she realised the others were staring at her. "That's not funny!" She snapped. "That's not funny at all…"

199

The DeadBeats

Without warning the door suddenly burst open and a dishevelled Cowboy dashed through the gap, slamming the door behind him he used all of his weight to hold the door closed. "Guys, do not go out there, it's hell!" He cried breathlessly.

Eyeing the torn shirt and shredded jeans Mitch frowned. "What the hell happened to you?" He asked. "You get mugged?"

"Paparazzi! Cameras, hundreds of them everywhere; screaming teenagers for as far as the eye could." He paused to catch his breath. "It was hell out there man; they very nearly killed me in the crush! We live here now! We must never leave this room, ever again!"

"Oh, wait everybody!" Holly cried as she noticed the time. "A new episode of the Fame game is about to stream live." Opening her laptop, she pressed several keys and then sat back. "It's on!"

As the rest of the team gathered around the computer Cowboy slid down the door until he was sat on the floor. Removing his Stetson he groaned at its misshapen form, and then set about repairing it. "You guys just don't care do you?" He whined. "I could have been killed out there!"

"Pipe down in the cheap seats!" Holly said. "We're trying to watch something over here!"

"Ladies and Gentlemen it's time to play; welcome to the Fame game… In today's action-packed episode two of our competitors will battle it out in our purpose-built colosseum. That's right viewers you heard it right..! Two girls will enter the arena but only one will leave alive."

"I literally can't wait to put a bullet in that guy's face!" Mitch said in disgust and moved away from the laptop to sit on the couch. "I am not going to watch two young girls murder each other! Surely the tech guys can trace this dirtbag?"

"We have the best on it and they're doing the best they can Mitch, but this asshole is clever he knows how to cover his tracks!" Colonel Harker said. "We'll get him… We have to!"

"Sir, Mitch! Something's wrong! One of the girls was meant to be Brianne but she isn't there!"

"What do you mean?" Said Mitch as he rose out of his seat, still reluctant to witness the bloodshed he remained where he was.

The DeadBeats

"I don't know what's going on but that is definitely not Brianne, they're wearing Roman-styled armour but it's not her, she's not there!"

"Maybe she's already dead!" The normally quiet Tony offered his opinion.

The two Gladiators, one holding a long trident and a net and the other a short sword and shield, stood in the middle of the room facing the TV monitor. Beneath the leather and metal armour, both trembled and sobbed with fear.

The sudden sound of fake applause signalled the game was about to start. "Gladiators, congratulations on making it this far in the Fame game. Tonight, one of you will bask in glory and one of you... will not! This is a battle to the death- Claudia, Lena please turn and face your opponent."

Both girls complied, Lena, the smaller of the two visibly trembled. "I... I don't want to do this!" She sobbed. "You can't make us do this!"

Assuming physical superiority, Claudia looked down on her somewhat squat opponent with surprisingly less pity than she thought she would. "I'm very sorry!" She said quickly in broken English. "I must survive; I will have to kill you! There is no other way!"

"No... Wait..!"

"When the buzzer sounds you may begin."

Nervously backing away, Lena held out the trident as she attempted to keep her distance. "We don't have to do this... Let's just not fight!"

"I am sorry..!"

Suddenly the buzzer sounded and Claudia rushed forward swinging her sword wildly. Ducking, the other girl pivoted on her heel and then stumbled into the middle of the room.

"Just stop!" She cried. "This is stupid; they just want us to murder each other!"

"Stop talking and fight!" Claudia demanded through gritted teeth. "If you don't want to fight then lay down your sword and I will make it quick!"

Lena scowled at her opponent. "You'll make it quick?" She scoffed. "This isn't a film; this is real life and I doubt very much you'd know how to 'make it quick'!" An anger began to form in her stomach soon

becoming an uncontrollable rage. "You know, screw this and screw

you! If you want to kill me then come and try!"

"It's happening isn't it?" Mitch said. "He's getting them to kill each

other, and streaming it live to the world."

Cowboy nodded loath to take his eyes from the developing

spectacle.

"We have to stop him, he's a madman!"

"After this…!" Claudia growled, and then she smiled menacingly.

"After this, after I kill you I'll be famous. I'll have followers by the

millions, I'll be on the cover of magazines, and the whole world will

want to know who I am…!"

"You dumb bitch, win or lose you're never leaving this hell hole!

You'll die here, we both will!"

Tentatively jabbing with her trident, Claudia tried to force her

opponent back. "Not me, I'm getting out of here, I'm going to win the

whole god dammed thing! I'm going to be famous!"

"So, you kill me, you win this and you get out! What do you think happens then?"

"They'll want me on Saturday night live…!"

"No, no they'll want you in prison for murder! Oh, I've had enough of this bullshit!" Lena barked, then dropping her sword she quickly stepped forward, and brushing the trident aside punched Claudia in the temple as hard as she could. A look of shock momentarily spread across her face before she passed out and fell to the ground.

"Screw you and screw your dumb show!" Lena barked and Showed the camera her middle finger. "As if I'd kill anyone just for your stupid enjoyment!"

"No..!" Casper shrieked. "No, she can't do this! What is she doing? She must kill, doesn't she know she is ruining my show? Manfred, Manfred do something!"

"And what would you have me do sir?" The old manservant sighed wearily.

"I, I don't know! Something, just do something!"

"Of course, sir, right away!" Manfred said, and very aware the master was angry and likely to throw something at any moment he shuffled backwards out of the room. Once suitably out of earshot Manfred stopped, sighed wearily and leaned against the cold stone wall. "Dieser mann ist ein dummkopf!" He whispered in his native tongue. It was slowly dawning on the old manservant that despite promises to a boy's father many years before, he could no longer serve, advise or protect the master from his insanity; but maybe now was the time to serve himself for a change.

He knew the world would not allow this cruel game to continue for much longer, and soon the law would be breaking down the front doors of this once-happy and magnificent castle.

Chapter 14

As the image on the Laptop screen suddenly froze and then went blank Holly glowered. "They've cut the feed!"

"Don't know who that girl was, but she sure was brave and kinda cute!" Cowboy said. "Shame though, I got a feeling we'll soon be finding a body!"

"Her name is Lena!" Holly added sullenly and then turned to look at the Colonel. "Do we know who she is yet?"

Colonel Harker nodded. "Lena Bergstrom, she's a Norwegian astrophysicist."

"So, why'd he take her?" She's no celebrity I ever heard of!"

"As it happens, she's huge in Norway, she has her own TV show and is very outspoken on the old green issues!"

"Norwegian!" Cowboy grinned. "I ain't never been with no Norwegian chick!"

"Really!" Holly spat. "Is that all you think about?"

"That and beer Cupcake, that and beer!"

"Quit the squabbling you two, and get this room cleaned up!" Then he looked at his wristwatch. "Don't forget you're on that chat show thing tonight-So get some rest."

"Are we performing?" Mitch asked. "I was thinking we could maybe sing something other than…!"

"Nope, it's a chat show! So, make sure you know your covers and don't screw it up!"

The silence was deafening and seemingly endless, Martello took a sip of his coffee and returned to the stand-off. Either Ike didn't understand the offer being made to him or he was just plain dumb. "Ok Ike, what's it going to be? As I see it you're looking at life without parole; jeez man you and your friends abducted an entire pop group."

"What if I know nothin'?"

"Look man, I know you wanna play the big man here and stay loyal to dumb and dumber in the next room there but I need to tell you Ike, those other two are brothers and they're being given the exact same

offer as you right now!" Martello said and picked up his coffee.

"Why, if I were them I'd throw you to the dogs! I'm offering you a

cushy jail and a cut in your sentence. Do yourself a favour man and

give me something I can use."

"If I do this I need something in writing!"

"Sure, that can be arranged; I give you my word!"

"Eat shit; you're word means nothing to me!"

Martello reached into his inside pocket and pulled out a white

envelope. "Lucky for you Ike I came here all prepared like." Placing

the envelope on the table he pushed it across to the prisoner.

"I can't read!"

"This letter states that your sentence will be no more than ten years

and you will serve your time in minimum security- But I ain't signing

nothing until you start talking!"

"They was south of the border; you know, Mexicans I guess, they

offered us twenty thousand dollars if we could deliver those girls to

them! We ain't never seen so much cash!"

"How many of them were there?"

"Two!"

"How did you meet them? How did they know you might be interested in doing the job?"

Ike shrugged. "I dunno, this guy just came up to us in a bar one night! They told us where the coach would be and exactly when it would be there!"

"Something went wrong, what happened?"

"We got the girls, that was easy; but Vince, well he kept wanting to touch them and he was making all these comments; There was this one girl, I don't recall her name, I think it was the blond one, well he just wouldn't leave her alone man. As time went on he just got worse. It was all Johnny and me could do to stop him raping her! I might be vermin but I ain't no rapist!"

"And then what happened!"

"I dunno, some guy came through the front door and kicked the shit out of us!"

"Dude, for me to sign this piece of paper!" Martello said and picked up the envelope. "I need something, it doesn't matter how small it is or how insignificant."

Ike frowned and shook his head. "Looks like we're both screwed because I can't think of anything…!"

It was obvious from his face that Ike did indeed know something and needed a little shove in the right direction. In a show of brinksmanship Martello stood, and then very slowly returned the envelope to the pocket from which it had come. "Five seconds and I'm out of that door, last chance! Come on man once I'm gone you're going back to jail, and you gonna spend the next twenty years as someone's little bitch!"

"Let me think man, stop rushing me… Maybe, maybe I have something? I think maybe they stayed at the Motel just outside town, and well there's a chance that… Well, they paid with a credit card!"

"How do you know that?"

"If I tell you, I don't want him to get into any trouble or anything! I know this one dude; he got this peachy little scam going down…!"

"Let me guess, He's skimming the credit cards!"

"Yeah man, he copies the cards and then leaves it for a few months before he uses them, you know? So, no one ever traces it back to him!"

"What's his name?"

"I'm no grass!"

"Well, the way it stands I can find this guy because you already told me where to look, and luckily for the law-abiding citizens who you may commit crimes against if you were to be free, I don't have to sign this piece of paper!"

"Hey dude! Come on man I gave you something!" Ike cried in desperation.

"I want a name and I want an address..! Now!"

Beyond the twilight, darkening skies and the threat of rain Culpeper emerged from behind the woods and fields of DC's rural backyard. Checking the maps application on his iPhone Martello began looking for somewhere to pull over where his car would be out of sight of the house; the target building was just two hundred meters ahead. Pulling over well short, he waited and watched and allowed darkness to descend before exiting the vehicle. Cautious of prying eyes he carefully approached the front door and knocked twice before realising the door wasn't on the latch.

From somewhere deep inside a radio was playing a tune. "That goddam song is everywhere!" Martello whispered. "Hello inside!" He said loudly. "Is there anyone home?" Hardly waiting long enough for a reply he pushed the door open and stepped inside, and was immediately hit square in the nose with the only too familiar scent of blood. A sudden surge of adrenaline saw him unholster his weapon, as his eyes adjusted to the darkness within he noticed the room had been ransacked.

slowly covering his arcs and tingling with anticipation he crept forward, moving to what he eventually found to be a kitchen, or at least what was left of one. The scent of blood was strong in this room, something terrible had happened here.

Moving quickly to the small staircase he stopped and listened, but was met with only silence. Pressing on, he took the steps two at a time climbing to the first floor, all the while conscious of what could be awaiting him. As he walked along the landing he noticed the carpet seemed sticky, he could only guess at what the substance was. He paused at the first bedroom and took a breath composing himself before pushing the door open.

The DeadBeats

The view that met his eyes was incredulous; a bloody mangled form which had once been a man lay sprawling naked on the bed. Martello's hand instantly moved to his mouth to stifle his gag reflex, taking a breath he moved closer and took in the whole awful scene. The victim's left arm was broken and laying at an odd angle and each hand was missing two fingers; the latter and all of his teeth lay scattered on the bed; his chest and stomach had received many lacerations and stab wounds and the offending weapon still lay embedded in his left kneecap.

Placing his iPhone to his ear he waited for the ringtone to stop. "He's dead!" He said and replaced his pistol to its holster. "Looks like he's been tortured; I want forensics and a search team down here as soon as possible!"

None of it made any sense, Martello knew he could get the credit card details from the Motel anytime and assuming he was dealing with professionals they also knew the same; that can't have been what they were after here. A thought suddenly occurred and seemed to leak out of his mouth. "It's loose ends, they're tying up loose ends." He paused as his mind stitched all the ideas together to form one thought. "Get someone down to the penitentiary now! He's gonna try to kill Ike and the brothers Grimm!"

A terrible feeling suddenly overtook his senses dashing out of the house he sprinted for his car. Jumping in he gunned the engine and surged forward in a cloud of burning rubber; driving at breakneck speed he raced the few miles to the motel, swinging into the parking lot he skidded to a halt.

Dashing into the reception, his worst fears were realised, still sitting at her desk the receptionist sat staring blankly into space, a single bullet hole in the centre of her forehead.

"God dam it...!"

Touching her cheek, he noted she was still warm, and the blood seemingly fresh; her death was very recent and her killers were possibly still in the area. Wiping a splash of blood from a tag on her blouse to see her name Martello looked at her young face. "Well Debby, I'm Sorry I couldn't get here any sooner!" He said and reached into her top pocket retrieving the master key card. "If you don't mind, I'm just going to borrow this!" He smiled at her and then once again unholstered his pistol. There was no way to know if in fact, the killers were still here or which room they were in, then Martello noticed the computer and turned the screen to face him. "Bingo!" He said, Only six of the fifteen rooms were occupied but tellingly a key card had only been used on one door in the last twenty minutes, room eight.

Cold with anger and full of vengeance for a young girl he had never met, Martello strode into the corridor leading to the apartments.

Loose ends, this was all about tying up the loose ends and covering their tracks; They were disposing of any witnesses and sanitising anywhere they had lingered.

Room eight was at the end of a short corridor on the right, and the approach had no discernible cover should anyone exit the room shooting. Martello didn't care, he was in no mood for the pleasantries of a shootout. Only stopping momentarily at the door to push the card into the slot, he heard a soft click as the locking mechanism opened; turning the handle he pushed the door open and raised his pistol ready for trouble.

Stepping inside the brightly lit room he stopped and listened, Someone was home, noises coming from the bathroom told him as much. "You inside there, come out with your hands up! The building is surrounded you have no hope of escape!"

The noises immediately stopped and exactly four seconds later the door slowly swung open. Martello braced himself, in his experience professional gunmen rarely surrendered, it just wasn't in their nature.

"I'm coming out, please don't shoot me!"

Martello frowned; he was not expecting a woman's voice, especially an elderly woman's voice. "Ma'am, step out of the bathroom please, with your hands in the air!"

"I'm coming dear." She said. "Just a moment, I'm not as mobile as I used to be! It's my hips you know!"

As the small, stout woman stepped into view Martello doubted himself and double-checked the room number. She was old, maybe seventy or so, complete with grey rinse and a pinafore whose one large pocket seemed stuffed to overflowing with rags and cloths. "Who are you!" He asked.

"Why dear, I'm just the maid; it's my job to clean these rooms- May I lower my hands please, I have arthritis in my shoulders?"

Martello nodded dumbly. "Anyone else here?" He asked and glancing down at her shoes noticed the smallest droplet of blood on her left heel.

For an elderly lady her eyes were just a little too bright, and her gaze just too fixed.

"No, just… Just little old me."

The sudden change in tone of her voice told Martello that she had realised very quickly that he had seen something incriminating.

Giving her reason to react he began lowering his pistol, their eyes met in a fleeting stare off and Martello watched in slow motion as she suddenly reached into her apron pocket, pulling out a silenced pistol. He reacted instantly, shooting her three times in the chest; she fell to the ground as frothy air fill blood began oozing from her mouth.

Taking three steps he bent over and took the pistol from her hands and then looked down on her as she gasped her last dying breath. "That was for Debby!"

Then he took out his cell phone and grimaced as he wondered what the hell he was going to tell the boss.

The applause cascaded through the studio mixing with the adoring screams of the young female fans. Leading the group from the stage Mitch waved at the audience which resulted in more applause and more screaming. "Let's get outta here before they riot!" He cried. "Well done, great performance guys!"

"Man, that was cool!" Cowboy cried as he wiped the sweat from his forehead.

Holly just giggled and then let out a small scream as Scot swept her up in his huge arms. "God, I love this shit man!"

"Ok, guys!" The Colonel said and clapped his hands three times. "Straight outside and on the coach, we got another performance across town!"

"Dude!" Tony cried. "I'm starving, I need food man!"

"There's food on the coach, less talking and more walking! Come on let's hustle!"

Moving quickly along the warren of narrow and dark corridors Mitch was first out into the storm of screams and shouts, and the barrage of camera flashes.

The DeadBeats

"Keep moving!" The Colonel shouted as loud as he could. "Don't stop, push through!"

Towering above the throng Scott noticed a group of five teenage girls all singing his rap section of the song; he couldn't resist breaking ranks and pushing through the crowd until he was right in front of them, Who noticing him, began screaming hysterically.

"Hey cool it -Sing the song girls, I wanna hear it!" Scott hollered. "You just sounded great!"

A sharp jab in his back reminded him the coach awaited. "I gotta go girls, it was great meeting you guys!"

Turning his back, he left them to shrieks and shouts of "We love you Scott" and then they began singing again.

"What the hell were you doing back there!" The Colonel growled.

"I was conversing with my fans, Sir!"

"Scott! Do not wander off like that again! These girls will tear you apart given half a chance!"

"Just got caught up in the moment Sir, sorry it won't happen again!"

"See that it doesn't- Ok guys now we're all on the coach settle down, get something to eat and take a break. We'll shortly be arriving at BBC studios for the Harry King show!"

"She was very thorough Agent Martello; this place is spotless!" The Crime scene Investigator said, but from the twinkle in her eyes, Martello knew there was something. "But these cleaners always forget things like the bath plug and under the toilet seat- Fortunately I don't! I've lifted several prints which instantly lit the whole system up!"

"You're kidding!" Martello was aghast, he hadn't expected any results! "Good work! So, who are we looking for!"

"We have two hits the first is this man!" She turned her tablet so Martello could see the screen. "One Manuel Gonzalez, known professional hitman, works as an enforcer for the cartel."

"And then there's Carlos Estefan, another mob heavy, same story, I've put out an all-ports bulletin, but it's unlikely we'll be catching up with them tonight!"

"Can you do anything else with that tablet?"

"What like, could you cross-check any credit cards used here in this motel with say other places they may have been used!"

"I'd need a time frame!"

Quickly doing the maths in his head Martello worked out the date Mitch had rescued the girls and then estimated the dates the killers were staying at the Motel. "At a guess, I'd have to say they arrived here around the fifteenth and stayed no more than two days; you can go a little either side of my figures."

"I'll have to make a phone call to one of my colleagues, If they don't already know you're onto them and they're actively using the card, he'll find your guys!"

After exchanging contact details, Martello returned to his car. Whoever was running the Fame game had some serious power and some very credible underworld connections. Even if he could somehow catch up with the Mexican contingent it was imperative he didn't kill both of them, however difficult that may be.

Suddenly realising how tired he was, he figured he'd find a hotel that didn't have dead bodies littering the place, take a shower and get some sleep. But fate had other ideas, no sooner had he gunned the engine than the CSI agent was tapping on the passenger side window.

Winding the window down Martello Absentmindedly twisted his neck, as he tried to remove the stress which had built up during the events of the day. "What is it?" He said wearily.

"Guess what? They used the card!"

"What?" Suddenly he was wide awake. "Where? When?"

She grinned. "Twenty minutes ago, at a gas station in Jacksonville; We even have CCTV- Including make, model and colour of the vehicle they're driving!"

"You guys are incredible! How the hell did you do that so quickly?"

"That would be telling!" She smiled. "There's more, one of them used a cell phone inside the gas station, we're now tracking that phone; They're currently seventeen miles south of Jacksonville!"

"Can you send everything you got to my cell phone?" All of a sudden the game was very much back on; the only problem was the huge head start the bad guys had on him. "Now all I need is a chopper and a military satellite!"

She laughed. "A military satellite?"

"Yeah, I got some friends in high places!" He said and took out his cell phone. "Thanks for everything, I'll let you know when I catch up with them!" With that, he waved and set off at speed for the nearest airfield.

"Where the hell are we?" Holly said and yawned. "I'm beat! And these seats are so dammed uncomfortable!"

Mitch shook his head. "I have no idea! I lost track after Manchester! What is it with all the dammed roundabouts- People in this country must spend half their lives in a perpetual state of dizziness!"

"I think we're back in London!" Tony said and then he too stretched and yawned. "I'm pretty Sure, we just went over London Bridge!"

"How many performances have we done today? Is it six or seven?" Scott said as he tried to remember the answer to his own question.

"Gotta be more than six."

"It's six!" The Colonel said. "And you got one more, it's in a top London nightclub. We get in, do the gig and get the hell out!"

"And then what!" Mitch asked.

"Paris! And the circus begins all over again!"

Chapter 15

"Manfred!" Casper barked, for the seventh or eighth time and banged his fist on the table, causing a bone China cup and saucer to fall to the floor where they smashed into several pieces. "Where are you, old man? Look what you have made me do!"

"I'm coming as fast as I can master!" Manfred cried wearily but made no effort to move his Zimmer frame any quicker.

"Do hurry! I must speak with you urgently! Where were you? What were you doing?"

"You called Sir?" He said ignoring the questions, as he entered the master's bedroom.

"I've decided that I don't like the game anymore, it's not big enough! Tell our contacts more girls, more games; bigger and better games. More blood, more death… More everything!"

"Yes sir!"

The DeadBeats

"My fans deserve bigger and better; I want a live stream every day until we have a winner."

"And what would you have me give the winner sir?"

"Why, Manfred my man she wins her life and eternal fame! She'll forever be known as the girl who won the Fame Game!"

"Yes sir, quite!"

"The girl who refused to fight last night, have you taken care of her?"

"Yes sir!" Manfred said. "Lena left us this morning."

Casper turned from looking at himself in the mirror and glared at his manservant. "She left us this morning? Dead, she had better have been dead!"

"Yes sir, she was very dead!"

"Did she feel it? I…I wanted her to feel it! I wanted her to feel it with every last nerve in her wretched body.

"Oh yes sir! She was screaming with wretched agony!!"

"Did you drain the life out of her slowly and very painfully?"

"Yes sir, one could not have died in any more pain than she!"

"Good… Good! Now off with you and make preparations!"

Manfred bowed, turned and left the room; taking hold of his Zimmer frame he shuffled along the corridor until he reached the stairs down to the ground floor, at which point he once again parked his walking aid and gingerly headed below.

Moving beyond the ground floor he soon found himself deep in the dungeons where all the contestants were being housed. Pausing for a second to catch his breath Manfred took hold of a second Zimmer frame and began moving toward an alcove where an armed man sat at a desk.

"Good morning Jurgen, everything is as it should be I presume?"

Jurgen nodded. "Everything is secure!" He growled. "I have been here five hours without food, I am hungry! Why have you not brought me breakfast!"

"I apologise, the Master has asked that I take a watch while you go to the kitchen and help yourself to food! Have what you want, take anything!" Manfred lied, and then watched as the huge Austrian glared at him before rising slowly from his chair and quickly heading up the steps.

The DeadBeats

After waiting for the sound of footsteps to disappear into the distance Manfred turned and slowly headed to the far end of the corridor. Where, once there he reached up and twisted an old, unused candle stick holder. Checking over his shoulder to make sure Jurgen or none of the other security team were about, he yanked on the rusty metal and immediately a section of what appeared to be a stone wall suddenly swung open slightly. Pushing the door open he stepped inside. "Good morning Lena; I trust you slept well?"

Swinging her legs around and off the bed she sat up. "What's happening?" She said fearfully. "Are you here to kill me?"

"NO..! What's happening is that you are already dead, you died in terrible pain and your body was dumped on the mountain- or so I would have the Master believe!"

"Why have you done this? Why are you helping me?"

"Young lady, I have never willingly lied or been disloyal to the Master or his father before him in over fifty years of proud service. But now…!"

"But now what?"

"But now..!" Manfred paused and shook his head sadly. "I realise he is quite irreversibly insane!"

"Will you help me to get out of here?"

Manfred grimaced; the pain of betrayal was almost too much to bear. "I am but an old man, almost all of my many days are far, far behind me." His voice weak and shaking, he paused to clear his throat. "I must confess this building has… Has seen some terrible things of late, things I am deeply ashamed of. I am as guilty as he and sad to say have gone along with the madness as far as I can but it seems to me that what is taking place here is wrong, and I fear soon men with guns will come and stop him…!"

"So, that's good, isn't it? We'll all be rescued!"

"So, I do not wish to die here… Or spend whatever time I have left rotting in a prison cell."

"Why can't you just call the cops and tell them where we are? I'll tell them you helped me, that you saved my life!"

"No… Not yet! And besides, whatever you say I will still go to prison, and quite rightly so!" Manfred licked his dry lips as he thought of his next words. "You know, his insanity knows no bounds, he demands more girls, more death and more blood!"

Manfred shook his head in sadness. "I cannot allow any more innocent girls to be murdered in the name of entertainment!"

"Call the police, that's all you have to do- Just call them!"

"What? And have them destroy this most ancient of castles! No… No that is not the way, I will not do that! This glorious building has been my home for as long as I can remember."

"The castle is just cold hard stone, it will survive, we may not!"

"Of course, you are right, but I am an old man and I am very tired; I would not survive long in prison. I feel that I would very much like to end my days sitting on a beach somewhere with a drink in my hand and the ocean lapping around my feet. When the time is right, I will help you to live and you will help me with my retirement plans- That is the deal?"

Lena nodded.

He began to close the door but stopped short. "There is another girl, her name is Brianne; she is sick, I will move her in here with you. Take care of her, and be quiet; there are bad men here who will kill you on sight should they discover you!"

"Manfred, thank you!"

Holding the shotgun tightly into his shoulder, Martello remained out of sight using an old pine tree as token cover from the steady drizzle. "Any time now guys!" He shouted and almost right on Q the headlights of Pickup approaching at speed, lit up the country road. Chambering a cartridge, he gave a nod to the local Sherriff who immediately turned on his red and blue flashing lights. "Ok guys this is it, nice and easy I want at least one of them alive!"

As the Pickup drew closer it began to slow, stepping in front of his car the officer held up his hand ordering the vehicle to stop. Then he quickly walked up to the driver's side window. "Hi guys, I tell you you're a sight for sore eyes. There's been a bad accident, I wonder if you men could step out of your vehicle and help remove the lady from her car?"

Eternally suspicious, the driver first checked his rear-view mirror and then tried to peer into the brush on each side of the road. "I don't see no accident Officer!"

"It's just down the road! Seriously guys she's gonna die for sure if we don't get her out right now!"

231

The DeadBeats

Nervously glancing at his passenger, the driver desperately tried to think of a good reason why they couldn't help, but nothing came to mind and feeling backed into a corner he relented. "Show us the lady, we help you!" He said reluctantly but a second glance at his passenger and unspoken words told him they would kill the Sherriff and leave the woman to her fate.

Slowly leaving the vehicle both men moved toward the lights of the Police car, unaware that behind them Martello and four deputies had stepped out of the darkness and were currently levelling their weapons at the back of their heads.

"Stand still, and raise your hands in the air!" Martello cried. "Move a god dam muscle and I'll blow your heads clean off your shoulders!" Then he moved up behind the shocked hit men and removed pistols from both their waists, tossing them on the floor. "Ok Sherriff, let's get this shit off the highway before we get a ticket for littering! they're making the place look untidy!"

The motorcade swept out of the airport with a police car leading the way and was immediately stopped in its tracks as thousands of screaming fans surged through the police cordon in a desperate attempt to catch a glimpse of their idols.

"Jeez man, this is crazier than London!" Scott cried.

"I'm not sure I like this very much!" Holly said and lowered her sunglasses slightly to get a better look, and then waved at a young girl who looked like she was about to be crushed.

"It comes with the territory people! You should have seen what the last guy had to put up with, he couldn't go to the can without some kid hiding in there waiting for him."

"Sir!" Mitch said and held out the newspaper he had been reading for everyone to see. "How the hell are we going to do our jobs with this kind of scrutiny? Hell, there's some woman in Montreal who says I fathered two of her five kids!"

"Well, did you?"

"Hell no! I've never even been to Montreal!"

"If that was Cowboy they were talking about I might believe it!" Holly laughed and gently punched him on the shoulder.

"The only woman having my kids is you Cupcake!" He said and then pulled a face at the thought.

"Never happen shit face!"

"I must admit your song has grown far bigger than I ever anticipated, and it does complicate things!" Harker said. "Hell, you guys are bigger than Elvis was…"

"We ain't never gonna be bigger than Elvis boss!" Cowboy said. "He was the king of Rock and Roll!"

"He was a dick, and he's still a dick! You're just lucky you don't have to deal with that old-timer's demands like I do! But sure, you're certainly bigger than the last guy! You already sold more records than he did… Oh wait, hang on a second!" On hearing his iPhone bleep a notification Harker reached into his open briefcase and retrieved the gadget. "I got a text message here from Agent Martello! Good news people, they've apprehended the Mexicans and they're singing like canaries… He's flying over to meet us, where he will give us a briefing, he'll be here in the early hours."

Suddenly the coach began moving again as dozens of riot police forced the crowd back, and soon the cavalcade was moving freely along the capital's highways.

"Sir!" Mitch said. "I know we're not a real band and everything, but this one song is not going to be in the charts for very long and to be honest I think I speak for everyone when I say we're getting real tired

of singing that same song over and over..."

"That's just the way it is kid!"

"What I'm saying is Sir, I have other songs; Scott has some lyrics

he's working on maybe while we're hanging around and doing these

dumb shows, maybe you could give us a couple of days and some

studio time!"

Harker stared back at Mitch while his brain computed the reply.

"Funny you should mention that! You guys need a short break and I

think we'd all like to get away from the crazy fans for a while- I

guess a couple of days down at good old Ramstein Airforce base

couldn't hurt non!"

"Ramstein Sir?" Mitch frowned as he suddenly realised the Airbase

was already on the itinerary. "You mean, Ramstein the Airforce base

where we're likely to launch a rescue mission from?"

Harker nodded and grinned. "Sure, I'm going to send the roadies on

to Berlin to set up the concert, as you're supporting Strawberry Island

on this leg of their world tour we're going to be needing those songs

from you- So, you guys are flying south tonight;

The DeadBeats

"Why do I get the feeling there ain't going to be much resting?"

"Well, you know what they say, a change is as good as a rest!"

Colonel Harker said and then turning in his seat picked up a

newspaper. "And besides as of thirty minutes ago you're on one

hour's notice to move on a rescue…"

"And of course, while we're there you'd like us to go through our

gear, which just happens to be waiting for us in some quiet little

hanger on the edge of the airfield!" Holly Said.

"Amen to that!" Cowboy added. "I haven't laid eyes on my Colt 45

in weeks, I'm beginning to have withdrawal symptoms!"

"Oh, and by the way, you have a number-one track in eight different

countries and a mob of very annoying fans, so don't tell me you're

not a real band!"

"Manfred..!" Casper shrieked. "Manfred, I need you! Come here at

once!"

Rolling his eyes, Manfred sighed heavily. "I'm right here master!

How can I be of service he said and stepped into the room.

"I've been calling you! Where have you been?"

"I'm here now sir!" Manfred said calmly; Knowing only too well what was about to come.

"Close the door, so they can't hear!" Casper whispered and then placed a finger on his lips telling his manservant to hush.

Manfred closed the door. "May I enquire as to whom is listening, sir?"

"All of them… They're all listening! They're watching me too..! And they're talking about me! Tell… Tell them to stop it at once!"

"Who is talking about you sir, there is no one else here!"

"Not here you… You fool! Downstairs, the guards they're talking behind my back- They're laughing and plotting!" Casper said and nervously looked around the room, and then he whispered. "Plotting..! They have gadgets, they know what I'm thinking- They want to kill me and take my show- They want the fame game for themselves."

"I'm sure that isn't the case sir! The men and I have the utmost respect for you!"

"Oh no, not you as well!" His eyes widened in terror, he took a step backwards and then placed a hand on his chest as he began to hyperventilate. "It's you, isn't it? You're one of them!" He cried

breathlessly. "Oh my god, my most trusted man has turned against

me! Who will help me now? Help, someone, help me!"

"Sir… Sir, you need to calm down; you're just having one of your

attacks! Just relax and let me pour you a drink.

"Don't tell me to calm down! I'm the master…!" Casper barked.

"You do as I say; Now pour me a drink. I seem to be having one of

my attacks!" Taking another step backwards Casper collapsed in a

heap on his bed and began to sob. "Manfred my pills, fetch my pills

at once! I'm dying, I'm really dying this time!"

"No sir, you're not dying, it's all in your mind, remember what the

doctor's said." As Manfred turned to leave the room he took a

lingering look at the portrait of Casper's father over the fireplace. "I'll

be back just as soon as I can!" He said and smiled.

"The show must go on Manfred; the show must go on!"

"Quite, sir! That it must!"

"Ok guys, I'll make this quick; I know it's late and we all want to get

some sleep!" Martello said.

"Sleep?" Cowboy scoffed. "I thought we were all going on to a club!"

Rolling her eyes Holly shot Cowboy a look of derision. "I don't think the beefcake quite understands our lives now! Cowboy, we ain't never going out in public again! We're like circus animals that are kept in a cage and only let out to perform!"

"Anyhow..!" Martello continued. "Between the brothers Grim and the two Mexicans, we're beginning to paint a picture of the organisation behind the abductions and the so-called Fame Game! Whoever is behind this is seriously wealthy and well-connected to all of the world's criminal organisations; all communications are made via the so-called Dark web and burner phones. Payments are made in untraceable cash or gold and from what I gather, it's all very simple a contract goes out the girl is taken and shipped to a central collection point in Munich before being moved on to the site of the games."

"And where might that be?" Mitch said as a sinking feeling began to form in his stomach.

"Well, we don't quite know but believe me the net is tightening!"

"Jeez Agent Martello!" Holly said. "It's a castle somewhere in Europe… How many castles can there be?"

"Obviously, more than you think… Arrests have been made on several continents and these people are being interrogated as we speak, and now I'd like to hand you back over to Colonel Harker!"

Standing, Harker moved to take Martello's place at the front of the room. "ok people, there will be no clubs and zero sleep tonight… This is it! We got spy planes over Munich and intel tells us there's increased activity in and around the site!"

"What is the site, sir?" Mitch asked.

"It's a warehouse complex on the north side of the city; We have a green light so get your gear and I'll see you on the choppers! In ten minutes!"

"What about mission parameters or a plan Sir?"

"We'll wing it!"

"Wing it..? You want us to wing it?"

"Alright, I'll give you a plan! We go there, and kill most but not all of the bad guys; Yes Cowboy that statement is aimed squarely at you! We mustn't kill them all as I'd like to speak to at least one of them… oh and it would be helpful if you could rescue all of the hostages without any of those people dying! Come on guys it'll be fun; it's what your all trained for, it's what you've all been waiting for"

"Hell yeah!" Cowboy cried and jumped to his feet. "Let's go, guys! I get to kill me some bad dudes tonight!"

"Has anyone seen my other blades?" Tony said. "I haven't seen them since... Well, since I don't know when."

"Blades?" Holly said. "What do you mean? Like knives or something?"

"My legs... I'm talking about my legs." He said as if talking to an idiot. "I have this pair that I wear all the time and I have another pair for operations."

"Is there like, a difference? Do the other pair let you run faster and jump higher? You know, like Steve Austin in The Bionic Man?"

"No Cowboy, you dumb shit; My operational legs are... Green!"

"Jesus Christ!" Harker moaned. "What the hell did I do to deserve this gig, It's like working with children!"

The DeadBeats

Chapter 16

As the Black Hawke helicopters began to level off at fifteen

thousand feet, Colonel Harker tossed a bag onto the floor. "There's a

good chance you guys could be recognised." He shouted over the din

of the engines. "And we can't be having any of that nonsense. So,

there you go a little present from Uncle Sam!"

Reaching into the bag, Mitch realised straight away what was in his

hand, looking at Holly he grinned. "Sorry about the hair." Then he

tossed one of the items to her.

"No..!" She whined. "Balaclavas, really sir! Is this necessary?"

"This is not a beauty contest Marine! It was either this or a

respirator, I thought I was doing you a favour!"

"So, what's the plan, sir?"

"We have a green light for a kill or capture mission! The local law

enforcement has cordoned off a six-block radius, no one is getting in

243

or out! Cowboy is in the other chopper he's going to fast-rope onto the neighbouring building and give us top cover; once he's taken out any armed guards Scott and Tony will enter from the north side and you two from the south. Your mission is twofold- One, release any hostages and two, kill or capture the people in charge!"

"Sounds easy when you put it like that sir!"

"It's going to be a walk in the park! Now mask up, five minutes and you're out the door!"

As the helicopter slowed to a hover the buffeting became more manageable, stabilising his legs against the Black Hawk Cowboy held onto the rope and readied himself for the descent. Suddenly Colonel Harker's voice crackled in his right ear. "We have a green light; Go, go, go!"

"Roger that, moving now!" Wrapping his legs around the rope he began his controlled descent. Hitting the roof three seconds later, he knelt until the pilot had moved away. "I'm down and moving into position now!" He whispered into the throat mic.

Without waiting for a reply, he quickly drew his sidearm and chambered a round before re-holstering the weapon. Then he remained still and silent, absorbing the atmosphere and sounds of the night, as he awaited the tell-tale signs that his presence was known, once satisfied he unclipped the M22 sniper rifle from his shoulder fitted the silencer, removed the sight lens covers and quietly fed a round into the breach.

"In position in thirty seconds, wait out!" Moving quickly but silently he made his way to the western side of his building, Where after identifying a suitable fire point where he could see the whole of the target building, he got down in the prone position and made himself comfortable.

Lifting the butt into his shoulder he peered down the sight and scanned the building opposite. "In position boss!"

"What are you seeing Cowboy?"

"We have two... No three heavily armed targets at the main entrance, one in an external second-floor stairwell and I see two on the roof- They look like Mercs to me boss, from the way they're holding those AK47s I'd say ex-military!"

"Standby Topcover!"

"Roger that!"

"Sabre two, sabre two this is Sunray!" Colonel Harker said into the mic. "Proceed on mission! I say again proceed on mission!"

"Roger that!" Scott replied and two seconds later both he and Tony were fast-roping to the ground."

Once down they both remained in a crouching position until the chopper had lifted out and then chambered rounds in the MP5s.

"Sunray this is Sabre two, moving toward the target now, wait out!"

"Sabre two this is Topcover welcome to the party, the bad guys are out and about, so watch your six!"

"Roger that Topcover!"

Covering their arcs of fire Scott and Tony began a tactical advance toward the target building.

"Ok you two, get going and good luck!" Harker cried over the din of the rotors. "See you on the flip side… And try not to die I hate writing those letters!"

"Thanks for the concern sir, I always knew you cared!" And with that Mitch and Holly headed down to the ground,

Kneeling they waited for the chopper to go airborne, once it was away they chambered rounds and made their weapons ready. Then they quickly moved toward the cover of shadows and darkness beside the buildings,

"Sunray this is Sabre one, moving out now!"

"Roger that! Watch your twelve, we have Goons overlooking your approach!"

"How long until the power is cut?"

"You have three minutes to make your start position!"

"Roger that"

Covering their arcs of fire, they silently began to edge forward; each one covering the other's advance as they leapfrogged each other's position. Soon they were moving smoothly yet rapidly as if in a highly choreographed dance. As the target building finally came into view Holly signalled Mitch to stop, then she slowly melted into the shadows and pointed to the roof.

"Sunray this is Sabre one, two hundred meters to the start position; we have eyes on!"

"Roger that, Top Cover we go dark in sixty seconds, you have a green light to take out both targets on the roof!"

"Roger that Sunray!"

"Thirty seconds!"

"Fifteen seconds!"

Every light in a four-block area suddenly went out. "All Callsigns you have a go!"

Settling his breathing Cowboy rested the cross hairs of his rifle on the chest of target one and squeezed the trigger, without waiting to see if the man had fallen he located target two who was further away, slightly adjusting his position he once again controlled his breathing and held his breath just as he pulled the trigger. "Sabre One, Sabre Two this is Topcover the runway is now cleared for take-off, enjoy your trip!"

"Roger that Top cover we'll take it from here!"

Switching to night vision they were now out in the open and moving quickly. Mitch and Holly soon found themselves approaching a fire exit, reaching into Holly's rear right pouch Mitch took out a shaped charge and a small cigarette-shaped detonator. Fixing it to the door he inserted the detonator and they both moved a short distance to take cover from any fast-moving debris.

The explosion was little more than a flash and a dull thud but the desired effect was evident as the blast turned the heavy door into splinters. Ready for a firefight they rapidly filed through the freshly made, and still smoking, hole. The room was windowless and empty and looked like it hadn't been used in decades.

"Sunray, Sabre one we are in!"

Having used an external metal staircase to gain access to the first floor, Scott hauled his huge frame through the open window and followed Tony inside. "Sabre two, we're in!"

Pointing to some concrete steps which led down to the ground floor Tony signalled Scott to listen and as they both stood in silence distant voices began to drift up from below.

The DeadBeats

A mutual nod was all it took for them to quietly begin their descent, halfway down the steps turned ninety degrees, and, leading the way Scott suddenly held up his hand and stopped dead in his tracks. Even without seeing or being told Tony knew from Scott's body language there was a guard in the doorway below and froze.

Taking out his knife he held it aloft for Tony to see, this was a sign Scott would take the guard out silently. Leaving his partner behind, Scott stealthily continued down the steps, as he neared the guard he ceased to breathe from fear his breaths would be heard.

Loath to kill needlessly, he re-sheaved the knife and moved close enough behind the mercenary that he could smell his stale sweat, and oddly Scott thought his rather flowery hair product. In one explosive, fluid movement he reached around covering the mouth and violently dragged the man back into the pitch darkness, beating him senseless and knocking him out cold.

Crouching beside the guard's unconscious form he tie-wrapped the hands together and then the feet. "Sunray this is Sabre two stairwells clear and one very bad dude hog-tied and sleeping like a baby!"

"Roger that Sabre Two, Topcover reports activity outside, He'll take them out as they bear! probably trying to figure out why the lights have gone out! I don't think they're onto you but watch your six!"

"Roger that, moving now, wait out!"

Cracking the door open just enough to see out into the huge void of the near-empty warehouse, Mitch found himself only thirty meters from a beat-up old transit van; the driver, unaware of the impending danger stood in the open door rummaging around in the glove compartment.

Beyond, Mitch could see a container where most of the voices seemed to be coming from. Somewhat surprised to hear someone shouting for a torch in English he realised they would have to make their assault whilst the bad guys were fumbling around in the dark.

"Sabre two, you in position?"

"Roger! Ready to go when you are!"

"Let's do this guy's GO, GO, GO!"

Weapons in the shoulder they filed out, quickly covering the short distance to the van. The driver having failed to find a torch and hearing footsteps half turned, but in the pitch darkness saw neither Mitch or the MP5 butt which smashed into his skull, knocking him out cold. As the body crumpled to the floor Mitch and Holly were already moving around to the back of the container, where they saw Scott and Tony approaching from the other side, momentum and surprise on their side they pressed home the assault.

Only now as time seemed to stand still in the inky darkness did it begin to dawn on the three Mercenary guards something was wrong, they would never know what it was or why they raised their weapons, or why one of them fired his AK47 wildly into the void.

Instinctively returning fire by way of a double tap, Holly hit the offending guard square in the chest. His weapon clattered to the floor as he staggered back two steps and fell dead.

Moving quickly to place himself between the hysterical screams and shrieks of the captives and the gunmen, Mitch fired two rounds dropping one target while Tony pole-axed the last one with a single punch to the temple.

"Sunray this is Sabre One hostages secured!"

"Roger that, Topcover reports all external threats neutralised! Well done guys standby to receive local law enforcement!"

"Roger out!"

As the lights returned Mitch switched off his night vision, and while Scott and Tony disarmed the mercenaries he made his way into the back of the container, where he found Holly untying the six hostages. "US Marines... It's alright you're safe, no one is going to hurt you now!" She cried above the sobs and pleas for help.

"Is anyone hurt?" Mitch said and took the lack of a reply as his answer. "OK local plod will be here in three minutes; I want to be on the chopper in two! Let's move people!"

"Ex... Excuse me!"

Mitch turned to meet the voice, and despite the bruises and running mascara probably one of the most beautiful women he had ever seen. For the shortest of seconds, he was dumbstruck.

"This... This whole thing isn't real is it?" She said meekly and dared to glance down at one of the dead bodies. "The producer said it was a hostage reality show...But I think some of you actors are overdoing it a little!"

"What..? What are you talking about?"

"It's just that I really need the makeup girl..." Then she moved closer and lowered her voice to a whisper. "And I need you to tell me where the cameras are... You know, so I can show my best side!"

"Madam, I don't think you understand what's happening here!"

"Oh, and could you be a sweetie and ask the producer for some water and maybe some food? We're all shivering it's very cold in here!"

His mind now scrambled from the short conversation Mitch found himself almost speechless. "Sure thing... Err I'll go speak to him right now!" He said and simply walked away from her.

The sound of sirens and approaching vehicles hurried their departure, leading the team out the way he had come Scott collected the unconscious guard, and heaving him up onto his huge shoulders made his exit.

"What the hell you taking him for?" Tony asked. "Put him down, you don't know where he's been!"

"Souvenir for Agent Martello, thought he might want to ask him some questions! And besides I saved this guy's life he owes me!"

"What do you mean 'you saved his life'?"

"Well, the dude ain't dead is he?"

"There is something seriously wrong with you man!"

Folding the white cotton shirt precisely, Manfred added it to the pile

of five precisely folded white shirts, then carefully picking them all

up he placed them in the suitcase beside the pile of immaculately

pressed trousers.

Slowly and deliberately, he made his way over to the chest of

drawers and opened the top drawer, where he removed six pairs of

socks and six pairs of white cotton Y fronts. Gathering them up he

returned to his bed and placed them all in the suitcase.

Satisfied with his work so far he closed the suitcase and placed it

back under his bed. There was much to do and little time, the secret

to his success would be travelling light, which meant only taking the

most valuable gems and highest denomination notes, but the girl

would help… For a price.

As he meandered through his thoughts and plans the bell

summoning him along the corridor to the Master's bedroom suddenly

began ringing. Manfred dissed and then sighed, he wondered what the master's mood would be today, lately it could change with the wind.

"I'm coming..! I'm coming!" He said with the weariness of the put upon and then took hold of his walking frame.

"Manfred... Manfred, It's happening!" Casper cried breathlessly as he clutched his chest. "Manfred, it's my heart; I'm having a heart attack! Manfred, I'm scared! Help me!"

"Sir!" Manfred said louder than he possibly should have. "Master, you're experiencing one of your panic attacks- Just sit down on the bed and breathe deeply!"

"No... No, look at the monitor man! Read the message!" His voice trembling with fear and Panicked to the point of abject terror Casper's eyes darted anxiously around the room. "I'm doomed... They're coming... It's happening!"

Doing as he was told Manfred moved closer to the computer. "I'm not sure that I understand sir!"

"What do you mean 'you don't understand'? You senile old fool! It's there..! There in black and white, they've killed my people..! In Munich!" He wailed. "My beautiful girls, the stars of my show are gone..! All gone! Those bastards are ruining everything!" The dawning of a realisation suddenly spread across his face. "Oh my god! Oh my, they'll be here next; they'll come for me! They'll kill me, they'll kill you! Oh my god don't let them in! Promise me you won't let them in!"

Although he wholeheartedly agreed with his Master's assessment, and quite frankly needed it to happen to make his escape, it was imperative that meantime he pacify him.

"Sir, you need to calm down and think rationally! There's no connection between Munich and here! Is there?"

"Oh god, I... I don't know, I'm not sure!" Casper began hyperventilating. "Don't...! Don't let them take me!"

"No one is coming sir! You're quite safe here!" Pulling a folded paper bag, the one he kept for just such occasions, from his inside pocket he handed it to his boss and said. "You know what to do sir! Breathe slowly into the bag! Just like you used to do when you were that sweet little boy I remember so fondly!"

As he began to calm down, Casper removed the bag from his face. "I don't understand." He said shaking his head. "What have I done that is so wrong? The Fame Game is loved, the whole world is talking about it! Do we not entertain them? Do we not bring

excitement to their boring and pathetic little lives? - Are we not

providing a service? Who else will rid this world of these vain,

vacuous and self-promoting fame whores?"

"If I may speak so candidly sir, perhaps with hindsight one might

not have allowed quite so many, if any fatalities- I suspect the

recompense one must pay for these acts may be more than one can,

in essence, afford. But as one may not, as it were, turn back the

proverbial clock one must see one's game to the end no matter the

consequence!" Manfred said, puzzling inwardly at his own words.

"In the end, we are nothing more than the sum total of our actions,

and we will be remembered for them; good or bad!"

Casper smiled. "You are indeed a wise old man!" Holding out the

bag he handed it back to his manservant. "Thank you Manfred once

more you have saved me!"

"Quite sir! Although one has mentioned on numerous occasions the

need for one to carry one's own paper bag!" Taking the bag from his

Masters's hand he first flattened and then folded it, and then tucked it

safely back inside his pocket. "Will there be anything else sir?"

"Tea Manfred..! One needs hot tea at times like these!"

"My thoughts exactly sir, I'll inform the kitchen immediately."

Leaving his master in a marginally better mental state than when he had arrived, the tired old man trod the slow and familiar path down to the dungeons.

First, there would be a visit to the kitchen but there would be no tea, for by now Manfred knew the master would be snorting line after line of that nasty white powder.

Quietly entering the kitchen, he collected bread, cheese and ham. After taking a bottle of water from the huge refrigerator he continued his journey without alerting the dozing cook to his presence; and once in the old dungeons he dismissed the guard, who was just relieved to go outside for a cigarette.

Before opening the door to the hidden room Manfred knocked and waited to be invited in. With no such invitation coming forthwith, he slowly opened the door, and with a cautionary look over his shoulder stepped inside.

Loath to see the fear etched across their gaunt faces, Manfred allowed his eyes to pass over the two girls huddled in the corner.

The DeadBeats

"This is quite the pickle we find ourselves in, isn't it?" He said softly and smiled if only to ally their distress. "This room once held the old Master's private wine collection you know." He said and sighed before placing the food he had collected on the floor. "All gone now of course! You should know that In the old days, this amazing building stood for something good! The castle was full of life, laughter and joy; In the old days, the Master and his Lady entertained everyone from world leaders to Hollywood stars… Charlie Chaplin once stood right where you are now and sampled what was at the time the most expensive bottle of wine in the world." Manfred paused lost in hazy memory, then he smiled again. "I sometimes wonder where it all went; It saddens me, the corridors and rooms are haunted by memories and the ghosts of better times … Sometimes I swear I hear the distant beat of a waltz coming from the great hall… Alas, all gone now! I fear this old fool has somehow become the servant of evil and now it is time to make amends!"

His sadness seemed contagious and all-consuming; Brianne waited for the old man to stop talking and then licked her dry lips before speaking. "Why are you doing this to us?" She said. "We just want to go home now!"

"And so you shall my dear, so you shall!" He earnestly replied.

"Now, eat the food, drink the water and keep as quiet as a mouse. If you two are discovered in here you will without doubt be killed!

"But..."

Manfred placed a finger on his lips to quieten her. "Shush, It won't be long now, the authorities are slowly but surely closing in! I shall endeavour to keep you safe!"

Approaching footsteps coming from the stone steps at the end of the passage cut him short. "I must go, quiet now!" And with that, he turned, closed the door and began his long trudge back up to his room.

Chapter 17

"Dieter Andreas Jurgens, thirty-six years old and something of a small-time crook!" Martello said in passable German and turned the page over to reveal nothing. He frowned at the man across the table. "Hardly Al Capone are we now Mr Jurgens? A little car theft here, a little burglary there but nothing like what you've gone and got yourself involved with now.

  The prisoner, aggrieved at his shoddy description leered back at his captor with abject hatred.

"So, tell me how did you get tangled up in this particular caper?"

"No comment!"

"So, it's going to be like that is it, you're going to play the tough guy?" Martello exhaled heavily. "Come on man! I just want you to answer a few little questions; Where's the harm in that?"

"No comment!"

"Mr Jurgens I'm not a gambling man by any stretch of the imagination, but I'm willing to wager you have literally zero idea what you've gone and gotten yourself into! Innocent Young women have died!"

"No comment!"

Leaning back in his chair Martello took a sip of a coffee which the Police officer now standing by the door had supplied. "This is my first time in Germany, seems like a nice place!"

Dieter Jurgens stared straight ahead and this time remained silent.

"I was wondering what your prisons are like here!" He paused to allow Dieter to comment, which when he didn't he continued. "If they're anything like ours I wouldn't want to be you. So, Dieter what sort of sentence do you get in Germany for kidnap, false imprisonment, trafficking and conspiracy to commit murder? Fifteen, twenty years or is it a whole life sort of thing?"

"Screw you, I was just a driver! You have no jurisdiction here! How are you even allowed to be talking to me?"

"Well, just so you know I'm part of an international task force! And I have permission from your government."

Dieter scoffed.

"But that's neither here nor there, it doesn't matter if you were just there to make the tea; That's why we call it 'conspiracy' to commit murder! You are as guilty as the ones who pulled the trigger."

"Just because you killed all the others doesn't mean you're pinning this whole thing on me!"

Taking a mental note of the fear in his voice Martello went on. "I don't want to pin anything on you, Dieter. But as you're well aware, the law is very complex. I can only imagine that German law is the same; mistakes can happen, the innocent go to jail and the guilty go free, these things happen occasionally! Foot soldiers like yourself take the wrap and the guy at the top gets to go home and screw his wife every night! There's always a need for a good scapegoat!"

"You're not listening to me; I was just the driver!" Dieter barked. "I drove a van; it was my job to move the girls onto the next place, nothing else! I didn't kill anyone! I wouldn't hurt a fly!"

"I hear you; I hear you… and I know you haven't killed anyone, but I'm not the judge and I'm certainly not the jury!"

"I'm not taking the wrap for this!"

"So just for the record, let me get this straight- The girls were kidnapped from various locations, transported to Munich in the container, they were about to be transferred into your transit van for the next leg of the journey but you got bumped!"

Dieter nodded. "Who were those people?"

Shaking his head Martello shrugged. "I don't know." He lied. "But they sure were scary dudes hey! So, tell me where was your destination? Where were you taking those girls to?"

"Screw you, I'm not saying nothing! I want protection for me and I want protection for my family! You people really don't know what you're dealing with!"

"Ok Dieter I've tried my best to help you, but you're not even helping yourself, so if that's how you want it, I'll simply have you released and then let it be known that you're helping us with our enquiries!"

Jumping to his feet, the German knocked over his chair. "No...!" He shouted angrily. "You can't do this! They will kill me; I'll be dead by morning!"

"So!" Martello said calmly knowing he now had his man in the palm of his hand, "Pick up the chair, sit down and tell us- What are we dealing with?"

"Salzburg...! I was to take them to Salzburg!"

"Where in Salzburg?"

"I don't know, but you idiots just killed Wolfgang and he was the only man who did!"

Suddenly interrupting, the policeman standing by the door spoke. "Wolfgang Friedrichs! We have his body in the cooler and crime scene investigators at his home address as we speak."

"How far away?"

"I can have you there by helicopter in less than thirty minutes!"

Martello nodded. "Let's do it!"

Landing just meters from two lit-up police cars which were blocking the road, Martello stepped out of the aircraft onto neatly cut grass. "Where the hell are we?" He said, speaking as he walked.

"Mitterfelden, just a few kilometres west of Salzburg!" The policeman accompanying him said in perfect English. "This is quite an affluent but rural area!"

"You don't say! This isn't what I was expecting, it's really quite beautiful around here!"

"Wolfgang Friedrichs has a small farmhouse just up this drive; he has been on our radar for quite some time now. His primary income seems to be from human trafficking and the movement of illegal immigrants! But he always covered his tracks very well and we could never pin anything on him."

"Who was home when you arrived?"

"Just the wife."

"Does she know he's dead?"

"Yes, we told her right after we arrested her!"

As he rounded a small copse of pine trees Martello got his first view of the typically Germanic farmhouse. "Wow, this is real nice! Looks like crime pays for some people!" Walking up some wooden steps onto a wide veranda he paused. "Is it ok to go inside?"

"Yes, my people have finished the search and unfortunately found nothing." He replied and opened the door allowing Martello to enter first. "What do you think you might see here?"

"I don't know! But I'll know it when I see it."

The entrance hallway was large with ancient weaponry, deer antlers and old paintings of hunting scenes adorning the walls. Beyond a large staircase with ornate wood carved bannisters, Martello could see a sumptuous living room complete with a very large L-shaped leather couch and a huge flat screen TV almost filling one entire wall. "This place is incredible! What's through there?" He said and pointed to a door almost hidden behind a life-sized wooden bear.

"That would be the kitchen back there!"

"Well, I guess that's as good a place to start as any," Martello said and held his hand out inviting the police officer to enter first. "I didn't ask you your name."

"Officer Gruber." The police officer said.

"Well, Officer Gruber I'm Agent Martello and I'm guessing old Ma' Friedrichs likes to bake." The modernity of the kitchen seemed almost out of tune with the glaring antiquity of the rest of the building. "She got all the toys, don't she? Nice to see your boys didn't make a mess in here." He said and noticing several photographs stuck to the refrigerator walked over to take a closer look. "Is this Wolfgang and the wife?"

Gruber nodded. "The young girl in the other photograph is his daughter, she's away at university. Studying criminology of all things."

"It's a strange, strange world!" Martello said and then noticed two postcards also attached to the refrigerator. "Well, well, well what do we have here?"

"They're just postcards, they mean nothing." Gruber said dismissively.

"Is it ok if I take them? This one..!" He held up one postcard with a picture of a snow-covered mountain on the front. "This one is from someplace called the Principality of Swartzstein! Where is that?"

"You telling me you never heard of Casper Von Swartzstein?" Gruber said and laughed loudly. "He's that idiotic multi-millionaire playboy prince! Surely you have seen him on TV!"

"Nope, never heard of him!"

The DeadBeats

Gruber surveyed his American counterpart with disbelief.

"Swartzstein is a Principality nestled in the mountains just above Czechoslovakia! Good skiing and great nightlife; It's world-famous; they call it the cold version of Monaco... Only more expensive!"

"Why would Wolfgang go there?"

"It's a frozen paradise! My guess is he goes for the skiing, or the climbing or maybe he just goes for the girls."

"Oh, I see it's like that is it? Just out of interest does this Swartzstein place happen to have a castle of any type?"

Once more Gruber laughed. "You really need to get out more! Maybe you Americans should travel to more countries instead of just bombing them!"

"You're a real funny guy, Gruber. But I get out just fine thanks!"

"I guarantee you have seen this castle a thousand times and you don't even know it!

"What..! Wait..! I don't understand, I think you're going to have to spell it out for me!"

Rolling his eyes in disbelief, Gruber began speaking as if to a child. "If you have seen virtually any Disney film, then you have seen

Prince Casper's castle. It is how you say 'very picturesque'! A real winter wonderland."

"Sounds a little on the chilly side for my liking! Ok, I've seen enough here; Don't suppose you could give me a ride to Ramstein - It's kinda urgent!"

Striding into the room Colonel Harker held up a hand for silence. "Settle down kids, Uncle Sam's wayward nephew here..!" He said loudly and motioned toward Martello. "Has got big news..!" Then he stepped out of the Secret Service Agents' way.

"Afternoon guys, I'll be as quick as I can... You'll be pleased to know we've located the exact site of the Fame Game! It's a castle!"

"I said it was a castle." Holly cried and punched the air with a clenched fist.

A look of disdain from the Colonel saw her curtail her celebrations and shrink back into her seat. "Sorry!" She whispered.

"Anyway!" Martello said and smiled ruefully at Holly. "As I was saying, it's a castle located in the principality of Swartzstein; but that's where our problems begin. It's essentially a small ski resort nestled in the far eastern Alps, we have no diplomatic presence and under law, we have no jurisdiction there. The castle was constructed on an outcrop on the side of a mountain, and consequently, there's only one way in and one way out..."

"Hell, Is there any good news?" Mitch said. "Surely whoever is in charge there has broken all kinds of international laws!"

"No, there's no good news! The Prince himself is a multi-millionaire and a failed reality TV show contestant- I haven't seen the footage yet, but he went through some kind of nervous breakdown live on TV; If rumours are to be believed he has what you might call a screw loose!"

"We're moving a satellite into position right now; we should have images within the hour." The Colonel added. "The whole area is like one big black hole; we have zero intel on this guy or his locale."

"Oh, there was one other thing you should know… The Russians pay the Prince millions of roubles a year.."

"And why would they do that?" Mitch said, but had a feeling he already knew the answer.

"Well, they use Swartzstein as their mountain warfare training centre!"

"Jeez!" Cowboy said. "So, what you're trying to tell us is that this nutjob lives in an impregnable castle and is surrounded by Russian Mountain troops?"

"Spetsnaz!"

"What now?" Holly said.

"They're Spetsnaz! Russian special forces!"

"Well, I ain't ever killed me no Spetsnaz before; make a nice change from the Taliban now, won't it!"

"Cowboy, you're here to rescue American hostages, not singlehandedly start world war three!" Martello said. "I would advise you not to kill Russian soldiers with US arms, for some unknown reason they don't like that kind of thing over there! Anyhow, I've told you what I know so I'll hand you back over to the Colonel."

"Guys, our hands are tied until the President gives us a green light on this thing; but having said that I don't think a little recon would hurt anybody. Mitch, Cowboy, how would you boys like a little skiing holiday..?"

"What about the rest of us?" Holly said, aggrieved at not being chosen to go skiing.

"Oh, what the hell… You can all go! Get the hell outta here! Just don't get caught and bring me back some good pictures, and when I say 'pictures' Cowboy I don't mean pictures of you naked, and drunkenly fighting with some floozy's husband!"

"I'll try real hard sir… But It would be remiss of me to promise!"

The further east the train travelled, the higher the mountains and deeper the snow became. "It's so beautiful here," Holly said as she gazed up at the snow-capped mountains. "It looks just like a Christmas card!"

"It looks dammed cold out there!" Cowboy said and exaggerated a shiver. "I hate the cold!"

"I got a feeling that I ain't gonna like this place!" Tony said. "I'm gonna spend half my time on my ass!"

"What? Why?"

"Holly, sweetheart! Look at my legs!" He replied with a pained grin on his face. "These are made from the same material as skis! I'll tell you what's going to happen- I'm going to get off this train and the first time these babies touch the white stuff I'm going ass over tit!"

"You think you got it bad?" Cowboy quipped. "Look at Scott here! Six foot five and two hundred and fifty pounds of solid muscle! If he goes down there'll be earthquakes and avalanches across the whole Alps, millions will die!"

"Shut up man!"

"Come on guys! We're going to a real-life winter wonderland; It's going to be great!"

"It's gonna be cold and it's gonna be painful!"

"Dudes! They drink hot wine; it's like their national tipple!" Scott said and scowled. "Why would you take a perfectly nice wine and put it in the microwave?"

Mitch laughed. "Scott, I don't think that is what they do!"

"Hot wine man! Who does that? - It's just not right!." A look of horror suddenly spread across his face. "Oh my God, I just had a thought- I hope they do burgers and fries here! I ain't eating me no reindeer!"

"Don't fret man!" Cowboy said faking sympathy. "If you don't like the old roast Rudolf you can always survive on the boiled cabbage!"

"Oh, thanks man! I needed that!"

"Stop it you two!" Holly barked angrily and then almost jumped out of her seat. "Look!"

"What!"

"Look; There on the side of that mountain- That's it, it's the castle! We're here!"

Barely visible behind low clouds and a thin veil of mist Schloss Swartzstein sat precariously on the side of what seemed to be a huge sheer cliff face.

"Jeez, man!" Scott said. "How the hell did they get that thing up there?"

Leaning across Scott to get a better look out of the window, Cowboy removed his sunglasses. "Wow, kinda epic ain't it? But I think the bigger question is how the hell are we gonna get up there?"

"There must be a road we can't see from here…!"

"Excuse me!"

The sudden and unexpected voice tore their eyes from the castle; they all turned at the same moment to find a young teenage girl nervously standing before them.

"Are you the DeadBeats?" She finally asked after staring at Cowboy for what seemed like an eternity. "It's just that my friend says you're not them, but I think you are- It's just that you look like him… Them! I mean them, you look like them!"

Realizing very quickly that their virtually non-existent cover was blown, and there was no point in lying Mitch held out his hand for her to shake. "Hi I'm Mitch and yes, we are the DeadBeats."

"I knew it… I knew it!" She cried excitedly. "Oh my god, it's really you! Can my friend and I have a picture with you? We're your biggest fans."

"Sure you can," Cowboy said with a big cheesy grin on his face. "Your English is real good; where ya' all from?"

Overwhelmed, the girl covered her mouth and just stared at Cowboy.

"Well!" Holly cried. "I think we all know which one of us is your favourite."

"We're both from Switzerland." She said just as her friend summoned the courage to join her. "This is my sister Anna and my name is Maria!"

"So, what ya' all doing on this train?"

"School term has finished, so we're going to meet our parents in Swartzstein for the holiday."

"You gonna get some skiing time in girls?" Holly asked.

Maria laughed. "No… No, skiing is so yesterday; only old people ski - We're here for the snowboarding festival."

"Yeh sure! We're here to snowboard too!" Holly, suddenly feeling her age lied. "Big-time snowboarding fan me- Just can't get enough of the old snowboarding!" Faking a smile, she made a mental note to learn how to snowboard. "So, you want this picture or what?"

After taking several photographs with the band the sisters politely thanked them and returned to their seats. "Guys!" Mitch whispered. "You know those selfies are going to be all over social media before we even get off this train!"

Cowboy slowly nodded. "So, what do you want to do- We can't abort now."

"I say we just go with it and see what happens! We're a rock band, taking a break in a winter wonderland- Ain't that what rock bands do?"

"No..!" Cowboy said. "No, it isn't! Rock bands go to Bali; they get a tan and they get drunk! Very, very drunk!"

Soon the train started to slow and the passengers began climbing to their feet and collecting bags from the overhead storage compartments.

"I guess this is us." Holly said.

Looking over the top of his sunglasses cowboy gave Mitch a cautionary look. "You know - We don't know what we're going to face out there! We may be in big trouble."

"I already googled the hotel, it's right across the street!" Holly said.

"If there's a crowd, we say hello, pose for a photograph or two and sign the odd poster! Then we get the hell out of there!"

"Ok, Mitch!" Scott said. "But just wait a while and let the other passengers leave the station first."

"Na... Let's just get our stuff and go! If I have to suffer then so should they!"

Slowly filing off of the train and onto the platform, they awaited the onslaught, but none came. Just employees and passengers going about their business. The station was small, with only two platforms, one ticket office and a stall selling newspapers by the exit.

"Ok, people get ready!" Cowboy whispered. "Any second now!"

Pausing and taking a deep breath Mitch pushed the door open and stepped out onto the street, and then breathed a huge sigh of relief. "Oh, no one here!"

"Hey man..!" Cowboy cried. "Where the hell is the fans and the paparazzi; don't they know we're famous!"

"Apparently not!" Scott said sullenly and began dragging his wheeled suitcase across the street, the rest quickly followed.

"Manfred..! Manfred come here quickly! I need you here, right now! It's happening! It's happening at last!"

"Oh, dear god!" The old manservant said under his breath. "Not again!" And then louder. "I'm coming sir, one moment!" Shuffling as quickly as he could push his Zimmer frame he made his way into the

Master's bedroom where he found his employer frantically tapping

the screen of his cell phone. "Yes sir! How may I be of assistance?"

"I can't breathe..! I..."

"Oh, that again sir!" Manfred said and reached into his pocket for

the paper bag.

"No, not that you old fool! I can't breathe because I'm so excited!

It's happened! It's happening right now! They're here, real-life rock

stars Manfred, rock stars are here, visiting our snowy little home!"

"Oh no sir, not those Rolling Stones people again; they were simply

dreadful sir, awful...Awful people! I never did get the dents out of

that suit of armour."

"God no, not them..!" Casper snapped. "Not after what Father found

one of them doing to Mother in the tower!" Casper suddenly drifted

off into one of his childhood memories for a moment. "She never did

explain why she was naked, Or why they were even up there...!" The

memory caused him to shudder and then he was back in the moment.

"Anyway, the DeadBeats are here for the Snowboarding festival;

they've just been photographed on our train. They're in the hotel right

now, my hotel..."

The DeadBeats

"A dead-beat Sir? One isn't familiar with a dead-beat?"

"Don't you know anything! They're world-famous rock stars, and they're right here! Right now!"

"Oh, sir..!" Knowing what was coming next Manfred sighed. "Is what you are thinking wise sir…? I'll have the Rolls Royce warmed at once..!"

"We haven't time for that man- Fetch my big coat!"

Opening the curtesy bar Holly balked at the contents. "Look at this, this thing is full of German Beer! Is there no food in these rooms? I'm starving."

"Yeh, me too," Scott said. "I could eat a diseased rat!"

"Beer?" Cowboy chirped up. "Did you say beer?"

"Shut up Cowboy, we ain't here to get drunk and Scott, you're always hungry, your stomach is like the black hole of Calcutta."

Hoping to put an early stop to the bickering Mitch grabbed his cell phone, stood up and said. "Come on guys; we can't sit in here all day, let's go down to the restaurant and get some food."

"Knodel!" Cowboy suddenly cried. "Knodel und Tafelspitz mit potato gulasch!"

"What now? Are you having a stroke or something" Holly cried.

"That was fluent Austrian, cupcake! What, didn't you bother to learn the language on the way here?"

"No... And neither did you! You don't even know what you just said? Do you?"

"Honestly... No, I have absolutely no idea, all I know is it sounds horrific!" He said and yawned loudly as he got up. "Truth be told I read it on the menu on the way up here; I don't know about you guys, but I've got a feeling I'm gonna be kinda hungry this trip..."

"There's got to be a MacDonalds in this town?" Scott said and followed Mitch out to the elevator.

"Come on guys, it won't hurt to try a few of the local dishes," Mitch said as the elevator doors opened. "And if it sucks there's an Italian restaurant just along the street!"

The restaurant was empty bar one little old man sat at the first table. With one hand on a Zimmer frame and the other clutching his heaving chest, he seemed in some distress.

"Poor guy, he doesn't look well at all!" Holly said

Cowboy laughed as he shot Scott a sideways glance. "The dude looks half past dead!" He whispered.

"Hello!" Holly said as she approached the old man. "Are you alright? You don't look so good; would you like me to get you some help?"

"No… No, my dear." He said breathlessly albeit in perfect English. "Just allow me one moment to catch my breath… You young people wouldn't be those singers, the DeadBeats? Would you?"

"Why, yes we are," Holly replied, rather shocked that the old man knew who they were, she frowned. "Were you looking for us?"

"My name is Manfred; I am the personal butler and man-servant to Prince Casper Von Swartzstein. He sends his greetings and extends an invitation for you to have dinner with him this evening at the castle."

Mitch couldn't believe this incredible stroke of luck and couldn't help but smile as he said. "Sure, the guys and I would love to have dinner with the prince, but I gotta tell you we don't have tuxedos and ball gowns!"

Surveying the group and what they were wearing, Manfred remembered the last time he had invited a famous rock band up to the castle. "It would seem ripped denim, sneakers and old cowboy boots will have to suffice sir." He said with some measured disdain.

"How will we get up there?"

"A car will collect you at nineteen hundred hours sharp, Do not be late the Prince does not like tardiness, it is seen as a show of disrespect in our little corner of the world."

"No problemo dude!" Cowboy said. "And the boots are vintage… Not old!"

"Yes, quite!" Manfred took one disdainful and lingering look at Cowboy and found himself oddly thankful the old master's wife was long dead, but it wouldn't hurt to lock the access door to the tower, just to be on the safe side. "Well gentlemen, madam if you would excuse me I have many preparations to make." Rising out of the chair Manfred gripped his Zimmer frame and slowly, very slowly headed back out to the car where Casper would be awaiting his arrival.

The DeadBeats

As soon as the old man was out of earshot, Cowboy turned to the others. "What do you say, guys? We could put this thing to bed tonight!"

"No, no I don't think so!" Mitch said. "I'll give Colonel Harker a call, see what he has to say, I doubt all the diplomatic pieces are in place yet for a rescue! If we act and just one of those girls dies we'd be crucified."

"It's just one hell of an opportunity, we'd be fools to pass it up!"

"No, I say we go up there, eat his food, drink his wine and play nice! Treat this as a covert recon, if we get a chance, we establish layout and try to take some pictures- If we can locate the girls all well and good but there can be no rescue tonight and when we're up there I don't want any of you trying anything dumb!!"

"Locate the girls? Are you kidding me? It's a big ass castle, Mitch!" Holly said incredulously. "Haven't you seen Beauty and the Beast, Sleeping Beauty or any other film containing a castle? These places always have dungeons, and I'd bet my sweet ass that's where the girls are."

"I'd bet your sweet ass too, cupcake!"

"Shut up, Cowboy!"

"Kinda stands to reason, Mitch!" Scott conceded. "Anyway, I'm still starving, so let's eat!"

Chapter 18

As the snowflakes slowly floated down from the twilight skies to settle on the sidewalks and freshly frozen roads, the town seemed to take on an eerie stillness. Like stars descended from the heavens, the lights of lodges and remote huts began to twinkle in the valley and up the mountainsides,

The ski lifts were still, suspended motionless and the skiers and snowboarders were long retired to the bars, and the town's singular strip joint. The only signs of life were piste bashers as they crawled up and down the mountainsides preparing the runs for the morning.

Holly pulled her woolly hat down over her ears in a futile attempt to fend off the cold. "I've never seen anything as beautiful as this!" She said through chattering teeth and plunged her hands deep into her pockets. "But jeez it's cold, why does it have to be so cold?"

Tony blew into his cupped hands and watched the steam from his breath dissipate. "Because if it wasn't this cold you'd be complaining that it's too wet."

"Well, it's nearly seven," Cowboy said looking at his watch. "Maybe the old guy ain't coming."

"Sure, he is!" Mitch said. "If I'm not mistaken that's the distant sounds of an approaching Rolls Royce Ghost."

As the car cruised into view Cowboy couldn't help but laugh out loud. "The dude drives slower than he walks."

"We'll have frozen to death by the time he gets here." Holly grumbled.

The car eventually rolled to a dead stop and Manfred opened the door, placing his Zimmer frame on the icy road he took his time to climb out. "Good evening." He said and proceeded to slowly walk around to the passenger side rear door, which he opened and beckoned them inside. "Please make yourselves comfortable, it is but a short distance to the Royal cable car."

The distance was indeed short but the journey impossibly long as the car barely exceeded five miles per hour. In what seemed like an age Manfred finally turned the car into a short tunnel, passing a single guard who waved them through and drove up the ramp before coming to a halt beside a black and gold cable car.

"Here we are he said, if you would care to wait one moment I'll get out and open the doors." He said.

"No… No!" Mitch blurted out. "We're fine, we're more than capable of opening the doors ourselves!"

Moving from the Rolls Royce into the cable car they sat down on the single wooden bench and awaited their escort. Manfred eventually joined them, closing the door behind him he pressed a large green button on the wall and the gondola immediately began climbing out of the building.

"Won't be long now!" He said and then smiled mischievously. "I do hope none of you are scared of heights; some guests find this part of the journey very frightening. But you're not to worry I've been doing this ride for more than sixty years man and boy, and no one has died yet!"

"Well, there's always a first time," Holly said feigning nervousness. "How high does this thing go?"

"The castle is two thousand eight hundred and fifty-two feet above sea level and one thousand seven hundred and ninety feet above the town… The highest inhabited castle in the world! He said proudly.

The Gondola climbed ever higher into the night, over the rooftops and the roads; soon the railway lines passed beneath and then the almost frozen-over river. Soon they entered low-lying clouds and the ground disappeared into a snowy abyss.

Catching something dark moving in the corner of her eye Holly jumped in her seat and grasped Scott's arm. "What the hell was that?" She cried.

Manfred smiled again. "Nothing to be alarmed about, just the other gondola on its way down dear; it means you're halfway there!"

The snow-covered mountainside slipped silently beneath the gondola, and as the tips of the towering pines brushed close enough to touch the glass Mitch was beginning to realise the difficulty with which the castle could be assaulted without alerting the guards. A climb from the valley would be near suicide and so would a helicopter fast rope insertion; finding a way to take control of the gondola seemed the likely route but loaded with risk.

Uncomfortable with the silence Holly spoke. "So, Manfred have you been to the festival."

"No miss, not for many a year; my duties keep me very busy, and I'm not as mobile as I once was."

"Do you ski...?" Once she'd said the words she blushed at their stupidity and immediately corrected herself. "I... I mean did you ski when you were younger."

"Oh yes my dear, the old master was a great skier and I would often accompany him; some days we would ski off-piste all the way from the east exit to the village bar... Where invariably he'd soon become inebriated."

Mitch's eyes lit up at that snippet of information. "So, there's another way up?"

Manfred smiled. "Oh no sir, not likely... One could ski down and think yourself lucky to survive, but one could never climb that route..." The distant rumble of an avalanche caused him to pause and gaze out of the carriage into the darkness. "And that my young friends would be the reason why!"

"What is that noise?" Holly asked.

"I think it's an avalanche!" Scott said nervously. "Am I right or what?"

"You are correct young sir! At this time of year, we are plagued…!" Suddenly the gondola swung and made a loud clunking sound as it hit a mechanism. "Nothing to worry about, we're just entering the castle and shall shortly be alighting."

"Err dude! Do we need to curtsy or anything when we meet your Prince?" Cowboy enquired.

"Girl's curtsy, boys bow you lumbering buffoon!" Holly said. "Jeez Cowboy didn't you ever go to school?"

"Not quite as much as my mother would have liked, cupcake!"

"It's perfectly acceptable for all of you to just shake his hand," Manfred said just as the gondola came to a halt. "You should refer to him as Prince or Your Royal Highness until he invites you to call him by his first name, which is Casper!"

"As in the ghost?" Cowboy laughed.

"Very odd!"

"Yes, he is very odd isn't he?" Holly scowled. "Cowboy's dumb, once you accept that it gets easier to deal with him!"

"No!" Manfred said, his eyes staring into the night lost in a distant memory. "The lead singer of the last rock band that visited us said exactly the same thing... I never did get the joke!"

"Don't you ever watch TV?" Cowboy asked.

"No sir, my duties don't allow time for such frivolous activities." Suddenly the Gondola slowed to a halt and the door opened automatically. "Ah here at last, if you would care to follow me."

As soon as Manfred's back was turned Scott and Cowboy threw each other pained looks.

"Wouldn't you be better off with a nice little wheelchair Manfred?" Holly asked. "It must take you forever to get anywhere."

"No madam, not with all the stairs in this place... And besides, walking keeps me fit!" After taking an age to manoeuvre out of the Gondola he began shuffling toward a doorway. "Unfortunately, one isn't as spritely as one was in his seventies."

"Shucks dude! Have you ever thought about retiring?" Cowboy said and leaned against the wall as he waited for the Prince's manservant to cover enough ground to make it worthwhile following behind.

"Me sir? No, never!" He said and smiled. "What on earth would an old man like me do with himself all day?"

Leading the way Manfred ushered them into the great hall, where the longest and most beautifully laid table Holly had ever seen awaited them. Awash with silverware, flower arrangements and golden plates; the sight took her breath away. "Wow, Is all this for us?" She asked. "It's incredible! Guys this looks expensive… Try not to break anything!"

Cowboy looked worried. "I'm not sure I can promise anything!"

"Me too!" Tony whispered to Scott who chuckled. "Dude, what's with all the knives and forks?"

Scott shrugged. "Beats the hell out of me!"

Realising the guests were about to take their seats Manfred waved them on. "Follow me!" He cried. "Dinner will be served after you have been presented to the prince." Leading his visitors into the study he waited while they all filed inside and then closed the door. "If you would care to make yourselves comfortable drinks shall be served promptly." Then he turned and left the room.

"This place is incredible." Holly gushed. "It's everything I thought it could be."

The DeadBeats

"Just remember why we're here," Mitch whispered. "The whole place is probably bugged, so stay alert and watch what you say."

Suddenly the door opened and Manfred stepped inside. "Ladies and Gentlemen may I present…!"

"Oh, Manfred my dearest man, there's no need for all of that..!" Casper cried excitedly and eager to meet his famous guests pushed past his manservant and flounced into the room. "Oh my, it's really you! I'm so very pleased to meet you all..!" He said and rushed up to Mitch threw his arms around the befuddled singer and hugged him. "Mitch Calvert; great singer and an even better songwriter." Releasing Mitch, he moved on to Holly. "Holly Lightfoot, you are an incredible drummer and so beautiful to boot.." Next, he threw his arms around Scott. "So… So poetic and so big… I didn't expect such a huge individual."

Embarrassed, Scott blushed and grinned nervously.

"And who do we have here? Tony Right? You're great on the keyboard… Just incredible; and all of that with two prosthetic legs- You'll be a hero to all those young people in the same situation!"

Tony simply nodded and forced a smile.

As the Prince turned to Cowboy the American put his hand up and took a half step backwards. "Not a hugger dude!"

Taken aback by his visitor's abruptness Casper paused as his brain tried to compute what his response should be. "Oh... Oh ok, I'll just shake your hand then."

"Sure, that's something I can do!" Cowboy said and shook the Prince's hand.

"I'm so excited to meet all of you, when I heard you were here in my little town I just had to invite you to my humble home... Please Manfred, aperitifs now I think! Friends, please enjoy my finest champagne."

The old man promptly opened a globe-shaped drinks cabinet and after using a short sword to ceremonially de-cork a bottle he poured each of them a glass and proceeded to hand them out. "Dinner will be served in five minutes sirs, madam; please take your seats." With that, he closed the globe and left the room.

"Ignore him..!" Casper said. "When he says five minutes he means thirty minutes or sometimes even an hour. At his age, I should really put him out to pasture but he served my father and he's been here most of his life… To be honest I don't know what I would do without him."

"I just love your home, it's beautiful..!" Holly said.

"Thank you, we are very proud of it."

"It's just like you see in a fairy tale!"

"Quite, yes it is, isn't it! They say it was built by the Crusaders to hide their treasures, but we have never found anything… And believe me when I say, that I have looked."

"Do you have dungeons here? I would love to see them."

Once again Casper's brain raced for an answer, allowing this woman to see the dungeons and discover his contestants was out of the question. "I'm… I'm afraid that's… That's presently impossible..!"

"And why is that?" Cowboy said.

"Err… Well, they are being refurbished and there is err… Well, It's all to do with health and safety; all really quite boring- Now tell me what is it like to play on stage to thousands of adoring and screaming fans?"

"Yeh, it's kinda cool," Scott said. "There's nothing like it!"

"I am so jealous, you're all so talented and famous…"

"You're welcome to the fame it's not all it's cracked up to be!" Cowboy said. "You can't go to the shops, or a bar or even a public convenience without some asshole taking your picture and splashing it all over the next day's tabloids… It's a real pain in the ass."

"Oh no, I would give anything to have your fame…!"

"But you're a prince, you own your own little country; For goodness sake, you live in a castle!" Holly cried.

"Since my parents passed it's been a very… Lonely existence- It can get how you say? Very, very boring!"

"Oh, I'm sure you can find something to pass the time?" Cowboy grinned. "A good-looking guy like you, the town must be full of eligible young ladies… Why don't you get them up here and throw a party."

"No, no I don't think so…!"

Appearing at the door, Manfred suddenly rang a small silver bell. "Dinner will be served, if you would all like to take your seats."

"Thank you, Manfred." Holly said and smiled at the old man.

"My pleasure ma'am- For the starter course I shall be serving Tiroler Grostl this will be followed by a main course of Wiener

299

Schnitzel with seasonal potatoes accompanied by a side serving of salad."

"What's for dessert old dude?" Cowboy said trying to sound more enthusiastic than he really was.

"Black Forrest gateau young sir and thereafter Coffee will be served in the study."

"That sounds lovely." Holly said.

Soon after everyone took their seats Manfred began serving the meal and after watching Cowboy picking at his food he approached the big American. "Sir if I may?" He said and removed the plate, replacing it with another covered one. "At the risk of being over-familiar, I took the liberty of pre-empting your palate sir." He said.

"What's this? I don't understand."

"Double cheeseburger and French fries!" He said with a grin and then removed the cover from the plate.

"Oh dude, you're an absolute genius," Cowboy said with barely concealed delight.

"I presume to hope the rest of you young people try the meals before you…!" Suddenly the telephone rang cutting him off mid-sentence. By the time he'd reached the sideboard it had rung several more times; Picking up the receiver he listened intently before replacing it in the cradle. "Sir, it would seem we have two intruders on the south side, the security detail is in pursuit as we speak!"

"Nothing to fear, I hazard to guess the paparazzi heard you were here and tried to get one of those dreadful front-page photographs…"

"The Southside? Isn't it kinda dangerous down there?" Mitch said.

Casper laughed. "It's virtually impossible during daylight- At this time of night… And in this blizzard well, they're going to die but fortunately for us we have ringside seats." Operating a control App on his iPhone, a large painting of a Cavalry officer in full charge slid sideways to reveal a small cinema screen. The screen flickered twice before the image of a dozen skiers tearing headlong down the mountain only a hundred meters behind their quarry.

"Are those muzzle flashes I can see?" Holly cried. "Are they shooting?"

Grinning broadly Casper nodded. "Manfred my man- Do we have popcorn?"

The DeadBeats

The wind howled fiercely as Agent Martello traversed the treacherous terrain of the snow-laden mountainside. He was a well-seasoned skier but this was severely testing even his limits. The blizzard raged all around him, a swirling vortex of white, obscuring his vision. Pressing on he kept the lone target in sight, risking a glance over his shoulder he saw the dark looming shapes, of which there were many, lurking not far behind amidst the storm; some carried flaming torches and the others machine guns. With steely determination and a strong will to live he skilfully manoeuvred down the mountainside on his skis, every move was calculated and precise; one wrong step or misjudgement and he was a dead man.

"Who the hell are those two guys?" Cowboy mused. "Boy can they ski!"

"We will get them, we always do… Just watch!"

"I'm not sure your men should be shooting," Holly said worriedly. "Those two might just be vacationers who got lost!"

"No...! We have signs all around that area! Those signs say trespassers will be shot on sight! What kind of Prince would I be if I didn't keep my promises?" Suddenly the Prince erupted in a loud roar as three of his security detail crashed into trees as they came off a

jump.

"Oh my god your men are using machine guns!" Holly shouted

angrily. "Aren't you worried about an avalanche?"

"Worried? My goodness no- An avalanche would very quickly

solve the issue! Manfred more popcorn!"

The icy slopes toyed with his balance as rocks and boulders

appeared out of the darkness teasing him with certain death. His

quarry was a good skier and seemed to be navigating the off-piste run

with ease; catching them would be difficult if not impossible unless

he could rid himself of his pursuers. He had to know why that person

was lurking below the castle and exactly what they were doing.

The first burst from a machine gun shattered a tree just to his left

and another tore up the snow behind; spurred on he adopted a tight

tuck position and allowed the skis to find their limit.

The chasing pack seemed to be getting closer until Martello hit a

natural jump and found himself airborne, landing awkwardly he

regained his composure and skied on. Seconds later horrifying screams of pain told him that not all of the pursuing pack had made the jump.

The remaining assailants were relentless, their murderous intentions lurking behind the veil of the storm; they would stop at nothing to prevent his escape. As he weaved through the towering pines at breakneck speed he suddenly found himself on one of the lower-manicured piste's, jumping through one hundred and eighty degrees to ski backwards he fired off two double bursts from his pistol, if only just to give them something to think about.

Skipping around to face his front he spied the welcoming lights of the town and the hordes of partying snowboarders he could hide amongst. Heading for the melee he accelerated down the steep slope skidding to a halt barely inches from the crowd he sprayed them with snow, a second later he was out of his skis and rushing into the most crowded establishment that he could see. As soon as he was out of their sight he discarded the jacket and sat down at the first empty chair he saw.

"Ricky!"

Hearing his Christian name seemed almost alien and caused his heart to jump into his mouth. Turning to face the voice his mouth fell open with surprise. "Chloe? What are you doing here?"

"We're here for the snowboarding festival!" She said brightly. "What are you doing here?"

"Well, the same! Where's the rest of Strawberry Island?"

"We're opening the festival -They're back there getting ready!"

She already knew he was Secret Service there was no point in lying, and besides his life was in danger and he needed help. "Look, I'm kinda in trouble- There's some guys chasing me- Have you got a car or somewhere I can hide?"

"Too late, they're right behind you." She said and with that, she reached up and locked lips with him until the guards had passed by.

"Jeez..!" He cried. "A car would have been ok!"

"Come on I'll take you back to see the girls!"

Following close behind and keeping a lower profile as was possible she led him backstage to a small changing room. Once inside Martello found himself face to face with three very unhappy-looking young women; who simply stared at him in silence.

"What's this?" He said nervously. "What's with all the long faces?"

Suddenly a side door opened and a small stout looking woman wearing a trouser suit entered. She glared at Martello before speaking "Is this him?" She barked. with the authority of a very annoyed headmistress.

"Yes ma'am this is him." Chloe said.

"I... I don't understand! What's happening here?"

"What is happening here? I'll tell you what is happening here!" The elderly woman growled menacingly whilst glaring over the top of her half-rim glasses. "You just ruined an operation my department has been working on for weeks!"

"Wait, what now..?" Martello's brain seemed to stop working as he tried to comprehend the information. "I... I don't understand!"

"For Christ's sakes Martello... We're CIA!" Chloe said. "Except her; Carly's MI5."

"What..? But you're Strawberry Island! The biggest girl group on the planet."

"Strawberry Island is where we were recruited and trained!"

"Oh my god! But you were kidnapped, you were beaten black and blue, hell they were going to rape you... Mitch rescued all of you..!"

"We allowed ourselves to be kidnapped, you dumb ass! So that we could find out where the Fame Game was being filmed and put a stop to it, but Mitch showed up and ruined everything... And you just had to go and do the same thing tonight!"

"Oh, so that's what all the faces are about! So, are you telling me that was you I was chasing down the mountain?"

"At last, looks like the flash here has finally caught up! I'd Hardly call it chasing though! But I guess we can agree to say you were following me!"

Shaking his head in disbelief Martello couldn't help but laugh, then looking into her eyes he suddenly realised how utterly beautiful she was and blushed. "You were quite incredible up there... I mean, on the mountain!"

"I know what you meant!" Her eyes softened and Martello detected the tiniest of smiles. "You were kinda kick ass too!"

Suddenly the older woman forced her ample girth between them, pushing the pair of them apart. "That's quite enough of that- Time for you to leave Mr Martello! We don't expect to be seeing you again."

"No…! No!" The Prince raged. "They're getting away?" Jabbing furiously at his iPhone he changed the cinema screen so that it now displayed multiple CCTV images, showing every conceivable part of the town. "Where are they...? I want them!" Scanning the images intently and coming up empty handed he suddenly erupted in rage-fuelled despair. "Manfred, Manfred you stupid old man, this is all your fault!"

"Casper," Holly said gently. "Why don't you leave them and come enjoy the meal? They were just paparazzi or vacationers and they've gone now!"

Fit to burst with frenzy Casper glared furiously at his guest. "No, you stupid bitch! I'm the Prince this is my house! Don't tell me what to do in my own house! What are you even doing here anyway? You're just a stupid woman!"

"Hey dude!" Cowboy growled menacingly. "You don't talk to my friend like that! Now you calm the heck down and apologise to the lady, or Prince or no you and I will be stepping outside- Do you get my meaning?"

Suddenly breathing heavily Casper clutched his chest. "Manfred help... help me I need you; My bag, I can't breathe, I need my bag..."

Quickly taking his trusty paper bag from his inside pocket Manfred first unfolded and then handed it to the Prince. "That's right Sir, just breathe deeply; nice and deep now." Then he turned to face the guests. "As you can see the Prince is presently feeling rather unwell and perhaps now may be a good time to bid goodnight."

"I'm so sorry to hear that," Holly said sarcastically. "And we were having such a cool time watching your live hunt... But before we go I really do need the lady's room."

"Certainly ma'am, out of the door turn left and it's the third door on the left... Oh, FYI You may have to flush twice... It's a very old building."

Throwing Mitch a look as she departed told him everything he needed to know, Holly was going to take a look around, and there was nothing he could do without alerting his hosts, to stop her.

The DeadBeats

"Back in two minutes!" She said brightly and headed for the door before Stepping out into the tunnel-like passage.

Lit only by the flickering of sporadic candlelight, the Spartan corridor, in contrast to the living areas was icy cold and gloomy. All around the air hung still and heavy with the pervading scent of dampness and decay, mingling with the musty odour of history and age. The whole place reeked of neglect, decay and if Holly's nose was correct, rats!

Beneath her feet, the stone floor felt uneven and worn smooth from centuries of use. Overhead, cobwebs hung in clusters and stretched across the low ceiling and down the walls like discarded veils, their tendrils reaching out to infect the aged and faded tapestries.

Dark doorways and gloomy dead ends teased of secret rooms as shadows danced in hidden corridors. Suddenly she felt as if the eyes of a thousand ghosts had fallen upon her and a cold shiver shot up her spine causing the hairs on her arms to stand bolt upright; fear gripped her stomach but resisting the desire to return to the relative safety of the group she pressed on.

"Jeez, this place is the pits!" She said.

Quickly moving past the closet door Holly halted momentarily and listened for any tell-tale noises. Nothing but the distant sounds of dripping water and its accompanying echo reached her ears. Satisfied that she was truly alone she moved on. Assuming any prisoners would be situated in the dungeons she searched for a way down to the lower levels, which sure enough she soon found.

With her back hugging the wall she dared to peer through the door and into the inky black void which would take her below. Reaching out with her foot for the first step she shifted her weight and began inching her way down the stone staircase.

Quietened voices, too low to hear but loud enough to be carried on the draught floated up from somewhere below. Hardly daring to breathe she descended lower; the darkness seemed to lift and was replaced by a dull, barely conceivable light.

The voices were louder now, loud enough for Holly to know that she was hearing Russian.

"Where is the girl?" Casper said breathlessly. "She has been gone too long!"

311

"Well, you know what girls are like once they get in the restroom?" Cowboy said. "Put Holly in front of a mirror and she could be there all night."

"There is no mirror...! Manfred, go and see what is keeping her!" Folding the paper bag, he placed it firmly on the table. "And inform Chef the rest of the meal is cancelled; our guests will be leaving."

Manfred nodded with a look of resignation, the evening was always bound to end badly but at least nothing had been broken, no one had been threatened with a sword and most of all no one had engaged in acts of sex in the tower. "Yes Sir!" He said and made his way out into the corridor. When he reached the bathroom door he tapped gently on one of the aging oak panels. "Madam, is everything alright in there?" When no answer returned he knocked again but this time louder. "Madam!" Opening the bathroom door whilst a lady was doing her ablutions was unconscionable, and went against everything Manfred stood for as a proud Manservant. Nonetheless, she had failed to answer the door; reaching out the old man grasped the door handle and he began to turn but his conscience got the better of him so snatching his hand away, he knocked once more. "Madam..!"

Suddenly the door opened and Holly stepped into the opening. "Hi Manfred, are you waiting for the bathroom, you might want to give it a few minutes." She said channelling her best giddy blond airhead act and then giggled. "I think I had a little bit too much of your wine.

Manfred frowned at her coarseness and puzzled at her comment about the wine, she had barely consumed any. "Err no madam! I've been knocking and calling you!"

"Oh sorry, I had my earphones in; I couldn't hear a thing! I'm such a clutz!"

"The rest of your party is preparing to leave; would you care to join them!"

"Really, what a shame I was so looking forward to dessert."

"Quite madam,"

With his suspicions aroused Manfred turned his head to the right and peered down the corridor, a corridor used by him and him alone. He knew every brick, every speck of dust and every cobweb- And seeing several of the older cobwebs disturbed and broken he could tell that she had been down to the dungeons. Looking back at the guest, he was no longer buying the silly little girl act there was too

313

much intelligence behind those eyes, and he was now seeing her in a whole new and very different light. She was not what she claimed, and was in all probability much, much more. He smiled wryly. "This way madam." As he led her back to the dining room he wondered what all this meant, and how it would affect his plans. "One presumes Madam didn't see as much of the castle as one would have hoped."

Holly shrugged, there had been too many armed guards at the entrance to the dungeons forcing a hasty retreat. "Never mind!" She said genuinely disappointed. "Maybe next time!"

"Speaking of 'next time' madam, may I suggest the views from the eastern parapet ground floor doors, they are most enlightening."

"Thank you, Manfred, I'll try to remember but I fear it may be some time before we get a return invite."

"Quite madam!"

Chapter 19

Mitch showered early and left the hotel carrying his skis, making his way to the Swartzstein Bahn, the principalities main ski lift, he bought a pass from the machine in the entrance and then queued behind a chattering gaggle of teenage snowboarders.

As the winter sun rose over the mountains and caused the light to glisten, bounce and dance across the lower slopes, the sense of excitement in the air began to rise as skiers and snowboarders of all ages, bundled up in colourful winter gear chatted and laughed sharing their anticipation of the adventures ahead.

Spotting Martello further along the queue, Mitch made his apologies as he pushed his way through. "Didn't think you were going to make it!"

"I almost didn't!" Martello said and grinned. "I bumped into a couple of your old friends last night." He said just as the ski lift door slipped open and the first batch piled in. "I'll tell you about it later."

"Did you get breakfast?"

Realising Mitch was just making small talk for the sake of any listening ears, he joined in the act. "Yeh I had a bite, I was kinda eager to get on the slopes before there's too many people up there, you know how it gets mid-morning."

"A friend of mine advised me to take a look at the slopes on the 'eastern side', she said it may be quite illuminating!"

"The eastern side, sounds interesting; do you mind if I tag along?"

"No problem."

Soon it was their turn to board the cable car that would take them up to the pists at the very top of the mountain. As they ascended, the awakening ski resort revealed itself in all its majestic beauty, the panoramic view breathtaking, with pristine slopes stretching out as far as the eye could see. Early bird skiers eager for the very freshest of snow, carved elegant arcs down the mountain, leaving trails of powder in their wake.

They sat in silence for the entire journey, both men's eyes trained on the fortress-like castle and all its approaches. Mitch knew Martello was probably thinking the same as he was; any incoming assault would be spotted miles away, and the element of surprise would be gone.

Before too long the cable car glided to a halt and the passengers began to get off. disembarking, both men clipped into their skis and then waited for the bustling crowd to disperse before speaking.

"So, what was all that about the eastern side?"

Pulling his gloves on Mitch looped the ski poles around his wrists and then pulled his goggles over his eyes. "The butler, an old guy called Manfred, told Holly that she should see the views from that side. She couldn't be sure but she said it was almost like he was trying to tell her something."

"Well, I guess that's where we're headed then!"

Pushing off they began to glide down the slope judging their route as they went. As the slope began to steepen they began to ski in wide arcs, carving up the virgin snow as they made turn after turn. Soon

317

they were plummeting ever faster, a choreographed dance between men, snow and mountain.

Spotting a track leading off into the pine forest from the main piste, Mitch leaned into the turn. Feeling the edges of his skis bite into the snow he expertly avoided barely visible rocks and dangerously low branches.

Gliding to a sudden halt he waited for Martello to fall in beside him. "Well, that was a whole lot of fun!"

Martello answered with a grin.

"Look!" Mitch said and pointed across the valley. "That's it! That's the eastern approach, I'm not sure we want to be getting much closer."

"They're bound to be feeling a little edgy after last night's adventures in the dark. "Martello said and pulled a small pair of binos out of his ski suit. "So, what are we looking for here?"

"I don't know, maybe a low window or a door."

Scanning the approach Martello settled on the base of the parapet. "Looks like the butler's come through for us." He said and handed Mitch the binos. "You got great cover navigating the valley and that door looks like a little C4 will blow it off of its hinges."

Mitch scanned up the entirety of the castle and lingered on the roof.

"The castle is far too close to the cliff face to get a chopper in, and what with the up draughts a fast rope assault is out of the question..." scanning higher he suddenly stopped. "Oh, wait a second, there's a ledge about two hundred feet above the castle, maybe we could climb down from the top."

"How do you get on the ledge? They'd hear the helicopters five miles out, there's gotta be another way."

"This is going to be tough man! And no it's not just the getting in, it's the getting out as well- How the hell do we exfiltrate with a bunch of hostages in tow?" Mitch frowned. "Let's just take some pictures and get the hell out of here before we're spotted."

"I think I need to take a better look at that royal cable car of his- It's going to be the only way out."

"We were there last night, there's one armed guard and CCTV!"

"Still, I'd like to take a look!"

All across the valley the air suddenly turned frigid as dark, heavy clouds slowly passed in front of the sun. Tiny, delicate snowflakes fluttered earthbound, a prelude to the blizzard which followed;

visibility diminished to mere feet as the snowfall intensified, forming a relentless curtain of white. Trees began to bow under the weight of accumulating snow, their branches bending and creaking in protest.

The howling winds carried with them a bone-chilling cold, gnawing at exposed skin and causing every breath to form a frosty mist. Ski tracks were swiftly devoured as if the storm sought to erase any trace of human presence.

Unable to take any more photographs, they skied down to the cable car and then leaving Mitch to ride the car down Martello decided to Ski the narrow winding track that led to town.

Skidding to a halt beside a restaurant full of chattering people hiding from the storm and drinking coffee on a low balcony, Martello sat down on a nearby bench. First, he removed his rucksack and took out a pair of walking boots placing them on the bench beside him, he then removed his ski boots and placed them into the rucksack. Once his walking boots were on and the laces tied he sat for a while people watching, ensuring he wasn't being observed or followed. Once he was satisfied that no one was taking any undue notice of him he got up and headed into town.

The mid-morning storm saw the lower slopes empty, and the streets only got emptier as Martello cautiously headed into town. Pausing at a news outlet to pick up a newspaper he pretended to read a story on the front page, whilst all the time using the reflection in shop windows to ensure that he wasn't being shadowed.

Obsessive-compulsive paranoia came with the job but even he had come to realise long ago that it was becoming a problem; he couldn't even sit in his mother's dining room without facing the door. But what the hell, it had saved his life on more than one occasion.

Strolling into a coffee shop across the road from the entrance to the Royal cable car, he ordered a latte and took a seat at the back by the window. After barely two minutes of watching the building it became obvious that no matter how the assault went down, someone was going to have to take control of the guard, the car and the building if the team and all of the hostages were going to make it down alive.

A vertical hydraulic post in the middle of the entrance ramp, controlled by the security guard meant it would be impossible to just ram the place, the guard could hit the alarm and fire off a burst of machine gun fire at the first sign of trouble and the assault would be over before it had even begun.

The coffee was far hotter and stronger than he might have expected, so raising his hand he called the waitress over. "Could I get more milk and maybe some sugar over here please?" He asked in German and smiled dumbly; he wasn't quite sure which language they spoke in Swartzstein but guessed she'd understand German. Sometimes the best way to get information out of people was to act dumb and play the redneck tourist. "Say, sweetheart! That building over there- That writing over the entrance, what..? What does it say? Is that the cable car I should take if I want to get right to the top of the mountain?"

From the look on her face and general demeanour, he could see that she wasn't a woman who was overly happy in her work and had very little regard for the tourists who paid her wages. She sighed before saying in perfect English. "It says Konigliche Gondel, it translates Royal Gondola and no you can't ride in it..!" She stared at him with all the graces of someone who had been asked the question many times before. "That one takes you up to the castle, that's the cable car you take if you want to get beat up or even worse, shot... No one is allowed up there!"

"Oh wow, is that the prince... What's his name? Prince Casper von something or other rides?" He cried, faking excitement. "I'd really like to take some photographs; you know to show the folks back home. Do you think they'd let me in there?"

"It's Von Swartzstein and no they won't let you in there!" she said wearily, and taking a long hard look at the clock on the far wall made a mental note that it was almost the end of her shift. "If you go around back there's a chain link fence you might get a photograph of him if you wait long enough, we haven't seen him in years though, or then again you might just get shot! Do yourself a huge favour and stay away, these are not nice people!"

"Thanks, I'll do that!"

Collecting his skis from the rack outside the coffee shop Martello looked just like any other tourist going about his business, but that was kind of the whole point. Going unnoticed was relatively easy if you knew how; A few simple rules had kept him alive this long. Rule one act like you belong and blend in, rule two don't draw attention to yourself, and rule three and probably the most important don't make eye contact in passing- Strangers only seem to remember you if you

323

make eye contact. In general, most people either don't notice much of what's going on around them or forget after a few minutes. The final rules and probably the most useful, if caught out act dumb, nobody ever questions stupid, and if questioned never lie outright it's much better to tell half-truths than white lies.

Ducking into a narrow alley, he squeezed past two garbage bins and then leaned his skis up against the wall. The alley was short and deserted, the only door, leading into an adjoining shop was firmly closed and from the lack of footprints in the shin-deep snow, hadn't been used in a while. Moving quickly to the rear of the building he stopped and peered around the corner, satisfied he hadn't been seen he stepped out into the open and walked up to the chain link fence securing the rear of the cable car, there were no guards at the rear and seemingly no CCTV.

The six-foot-high fence was barely an obstacle, it could easily be cut or climbed in seconds and once inside the lone security guard monitoring the front of the building could be neutralised with relative ease. Taking out his camera he took several photographs before collecting his skis and quickly leaving the same way he had come.

"Darn it man!" Scott said finally after several hours of group silence. "We were right there, probably no more than fifty feet away from those poor girls… We could've got them out!"

"What, with no weapons and a castle full of mercenaries!" Mitch said. "We'd be dead by now and so would all of those girls!"

"That piece of shit would probably have live-streamed the whole thing too."

Stirring from her slumber Holly looked out of the window and stretched. "I'm beat!" She said.

"Well, looks like we're home!" Cowboy said as the minibus which had collected them from the train station swept through the open gates and into Ramstein Air Force base.

As the vehicle slowed to obey the base's speed limits a military police officer stepped out into the road, as soon as they halted he marched up to the driver's side window. "Colonel Harker wants to see you all right now, he's in conference room two."

The DeadBeats

The driver nodded and drove on before pulling up outside a large building. "We're here, if you want to grab your gear conference room two is on the first floor."

Leaving their skis and bags in a pile they filed inside and up to the conference room in glum silence and sat down facing a lectern and whiteboard; Colonel Harker was waiting.

"Ok people, settle down." He said. "I'll try to keep this short and sweet; At this moment in time the mission is not a go. Both the Austrians and the Czechoslovakians are refusing to play ball, although the word on the grapevine is they're both close to an agreement- Meanwhile, we carry on and we plan, so to that end I want full reports from every one of you, everything you saw, heard or sensed; I want floor plans of every room you were in and we'll compare them to the sixteenth-century building plans one of the intel guys dug up- Any questions?" He paused waiting for someone to raise a hand or speak, but no one did. "Don't forget you're playing Munich tomorrow night, so get some sleep and I'll see you all first thing in the morning."

As a crescendo of deafening screams and cheering drowned out the final verse of the song, fireworks all around the stadium surged skywards exploding in a myriad of colours. Mitch applauded the audience and then waved to some of the younger fans in the front row. "Munich, you've been incredible-We'll be seein' you all real soon." He cried above the din, then he bowed and followed the rest of the band off stage.

"Oh my god!" Holly shrieked. "That was better than sex!"

Cowboy grinned. "If that was better than sex either you ain't doing it right or you need a better man!"

"Did you see that crowd? Did you see what most of them were wearing? Jeez Cowboy you and that stupid hat of yours have only gone and started a freeking trend."

"Maybe you should all start wearing a Stetson just like mine…!"

"Hey, Mitch," Holly shouted. "What do you think? Are we all gonna wear a dumb hat next time out?"

Mitch frowned. "There's only room for one Cowboy in this band!"

"Maybe we could even change the name of the band to 'the Rednecks' or even better still 'Cowboy and the dumbshits'!" Holly said and punched Cowboy softly on the chest. "Hell, we could even start singing good ole' country and western songs!"

"Can you imagine Eminem rapping over a Billy Ray Cyrus song?" Scott said and screwed his face up in horror. "Or Dolly Parton singing backing vocals for R.E.M!"

"Ok, assholes!" Cowboy barked feigning anger. "I'd appreciate y'all picking on someone else now- How about Tony? No one ever picks on him."

"There are two very good reasons for that…" Scott said. "Reason one, we like him and reason two he knows kung fu and could kick all of our asses!"

"It's Brazilian Jui Jitsu shit for brains!" Tony growled as members of another band pushed past on their way to the stage.

"Yeh, yeh..! Like it's not all the same,"

"Maybe so, but it also means I can kick you in that butt ugly face of yours!"

"Ok people, as of right now you are on three hours' notice to move!" The Colonel said as he approached. "Get your gear and get on the coach, all the fun and games are over, we got a lot of work to do!"

Carefully placing his guitar in its case Mitch closed the lid, tightly fastened the straps and then grabbed his leather jacket, checking his cell phone was in the inside pocket he took a quick look around the room and then made his way out to the parking lot and boarded the coach. Cowboy was already aboard and napping on the back seats so Mitch stowed his gear and sat in the next row. "You asleep?"

"No, but I was kinda working on it!"

"That castle, something else isn't it?"

"You sound worried dude!"

"That's because I am- You were there, you saw it. Getting in unscathed is going to be near impossible, then we have to find those girls! Even if we get that far there's only one usable way out and we'll have half the Russian army on our tails- I just don't see how we're all coming back from this!"

Sitting up Cowboy swung his feet around and placed them on the floor, then he tilted his Stetson up and looked at Mitch. "Well, the way I see it, as long as I get to put a slug in that murdering prick's face before I die, I'll go down a happy man!"

The DeadBeats

Climbing up the coach steps Scott squeezed his huge frame into a seat. "Is there any food on this thing?" He said grumpily. "I'm starving!"

"Just look at that- It's not so much that he's sitting on a coach as wearing it!"

"Screw you Cowboy; life ain't easy being this big. Have you any idea how hard it is to find a woman, and I mean any woman that likes a man to be as big as me?"

"Oh, you poor dumb shit it ain't cos you're big- It's because you're ugly!"

"And you're always starving," Tony added as he sat down. "What woman wants to spend her entire life shovelling food into you? It'd be like dating Godzilla!"

"Screw you too!"

"Are we all here?" Colonel Harker barked, making himself heard above the bickering.

"Her ladyship ain't here! I swear, that girl will be late for her own funeral!"

"I'll get her.." Tony said and began to climb out of his seat.

Mitch was already up. "I'll go- Come to think of it I don't remember seeing her since we came off stage!"

"Me either!" Cowboy added sensing Mitch's concern. "I'll come with you!"

"Yeah me too!"

"Scott, stay where you are; the same goes for you two! Mitch, sit down!" He said ominously and swallowed hard; they weren't going to like what he was about to say. "Guys Holly won't be joining us today- Driver, let's go!"

"What the hell is going on..?" Cowboy said and from the look on the colonel's face knew he wasn't going to like the answer.

"Yeh, boss what the hell?"

"Sit down Mitch- "He paused, preparing himself for what he was about to say. "Two days ago, intel hacked into something called 'the dark web', don't ask me what it is because I have literally no idea! Turns out your friend in the castle has put a two-million-dollar contract out on our Holly, he wants her in his game!"

"Why do I get the feeling you haven't taken her somewhere safe?" Cowboy growled as a feeling of dread began to rise in his stomach.

The DeadBeats

"Settle down Cowboy- This was all her idea- She volunteered for this!"

"For what?" Mitch said. "What the hell have you done?"

"Ten minutes ago, Agent Martello abducted Holly from her changing room and six hours from now, somewhere in Austria he will hand her over to representatives of Prince Casper. Whereafter Holly Lightfoot of the band The DeadBeats will be competing in the Fame game!"

"We need to go get her..! Right now!" Cowboy barked furiously. "If anything happens to that girl, so help me…!"

"Shut up Marine! Don't you forget who you are, what you are and why you are here! The same goes for Holly, she knew the risks and she volunteered anyway- And we needed someone on the inside!"

"She'll be ok guys!" Mitch relented. "Holly is more than capable of taking care of herself."

Biting his tongue cowboy seethed with anger… and fear; Up until now, this whole thing had felt like a fun game of soldiers. But now, suddenly it seemed like people might die, or worse still might be allowed to die.

Awakened by the violent shivering of her body, and the chattering of her teeth Holly groggily opened her eyes and winced at the cold as it seemed to penetrate her flesh, biting painfully at her bones. Her hands immediately went to her head to stay the pounding contained within, she had no idea what drug Martello had knocked her out with but promised herself that when this was all over, and if she survived they would be having words.

"Jesus Christ Martello!" She whispered through the pain. "What the hell did you do?" Looking down her body she realised that her clothes had been changed, she was now wearing military-style cargo pants and a red cotton shirt. "What the hell..?"

Slowly pushing herself up into a sitting position she surveyed her surroundings with an ever-growing feeling of dread; There was one tiny barred window, which was too high to look out of and one very heavy-looking door which she guessed was locked; Other than that, the room was empty, bar the old bed she was sitting on.

Swinging her feet around she placed them on the floor and stood up, and then waited a few seconds for a dizzy spell to pass.

333

The DeadBeats

The suddenness of the voice made her jump.

"Good morning Holly!" A computer-altered voice suddenly spoke from a hidden speaker somewhere in the room.

"It's ok Casper, you sad little man! you don't need to hide your true voice, I know it's you! I'd recognise the brickwork and cobwebs in this shit-hole of a castle anywhere." Holly said and smiled as she imagined his panic at being rumbled. She had no intention of bowing down or fearing this pathetic little narcissistic misogynist. "I'm not scared of you or your dumb little game! Like picking on girls do ya'... Well Princess, you picked on the wrong one this time!"

The silence seemed to last an age and then he spoke, only this time he used his own voice. "Clever little you! You found me out!" He said and chuckled. "It matters not Holly Lightfoot; you won't be leaving here alive!"

"So, what happened to you? You piece of shit; mommy not give you enough hugs?"

"You shouldn't speak to me like that; do you know who I am?"

"I sure do Princess! You live stream me in your dumb game and the first thing I'll do is tell everyone who you are and where we are! You might as well let us all go and give yourself up... Because this is only ending one of two ways- either you'll die or you go to gaol for the rest of your miserable life!"

"You're too cocky to be just a drummer in a band and this will only end one way for you!"

"What's up Princess don't you like strong women?"

Smashing the microphone repeatedly against the table Casper roared furiously. "Manfred!" He shrieked. "Manfred, where are you... Stupid old man is never here when I need him."

"Sir!" The manservant said from the open-door way. "How may I be of assistance, sir!"

"Oh, there you are! Where were you? I was calling!" He barked.

"I'm afraid I'm not as mobile as I once was sir!"

"Yes, well! Whatever...! Our new competitor! Holly Lightfoot!" He spat as if her name brought a nasty taste to his mouth. "She knows!"

"Indeed sir! One may presume having had her as a guest here just a few days ago could have contributed to her... Working things out, as it were!"

The DeadBeats

"State the obvious, why don't you?" Jumping from his chair Casper marched over to Manfred and thrust the microphone into his hands. "It's broken get it fixed- I hate her, I want her dead old man; but not just dead, dead! I want her flayed, I want her flesh pebble dashed on the outside of this castle, I want her bones…!"

Struggling with his compunction to scream at his boss, grab him by the lapels and ask him what the hell is wrong with him, Manfred simply smirked. "Yes sir, I get the general drift; may I suggest a nice little game of Russian roulette to start proceedings?"

Casper's eyes suddenly lit up with the expectant excitement of a child. "What, with a gun and some bullets? Yes, yes! The stupid woman will blow her head all over the wall, the fans will love it! Good man Manfred, I knew you wouldn't let me down!"

"Err, no sir; nothing so coarse- I've had a much better idea!" Manfred said, he had found Holly quite delightful during her time in the castle and there was no way he was going to allow her to blow her own pretty little head off. Somehow, he had to find a way of saving her or come up with a delaying tactic, things were not looking good for her. "One could say these young ladies drink far too much, perhaps a lesson in sobriety is called for! What if I were to say the words 'Russian roulette vodka'?"

"Oh, Manfred that's genius, that's just pure genius! Two girls, seven shots of Vodka... Only one of them isn't Vodka!"

"Indeed sir, one of them is very much not Vodka!"

"Make preparations we go live in two hours! If you need me I'll be in my room, I need to bathe, dress! And prepare for the show."

"May I suggest the green suit tonight sir, the sparkling of the green sequins will match your mood?"

"Yes the green will do fine and my blue silk cravats..."

"At once sir!" Manfred said and then almost as an afterthought added. "Which of our other guests will be taking part...?"

Casper shrugged with indifference. "You know? I really don't care, you choose!"

"A wise choice sir." Manfred said and turning on his heels, left the room.

The DeadBeats

With her hands deep in her pockets for warmth, Holly restlessly paced the room. "Could I have some room service please?" She shouted as loud as her lungs would allow her. "I need the maid service too? The bed sheets are disgusting... This place is the pits man- You just wait for my review, this dump ain't getting any five stars from me." Kicking the door angrily she turned and continued pacing. "The toilet is just a freeking hole in the floor! What the hell is that all about..?" Hearing the key turn in the lock she spun around and anxiously readied herself for what may come.

Stepping into the room Manfred smiled at her and then pointed to the walls, he then placed his finger across his lips indicating for her to be quiet. "I have food for you madam." He said and placed a tray on the floor, then taking three steps he handed her a note, which she read quickly before handing it back. "The Prince sends his congratulations on being selected for the Fame Game and wishes you the best of luck in your endeavours."

"Tell that asshole to go screw himself!"

"Tonight, you compete in your first trial, I strongly suggest you eat and get some rest- One of the guards will collect you shortly and escort you to the gaming area."

"Ok guys, get over here; It's streaming live right now!" Scott said and turned the laptop around so everyone could see the screen.

"Is it her?" Cowboy asked, already knowing the answer before it was given.

Scott nodded. "Holy shit guys, this ain't good, tonight's game is called Russian roulette!"

Mitch closed his eyes in barely concealed horror and then cast an accusing look at the Colonel. "What the hell have you done?" He mouthed

Remaining rock still, and barely breathing the Colonel suddenly became aware of how dry his mouth was and the barely perceptible trembling in his hands. This wasn't the plan; this wasn't meant to happen.

"I don't think I can watch..!" Tony said fearfully, and remained in his seat.

"You get over here right now Tony!" Cowboy growled. "If she dies, then she dies with all of us by her side!"

339

"This is bullshit man!" Scott barked and then lowering his voice said. "Guys, it's Hollybobs she'll be fine! She'll find a way!

Unable to listen to any more chatter Cowboy jumped to his feet. "Sir, we gotta stop this!"

"And just what the hell do you suggest marine?"

"An EMP burst above the castle, it'll knock out his power, and he won't be able to broadcast!"

"He's right sir, it could buy us time!"

"I'm sorry, it's too late for that! The missile would never make it in time!"

"So, she's dead, just like that!" Cowboy swallowed hard and clenched his fist tightly as he desperately tried to hold himself together. "Hey, how about that Colonel looks like your about to get yourself another name for that precious boathouse!"

Unable to look his men in the eye he bowed his head. "I'm sorry! I really am, it was not meant to go down this way!"

"You know something?" Mitch said. "I'm not convinced! You all know what she's like! If she was in danger Holly would fight! She'd be bouncing off of the goddam walls! Just look at her, she's calm, she's not dishevelled in any way and there's not a mark on her!"

"So, what are you saying," Cowboy said

"I'm saying there's something off about this whole thing and maybe we shouldn't be writing her off just yet!"

Chapter 20

"You touch me one more time and I'll gouge your freeking eyes out!" Holly barked as she Spun around to face her guard.

The masked and heavily armed man, towering above her simply looked down on her with the arrogance of a man who could easily rip her head off. "Move!" He said with a heavy Russian accent. "move... or I must break you!"

"Yeah, ok Ivan Drago I'm moving! I guess Rocky hit you one too many times hey... I must break you!" She said mocking his voice.

"Very as you say 'cocky'! Not so cocky when dead! Now move!" Once more the huge Russian guard pushed her, she stumbled violently through an open door, and as she regained her composure realised she was in a large room containing one single table with a chair at each side. "I told you not to touch me again!" She growled as she wheeled around and without warning grasped his scrotum and penis tightly in her right hand and twisted with all her might. For a brief second, she wondered if he'd even felt anything and then paralysed with overwhelming pain he suddenly and very slowly sank to his knees. "Not so big now are ya'!" She smiled and then head-butted him on the bridge of his nose. Releasing her grip, he fell to the floor whimpering in pain. "I must break you!" She mocked him once more.

Less than a second later two more guards appeared out of what seemed like nowhere and violently pinned her to the wall.

"Let her go!" Casper's voice boomed out of a loudspeaker and the men immediately obeyed. "Sort out your clothes and sit at the table! Any more trouble and you will be shot where you stand!"

Doing as she was instructed Holly sat at the table and waited less than a minute before another guard escorted a second girl into the room and barked at her to sit down.

Nervously obeying she sat down and fearfully avoided eye contact choosing instead to stare at the table. With her mascara and tear-stained face and ripped clothes it was clear the guards had been taking advantage and overstepping the mark.

The DeadBeats

"You fucking pigs!" Holly vaguely recognised the girl from some film or magazine story but couldn't remember her name. "Hello." She said gently. "What's your name?"

"Do not speak!" Casper barked through the speakers.

"Screw you asshole!"

Suddenly the room filled with riotous applause, as it faded away Casper's computer-disguised voice spoke. "Ladies and gentlemen welcome to tonight's edition of The Fame Game! And what a show we have for you- I can't even begin to tell you how excited I am, say hello to our newest contestant Holly Lightfoot of the rock band The DeadBeats and she will be going up against one of our longest-standing contestants the incredible Christi Temple- So without further ado, the game is called Vodka Russian Roulette; sat on the table between the girls are six shots of Russian Vodka but only one of them is laced with cyanide! You guessed it, people… Each girl will take it, in turn, you the public will choose which girl drinks from which glass. It really is quite simple people, the one who dies," He chuckled. "Will be leaving the show tonight! Should either of the girls refuse to drink they will immediately be shot in the head by the guard you can see standing beside them! So, lots of excitement

tonight and lots to talk about! Who are the winners and who are the
losers only fate will tell!"

"And we all know what the prick means by 'leaving the show'!"
Cowboy said. "I should've ripped his head off when I had the
chance!"

Mitch nodded. "There's a lot we should have done when we had the
chance!"

"Viewers, are you ready? Of course, you are! Girls, are you ready to
play the Fame game? Are you ready to reach for the stars!"

"He's just an insane and pathetic little man!" Holly said. "Don't give
him the satisfaction of your tears Christi! Don't let him see you're
scared!"

"But I am scared!" she sobbed. "We're going to die aren't we?"

"Look at me... Christi, look at me, you're not going to die! you'll be
out of here soon and that asshole and all of his goons will be dead!"

The DeadBeats

"Holly Lightfoot, the viewers have voted for you to drink first and they have chosen glass number...!" He paused for dramatic effect. "Number three!"

Picking up tumbler number three Holly held it up to the camera. "To all you sickos out there who watch this crap, cheers and bottoms up!" She said as cheerfully as she could muster and drank the liquid down in one gulp.

Realising that Holly wasn't showing any ill effects of poison Christi began to tremble and sob uncontrollably. "I can't..! I can't!" she spluttered.

"Christi, the viewers have been voting in their thousands and they have decided... you will drink from glass number... One!"

"Please, I don't want to die! I... I can't do it!"

"Christi..!" Holly said firmly. "If you don't drink it they will kill you anyway!"

With tears streaming down her cheeks, and trembling with terror she reached out and grasped the small glass; as she did so the guard unholstered his pistol, chambered a round and pointed the muzzle at her head.

"Come on you can do this!"

Christi, placing the glass on her lips stared down her nose at the clear liquid. Then taking two quick breaths she took the vodka into her mouth, paused and then swallowed. Dropping from her hand the tumbler fell to the table, and rolled off the edge before smashing on the floor. Christi barely noticed as her brain was on hyper alert for any physical signs of poisoning. "I did it!" she whimpered.

"Holly, it is now once more your turn- The viewers have been voting and they have chosen... Glass number four!"

Steadying herself she took the drink in her hand. "Well, here goes nothing!" She said and knocked the whole glass back in one swallow.

The effect was immediate, suddenly her chest tightened and as it became more difficult to breathe she began to feel dizzy. "I feel... I... I feel strange!" she said and began to cough. "What's happening... To me? " As the room began to spin she tried to stand and stumbled sideways collapsing in a heap.

Christi began screaming and only stopped when the guard pistol-whipped her across the back of the head; causing her to slump forward onto the table and knock over the remaining glasses.

"There you go, ladies and gentlemen, we have a winner; and a very worthy winner at that! Commiserations to the loser, who tonight on her first trial has left the game!"

Quickly standing, Cowboy snatched his chair up and violently launched it at the wall, missing Harker by inches. "This is on you Colonel, you son of a bitch; All on you…! I guess you're real happy, now you got another gad dammed name for your precious boathouse?"

"Cowboy!" Mitch warned. "Don't do anything dumb!"

"Screw you! Screw all of you!" He bawled and marched out of the room, slamming the door on the way out.

Leaving go of his Zimmer frame Manfred released the lever which opened the door of the old wine cellar, and stepped inside. "And how is our patient?" He asked.

Lena shrugged. "She looks dead to me!"

"Well, that would be the whole point wouldn't it?"

"What did you give her?" Brianne asked.

Manfred grinned. "Just enough Tetrodioxin to make her appear dead! This young lady could have fooled a doctor, been buried and no one would ever have known that she was still very much alive!"

"So, what now? Do we just wait for her to wake up?"

"Hardly," Manfred said and produced a syringe from his pocket. "This contains amongst other things Cucumbi Zombie; a drug which, with any luck should awaken our sleeping beauty here."

"Tetrodioxin!" Brianne suddenly said as if some distant memory had just been awakened. "Isn't that a poison derived from the Pufferfish!"

Manfriend looked at her bemused. "I'm very impressed!" He offered earnestly. "And how would madam know such a thing?"

"Before all of this, I was studying biology at Harvard."

He stared at her in puzzlement. "Harvard..! Really? One could almost wonder how one ended up here, in this unfortunate mess?"

"I ended up here because I got it into my head that I wanted the whole dumb celebrity lifestyle, fame money and men; the right men of course. I wanted it all and I didn't stop until my face and my opinions were all over social media! They call people like me an

'Influencer', I'm not sure who I'm meant to be influencing!" Brianne

shook her head in disbelief. "They use to call me Queen of the Trout

pout! How ridiculous is that?"

Unsure quite what a 'trout pout' might be Manfred was at a loss as

to what to say. "It sounds like one received very much more than one

expected!"

Lena rolled her eyes in barely concealed mockery. "You want to

know how I ended up with my fifteen minutes of fame? I dated a

football player for less than a month, I caught him in bed with my

friend and when I dumped him he posted what they politely refer to

as revenge porn all over the web! Before I knew what was

happening, I was a centrefold! I had ten million views on my Fans-

only account, and suddenly I'm more famous than Marylin Monroe

and God combined! I once had a guy recognise me by my tits but

couldn't quite place the face."

Manfriend could feel himself blushing, her words were infinitely

beyond his pay grade. "Yes, quite." He murmured and had to use all

of his many years of experience not to look at her breasts.

"Yeh well, if I get out of here things are going to change, I'll go

back to Harvard and I'll get my qualifications! Animal and fish venoms are incredible. We haven't even begun to tap into the potential for cures for all sorts of diseases and cancers, but I'm quite sure there is no known antidote for Tetrodioxin!"

"My dear not everything under the stars is known unto science! The voodoo practitioners of Haiti have long since used these drugs to great effect!" He said and kneeling pushed the needle into Holly's arm. "She'll soon awaken, she may suffer temporary paralysis and be confused, take care of her until I return!"

"When do we get out of here?" Lena demanded. "I can't take much more of this crap!"

"Patience child! Once this young lady wakes up I get the distinct impression it won't be long before her friends come looking!"

"Who is she anyway?" Brianne asked. "I don't recognise her."

Manfriend grinned. "She would have us believe she's just a drummer in a band... Which of course she is... But then I'm hoping, so much more."

The DeadBeats

"Welcome to Ramstein Airforce Base operations room Sir!" The officer said proudly. "Everything is ready for you now."

"Thank you!" Colonel Harker said and turned to his seated men. "Men, the gentleman to your right in the Whitecoat will now inject each one of you with a tiny pellet! The device will remain under your skin for the duration, not only does this tech give us real-time monitoring of your vital signs, but it is also a beacon, so we can see exactly where you are at any given time. While that work is being carried out!" He said and waved to the medical orderly to carry on. "I would just like to say, before Holly proceeded on her mission she was also implanted with this device; in the last twelve hours her body hasn't moved and no life signs have been detected. As a team, we have been dealt the most devastating of blows! I liked Holly, liked her a lot and her death lies with me, and me alone. This morning I tendered my resignation; it will be effective at the conclusion of this mission! I'd now like to hand you over to one of the intelligence guys for an overall situation briefing... Captain!" The colonel said and moved away from the lectern to allow the captain to take his place.

"Thank you, Sir!" He said. "Good evening, my name is Captain Jones of the inter-service intelligence regiment… As you are aware both known and unknown entities have kidnapped American citizens, they have transported them to foreign lands to take part in an illegal game where the competitors are losing their lives. Uncle Sam does not like this game and has tasked you good people, with returning these young ladies to their families. As of right now, you are all on thirty minutes' notice to move. After this briefing I suggest those of you who need to, gear up, get some food down you and then rest up – So to that end, Mission; You will assault Swartzstein Castle, rescue all captives and kill or capture Prince Casper Von Swartzstein!" He then paused before reading the statement again. "I repeat you will assault Swartzstein Castle, rescue all captives and kill or capture Prince Casper Von Swartzstein..! Are there any questions?"

When no questions were raised he continued. "Detailed outline- The team will be split into two groups and one solo operative. Tony, there's a chopper outside waiting to fly you back to Swartzstein, you will rendezvous with Agent Martello and he will supply you with the exit vehicle, at 'H' hour it will be your task to capture the street-level gondola control house and defend your position until the prisoners are off of the mountain!"

Tony nodded. "Yes sir!"

"Scott, you're also going back tonight, you will be teaming up with Agent Martello! Your mission is to traverse the valley by a method of your own choosing and ascend to the east door! You need to be in position and ready to blow that door by 'H' hour.

"Mitch, Cowboy you two get to have all the fun, you will be using the Hardwing! You will be dropped sixty seconds apart from thirty-five thousand feet, twenty miles inside Austria, by the time you cross the border you must be no higher than three hundred feet or you will be lit up on their radar- take note, there are several Russian SAM Missile systems operating in the area. Once on location, you are to climb to two thousand feet, jettison the wing and deploy parachutes- Mitch, You will land first on the small ledge just above the castle; it's imperative you clear your chute before cowboy arrives or you could both be in trouble. You will then abseil down to the roof, you need to be on location and ready to rock and roll, if you pardon my pun, by 'H' hour! Once you have the green light from Colonel Harker, you are to destroy any communication masts or antenna that you find on that roof; you are then to coordinate your entry with Sabre two and carry out the mission, are there any questions?"

"When is 'H' hour?" Mitch asked.

"That is yet to be determined."

"Once those hard wings go up to two thousand feet, there's a chance they'll know we're there!" Cowboy said.

"That is correct! Hopefully, they'll think you're a bird! If not, that's when the clock starts ticking! If you are killed or captured, you are on your own! we don't know who you are or why you are there!"

"You haven't mentioned extraction..?" Tony said. "How the hell are we getting out with a dozen or so girls in tow?"

"All simulations suggest this will be a hot extraction and we can't help you until you've crossed the border... I'm afraid guys, getting out is your problem to solve!"

Opening her eyes, Holly stared mindlessly through the dimly lit space above, at the ceiling. She wanted to speak, ask someone where she was and what was happening; but her tongue seemed somehow numb, and her lips wouldn't move. Forcing what little air she had in her lungs out; she made a noise; if only to tell herself she was still alive.

Suddenly, a face appeared above her. "She's waking up." It said, the face was stained with mascara and there was bruising under the left eye and along the jaw but it was still pretty, and young looking with long brown unbrushed hair. Holly wanted to ask her name, ask what was happening but darkness descended across her mind, she closed her eyes and fell back into slumber.

"Oh, she's out again!" Brianne said and sat back down on the floor.

"

The gentle knocking on his door came late in the night. Colonel Harker sighed heavily and placed the half-written letter to Holly's parents and an empty tumbler of whisky into his desk's top drawer. "Enter..!" He said and watched as a young female officer entered the room and stood to attention in front of his desk. "What can I do for you, Lieutenant?"

"Sir, I'm sorry to bother you at this late hour but there's something I think you ought to see!" She said and handed him a tablet computer.

One glance at the screen caused him to jump up. "When did this happen?"

"Just now Sir, it's like her heart just suddenly came back to life!"

"Could this be a mistake? How is this even possible?"

"I don't know but she's also now breathing! Should I tell the others?"

"No!" He said and paused while he gathered his thoughts. "Let them think she's dead! Revenge can be a powerful tool; They're about to go up against near-impossible odds; it just might give them the edge they need!"

Lena gently slapped Holly's face and then pulled back her eyelids and stared into her pupils. "I think she's waking up!"

"What..? What's happening?" Holly croaked, with her dry throat and parched mouth it was difficult to speak. "Who are you?"

"Lena and this is Brianne!"

"Brianne Masterson- Moore?" Holly said as she turned her head to look at the girl. "Your dad says hi!"

"My dad?"

"He sure has friends in high places!"

Lena offered a cup of water which Holly greedily gulped down in one mouthful.

"Just let me rest while I get some feeling back in my legs and we'll see about getting the hell out of this shift hole!"

"Are you insane? There are guards everywhere! And they'll kill us on sight!" Lena said as near panic spread across her face.

"Well, I guess we'll just have to kill them first then, won't we?"

"Lady, you're a drummer in a band? I don't think that's going to cut it here! These people are psychos! You will die!"

"I'm pretty tough when I'm angry and right now I'm very angry!"

"You got everything?"

Both Scott and Tony were dressed in white Arctic combat fatigues and were carrying large heavy looking rucksacks.

Patting the stock on his MP5 Scott nodded, hoping he hadn't forgotten some important piece of kit. "We got everything we need right here, Sir!"

"So, this chopper will take you as far as Schrattenberg and then the Austrian defence force will deliver you over the border on Skiddoos, Agent Martello will be waiting! Good luck gentlemen, it's been a pleasure working with you!"

Instead of saluting Scott and Tony both held out their hands for the colonel to shake.

"About Holly Sir!" Scott said. "None of us really think it was your fault and we've been talking and well we'd really like you to reconsider your resignation!"

"The place really wouldn't be the same without you," Tony added.

Harker smiled awkwardly; he'd forgotten about the letter of resignation. "Well, let's just see how the mission goes; You never know, there might be a few surprises along the way!"

Waving his men off, he watched as the Black Hawk helicopter lifted off and then he went back inside. Slowly opening his desk drawer, he tentatively retrieved the half-written letter to Holly's mother, then tearing it into confetti he tossed the pieces in the bin.

The DeadBeats

Barely skimming the treetops, the chopper flew in black-out mode, the pilot using all of his skill to navigate with night-vision goggles and GPS.

The flight through the darkness seemed to pass in no time at all before the passengers heard the pilot's voice in their earpieces. "Stand by, stand by; three minutes to touch down!"

Looking out of the door Tony spotted red flares on the ground forming the shape of a huge letter 'T', and patted Scott on the shoulder indicating the landing site. Both men began to gather up their gear and prepared to disembark.

The Black Hawk had barely touched down before the two men removed their headsets, tossed their gear through the open door and followed it out, landing knee-deep in freshly fallen snow. Moving clear they knelt and waited for the chopper to lift off and then moved off to the waiting vehicles.

"You got room for a small one on there?" Scott said and climbed aboard.

"Cover your face, unless you want frostbite." The driver said and handed him some goggles. "When we halt at the border you and your friend must remain silent... No speaking, many Russian patrols!" As soon as Tony was settled on the second Skidoo the two vehicles slowly moved off into the night.

The gale force winds raged in the mountains and heavily laden with snow charged, headlong down the valley, churning the flakes on a roller coaster of white noise to blanket the ground, rocks and trees.

Holding on for dear life Scott checked back over his shoulder and was relieved to see the following vehicle was still close on their tail.

Pulling off the track, the Skidoo suddenly came to a halt between three large boulders. The driver dismounted and signalled for them to be quiet. "This is the border; your guy if he's still alive, should be about two hundred meters in that direction!" He whispered. "Watch your backs, a Russian patrol came through here just this afternoon!"

Falling in beside Scott, Tony adjusted his rucksack for comfort. "You ready big man?"

"Ready as I'll ever be!" Leading the way, Scott took them out in single file wading knee-deep in powdery snow toward a large copse of pine trees.

The tempest drove the freezing snow hard into their faces, stinging any exposed skin and making walking and navigation difficult.

Suddenly halting, Scott slowly fell to his knees and signalled Tony to follow suit. Movement in the trees to their front saw both men drop to the prone position and quietly ready their weapons.

A single figure slowly emerged and moved out of the tree line toward them. Closing in on their position he waved them on. "You guys wanna get in the jeep? It's getting kinda cold out here!" Martello cried grinning.

Lumbering to his feet Scott made his weapon safe and headed over to the secret service agent. "How long have you been waiting out here?"

"Long enough to lose all of the feeling in both of my feet and I strongly suspect I may no longer be able to have children!" He said.

"So, this Jeep of yours, has it got any heating?" Tony asked. "Because I need some serious defrosting!"

"Come on!" He said and led them to a track where the vehicle was waiting.

Taking their rucksacks off, they tossed them in the back and then climbed aboard.

Navigating the treacherous rural tracks, they soon joined onto the main highway into town, remaining safely tucked in behind a snowplough until Agent Martello indicated right and began to turn.

"Where the hell are you going?" Scott asked. "Town is that way!"

"Your boss thought it best if we rented a lodge away from prying eyes! Somewhere we can lay low until it's time."

"Has it got beds and a shower?" Tony asked enthusiastically.

Martello nodded. "Trust me it's got everything! The place is stacked!"

"But has it got food!" Scott said seriously. "Because I'm starving, I could eat a scabby horse!"

"Sure Scott, I filled the refrigerator with you in mind!"

"Oh dude, you just made me so happy!"

Even though there probably wasn't a human being within two miles Martello still carried out his persec (Personal Security) drills. Two detours and one halt later he was more or less satisfied that they weren't being followed and headed toward the lodge.

Loathe to loiter out in the open, they quickly de-bussed, grabbed their gear and went inside.

"You guys want to stow your weapons and gear, and I'll light the fire."

Looking around the room with its large couch and sixty-inch plasma television, Tony grinned. "I must say this isn't quite what I was expecting!" And then he dumped his rucksack at Martello's feet. "Your fatigues for the assault! And you're welcome because that climb looks like a killer! Sooner you than me!"

"Well, If you take a look out of the back window you'll see I have something for you too?"

With a puzzled look on his face, he wandered over to the window and looked outside, and his mouth dropped. "What the hell, Martello?" He gasped. "What am I supposed to do with that old thing?"

"She's beautiful isn't she?"

Taking a look for himself Scott took a peek outside and found himself staring at an old yellow school bus. "Seriously dude! Is that what I think it is?

"She's our ticket out of here, room for us and all of the girls!" He said proudly.

"Where the hell did you get that thing? Does it even run?"

"Well, you might be surprised to know I borrowed it from the local school; Don't look at me like that- They're on half term, they'll never know! I'll have it back in a couple of days!"

"You stole a school bus dude! That ain't cool!"

After lighting the log fire Martello laid a large map of the area on the coffee table. "So, there's the route up to that east gate. Mitch and I recce'd it last week and it's going to be very difficult but not impossible...!"

"That's one hell of a steep descent into the valley!" Scott said as he took a closer look at the contour lines on the map. "And the climb up to the castle looks even steeper!"

"We could ski down and hope that if anyone sees us they just think we're Russians..."

"Or...?"

"It's the last night of the festival there's going to be parades, thousands of spectators and flares! I say we join in the celebrations and then snowboard down into the valley from the main piste in our civilian ski gear. It's the quickest route as the crow flies, once we're at the bottom and out of sight we get changed into fatigues and begin

the climb!"

"I like it!" Scot said thoughtfully. "I really like it … Now, on a more

important note, you said something about a fully stocked

refrigerator?"

Chapter 21

"Is she dead?" Casper asked eagerly. "Tell me she's dead! She must be!"

"I'm pleased to report that is very much the case sir!" Manfred replied

"Good... Good! Did you feed her to the pig?"

"Err, the pig? No sir..!" Manfred said with a slightly puzzled look on his face. "We don't have a pig! Your father had it butchered back in eighty- nine, after the crushing incident with your mother's cat... If you recollect he had old Barney turned into sausages!"

"Barney's Dead? Oh my..!" Casper wailed with tears filling his eyes. "Barney was my pet... Why did no one tell me?"

"If my memory serves me right you were away at boarding school at the time sir!"

Suddenly his eyes drifted away as he awoke to a distant and long-forgotten memory. "Oh my god, sausages! I remember now! Mother sent me sausages!" His hand shot to his mouth. "I… I ate Barney! I feel sick… Why would she do that? She knew how much I loved that pig."

"Yes, quite the quandary isn't it sir! Your mother did have the darkest sense of humour."

"I hate her, that bitch! If she wasn't dead I'd… I'd kill her!" He raged. "What is that disgusting smell then?"

Loathe to say that it was the stench of some thirty sweaty mercenaries and several dishevelled and half-starved young women Manfred lied. "I fear one may be suffering the consequence of firing most of the staff last year! The maids as you said, may have been useless commoners but they kept the old place clean."

"I sacked them?"

"Yes sir, against my council may I add!"

"What? All of them?"

"You kept the cook… Oh, and myself of course!"

"Oh, yes I remember now!" He said and wiped the tears from his cheeks. "I couldn't have all those people blabbing to all and sundry about the game… They had to go, Can you make a note to hire them

back when the game is over? Meanwhile, open some windows!"

"Yes sir! Was there anything else sir?"

"No, I don't want to be disturbed for the rest of the day; I'm in

mourning for my poor barney!"

"In that case, I'll take this opportunity to ask what one would like

for dinner?"

"Not sausages Manfred… Never again sausages!"

Nodding solemnly Manfred left the room, and once out of sight

shook his head and sighed. The time was drawing close and perhaps

now was the moment to complete the packing of his suitcase.

Climbing to her knees Holly checked her balance, and once

satisfied she stood up. "I think I'm ok now!" She said. "Right..! Have

either of you two had a look for a way out of this room?"

"No..!" Lena said and Brianne shrugged in agreement.

"Well, how does Manfred get out? Is there a key? Does he push a

loose brick, like in the films?" Holly said

This time both girls shrugged.

Marching over to the door in frustration she searched for a handle or mechanism but found none. "There must be something here?" She barked. "Next time that old man comes in here, we all have to watch him carefully and see what he does to get out."

"Maybe we should just hit him over the head and make a run for it!" Brianne said nervously, unconvinced by her own plan her voice was shaky and her eyes shifted tentatively from Holly to Lena.

"Nobody hurts the old man!" Lena said tersely. "He risked everything to save all our lives!"

"Yeh, she's right! I'm not about to start hitting pensioners over the head quite yet." Holly said. "And besides we won't get far just making a run for it! We need weapons and I'm not leaving here without the other girls!"

"What?" Lena barked. "Are you insane? We can't afford to worry about anyone else we need to save ourselves; get the hell out of here and call the police!"

"Lena! No debates! I know out there in the big wide world that for some reason you are some sort of celebrity! That you think you're more important than other people! But you're not in the big wide world right now; you're here with me and I'm trying to save your life so from here on in we do what I say and when I say it!"

"Or what?" Lena scoffed.

"Sweetheart! Mess with me and I'll make such a mess of your pretty little face even a dog wouldn't lick it!"

The sound of the door clicking open abruptly ceased the conversation.

"I don't have long the guard will be back shortly!" Manfred said breathlessly and then he nervously looked over his shoulder into the dark passage. "The time has come, we leave tonight; I'll try to return just after midnight!"

"What's happened? Why tonight?" Holly asked.

"His Royal Highness has as you Americans say 'lost the plot'! He's quite happy to carry out mass murder but he's up there right now mourning the death of a potbellied pig which died thirty years ago! I must go now I have much to do!"

"Wait!" Holly ordered. "If something goes wrong we need to know how to get out of this room!"

Manfred hesitated and then realised she was right. "Look there on the floor!" He said and pointed to a particular stone; Stand on that as you slide the door! Promise me you won't leave this room until I return."

"I'm not going to be making any promises I can't keep! I'm leaving at midnight with or without you!"

"I take it your friends will be joining us at some point!"

"You can bet your Lilly-coloured ass they will!"

"Friends? What Friends? What's he talking about? Brianne asked shakily.

Ignoring her questions Holly turned back to Manfred. "I need a weapon! Can you get me a pistol?"

"I'll see what I can do!" He reluctantly replied.

"Just who the hell are you?" Lena said.

"Who me? Why? I'm Just a drummer in a band sweety! Just a drummer in a band!"

Waking to the smell of strong coffee, Scot rose wearily and wandered into the lounge, where Martello and Tony were watching a cartoon on TV. "What time is it?"

"Just after eleven!" Tony said without looking up.

"What? Why did you let me sleep so long?" Scott barked as if he was late for an appointment.

"Chill man! Come and watch Scooby Doo with us."

"He's right!" Martello said. "Sit down, watch some TV. All the equipment has been checked, we cleaned all of the weapons! We all know our missions and what's expected of us! The parade doesn't start for another couple of hours so like the man said, chill out!"

"I say it's the lighthouse keeper?" Tony said and took a bite out of a ham sandwich.

"My money is on the son! Look at him; Always in the background, never says too much! And he's got real shifty eyes"

"What are you two idiots talking about?

"Scooby-doo!" Martello replied. "I'm sure those meddling kids will tell us soon enough!"

"I'm gonna take a shower!"

The DeadBeats

Over the space of two films and several cups of hot coffee a nervous energy began to fill the room as Scott and Martello began to get ready. Taking their time to don their arctic fatigues, carefully lace up their boots and check their gear for the last time. Once they'd pushed a full magazine into the housing of their weapons they Stowed the silenced MP5 submachine guns in their rucksacks and then slipped brightly coloured ski jackets over their whites.

"It's time!" Scott said as he checked his watch for the last time.

"So, I'll drop you two off in town…" Tony said. "And I'll see you on the other side! Try not to die!" After shaking hands with both men, he helped them carry their gear to the jeep.

Traffic was heavier than they expected and the carnival was well underway by the time they arrived there at dusk. The further into the resort they went the thicker it became with people.

"No point going any further Tony; just drop us off here!" Martello said and looked at Scott for his agreement which came in the form of a nod.

Climbing out they retrieved their rucksacks and hoisted them into their shoulders.

"Watch your backs and good luck!" Tony said and waved as he drove off into the night.

Mixing in with the excitable and chattering crowds they headed straight for the fun fare and illuminated market stalls. The air was cold, crisp and carried the scent of nearby pines.

As darkness fell orange flares began to be lit up on the pists and down the thoroughfare, twinkling lights adorned the stalls and burger bars. Face-painted children skidded past on their snowboards as parents vied to control their exuberance.

Alive with colour, the heart of the town was draped in a dizzying myriad of banners and flags. The mouth-watering aroma of burgers and deep-fried chicken now filled the air, teasing the taste buds and making Scott think about how hungry he was.

Passengers on illuminated fairground rides could be heard screaming above the sounds of horns and loud music. Somewhere close by a live band was performing on stage, their rhythmic beats and lively tune somehow familiar. "That's our song man- Those guys are stealing our tune!" Scott barked. "What the hell..?"

The DeadBeats

"They sound good!" Martello said as a huge mischievous grin spread across his face. "In fact, I'd go as far as to say they sound better than you guys!"

"They better not do my rap while I'm in earshot or so help me…!" Pushing through the crowd, Scott suddenly found himself faced with a DeadBeats tribute act performing on stage, and his eyes instantly fell on the drummer. The girl was slight of build like Holly, blond like Holly and drumming just like Holly and for a second Scott saw Holly grinning behind her drumsticks. "No way man, you can't do that… You shouldn't be…!" The big man said as his heart felt like it would burst.

"Come on man..!" Martello said and began dragging Scott away from the spectacle. "I'm sorry you had to see that!"

"It's ok, I'm alright! I'm fine!" Scott loudly and shrugged Martello off. "God, I wish she'd have been here to see that; She would have loved it! That girl would have been on that stage and dancing…!" His voice trailed off as his eyes fell on the dark shape of the castle silhouetted against the snow-covered mountain. "Come on, we got a mountain to climb and a Prince to beat the crap out of!"

Pushing through the crowds they made their way to the valley's edge and unstrapped their snowboards from the back of their rucksacks. Strapping them to their feet they launched over the edge and began plummeting down the near-vertical run.

Leaving the lights, music and carnival atmosphere behind, and just meters apart the two men plummeted near vertically as they carved a path through the trees and the deep virgin snow;

Deftly avoiding large boulders and skidding across the tops of others before landing back on the snow they descended at breakneck speed into the white abyss.

Adrenaline surged through their veins as they leapt ever higher over jumps and missed trees by mere feet as they hurtled past. Riding the crests of mini avalanches, they surfed the waves of snow until eventually, the descent became less severe. With the valley floor now in sight, they began to slow down, sliding to a halt under the protective canopy of some pine trees.

"Dude!" Scott said breathlessly. "I wanna do that again! That was one wild ride!"

The DeadBeats

Slipping out of their snowboards and rucksacks they place them to one side and then took off their over jackets in silence, digging a hole they buried them under a mound of snow and then carefully opened their rucksacks and took out their chest rigs, weapons and climbing gear.

Looking up at the castle Martello blew out hard. "We really need to be doing this in under six hours!" He said. "Or the party could start without us!"

"That's one hell of a climb!" Scott said as he finally finished fitting his climbing harness and clipped two ice axes onto his belt. Feeding a round into the chamber of his MP5, he checked the safety catch was on and then he slung it over his shoulder and began walking toward the base of the towering and very steep rock face. "I guess I'm leading? I'll put an anchor in every fifty feet or so! Look out for falling snow or rocks! If you fall, die quietly!"

Momentarily resting to catch his breath Manfred leaned heavily on his walking frame. "Yes! I'm coming, master!" He cried weakly. "I'll be there forthwith!" Pushing on he entered the Prince's bed chamber to see him sat at his dressing table applying makeup to his face.

"Manfred! Just the man I want to see!"

"Yes sir! How may I be of assistance" Manfred said and noticed several lines of cocaine on the dressing table.

"It's decided!"

"What's decided, sir?"

The prince looked at Manfred, his face alive with excitement.

"Tonight, is the night! Tonight, we shall create an extravaganza for the ages. To coincide with the closing of the snow festival in town I shall hold a podcast looking back over the whole Fame Game competition culminating in the crowning of our first champion and then I shall reveal my true self to the world!"

"Is that wise sir?"

"Fame and glory old man, fame and glory!"

"May I point out that several young ladies and one gentleman have lost their lives in this endeavour? You revealing your true identity could, as it were, cause some problems!"

Casper scoffed. "Like what?"

The DeadBeats

"Well far be it from me to say sir, but todays civilised society does tend to pour scorn on murder for entertainment!"

"No, no, no!" He barked angrily. "Everyone loves the fame game, just look at the viewing figures, this time next year we'll be on national tv, we'll be syndicated and I will be the most famous man in the world!"

"Quite sir! Quite..! I do sometimes wonder what your father would have made of all this!"

"My father was an imbecile... And my mother a whore! I care not of the opinions of dead people!"

"Yes sir! How would you like tonight's game to proceed?"

"Put all those little bitches in one tiny room and throw in a knife! The last one standing wins!"

"Genius sir! Quite genius if I may say so?" Inside, he was screaming.

"We go on air at midnight! Make the arrangements Manfred; oh, and the knife, make it a blunt one!"

"Blunt sir?"

Casper smiled maliciously. "Yes you blithering Imbecile a blunt knife, It'll hurt more, won't it?"

Waking with a start, Holly took a moment to remember where she was. Peering into the gloom she looked around the room but saw the sleeping figure of only one other person. "Brianne..! Wake up! Where's Lena?"

Sitting up Brianne groggily rubbed her eyes and yawned. "She's not here!"

"I can see that! Did you see her leave?"

"No, she must have gone when we were asleep! She's got some deal going on with the butler, maybe he came for her."

"What deal? What are you talking about?"

"I don't know! I think she is supposed to help him leave the castle!"

"Well, Lena or no Lena we're getting out of here right now!" She said and climbed to her feet. Placing her foot on the stone which Manfred had pointed out to her, she pressed and heard a quiet click as the mechanism unlocked the door. Opening the panel just enough to see out into the corridor, she looked and listened for the presence of any guards but there was nothing to see and no sound. "Come on,

let's go!" She said and slipped out through the gap with Brianne
nervously following.

Breathing hard, Scott hauled himself onto a small ledge and took a
deep breath before looking down to see Martello patiently waiting to
begin his ascent.

Blasted by icy particles carried on the freezing gale Scott unclipped
an anchor from his harness and pushed it into a crevice, giving it a
tug to ensure it was secure. He then attached the rope and tossed the
remainder down the cliff face.

Taking a firm grip of the rope Martello attached it to his rig and
placed his hands on the rockface. "Climbing now!" He whispered
into his throat mic.

"Roger that!" His breath visible in the cold and crisp night air Scott
climbed to his feet and set off on the next leg of his ascent. A rock
fissure made for easy climbing and gave some respite from the
tempest, he soon began to make good progress. Pausing once again
he attached another anchor to the rock face and secured the rope.
Taking a moment to check on Martello who was already hauling

himself onto the ledge some fifty feet below. "How are you doing down there?" He said.

"Not so bad, looks like you're about halfway!"

"Roger that! I'm traversing east there looks to be an easier route up... I think we might be able to get off the ropes and scramble the rest of the way!"

"Roger, I'm on the ledge, just moving into the fissure now, out!"

At odds with its surroundings and barely clinging on, a lonely pine tree sapling flourished on the extreme rock face. Climbing beyond there were more trees and larger ones clinging to a less severe scree slope. Quickly realising that the rope was now more of a hindrance than a help he unclipped, brought his weapon to bear and hunkered down to wait for Martello.

Certain as he could be that the prince was busy in the recording suite, Manfred led Lena to the study on the second floor. Placing his finger on his lips signalling he to be quiet, he entered the room and made straight for a large black safe standing in the corner of the room.

Without speaking the old man spun the combination dial and then stood back as the heavy metal door swung open.

Lena gasped at the sight. "Oh my god!" She said as her hand moved to cover her mouth.

"Shush!" Manfred barked in hushed tones. "Help me fill the bag!"

"You're stealing the crown jewels?"

"No, I'm saving them... But I am stealing the money, severance pay if you will! Now get over here and help me!"

Reaching into the safe she gently took a diamond-encrusted tiara from a tray of jewels and held it up to the light. "It's beautiful, I've never seen anything like it!"

"Yes, very pretty now put it in the bag with the rest and get the cash!" He said anxiously. "There's one of her ladyship's old coats hanging on the back of the door, now put it on and take the case."

Lena did as she was told and watched as Manfred closed the safe.

"There's a silk scarf in the pocket wrap it around your head, and let's just hope none of the guards recognise you.

"Wait..! What, like we're just going to walk out of here?"

"Sooner that than be carried, my child! If anyone asks you're the new maid."

Baulking at the very idea Lena rolled her eyes in disgust. "As if anyone would believe I was a mere maid?"

"Tonight, my dear, whether you like it or not, you are a maid! Now let's see if we can't leave this place without getting killed!"

Cautiously making their way out into the corridor Manfred led Lena down the back staircase to the Gondola control room. "Girl, I need you to find every ounce of courage you possess, if that guard doesn't believe you're a maid we're both dead!"

Lena nodded and taking a deep breath stepped out into the open. "Yes sir, tomorrow I will change the bedsheets and continue with the laundry!" She said making up a bogus conversation.

Alerted by the voices the guard stood up. "Who is there?" He barked.

"Only me!" Manfred said and waved. "Good evening Stefan!"

"Oh, it's you!" He replied with the misery of someone who hadn't seen a soul all day. "Who is she?"

"This is Clara, she's the new maid; she'll be coming up to the castle every day from now on."

Stefan smiled; this was a welcome relief from his monotony.

"I'm just escorting her down to the hotel, I'll be no more than twenty minutes."

The guard barely raised an eyebrow, but nodded sullenly and then took his place at the gondola console, indicating that they should climb aboard.

Once inside Manfred closed the door and turned to Lena. "One down and one to go?"

"What do you mean?" She said weakly, barely able to conceal the trembling of her lips.

"There's another guard at the bottom! Just be brave we are almost there!"

The Gondola lifted off jerkily but then the gears kicked in and it became smoother, gaining speed as it plummeted through low-lying clouds toward the distant lights of the town.

Cradling the steaming hot cup of coffee in both hands, Tony noticed the return of the phantom itch on the calf of his long-dead right leg; putting it down to the anxious wait and four cups of coffee he continued to surveil the Gondola entrance through the mostly steamed up restaurant window.

The last of the festival goers were wandering happily back to the hotels and lodges. The music and fairground rides long since quietened; only the diehards and drunks remained to claim the night as their own.

Gazing up at the imposing mountainside through the gently falling snow, he wondered if he had some binoculars would he be able to see the progress of his friends.

Suddenly, something moving against the darkness of the night sky caught his eye. Realising the gondola was imminently arriving at ground level he jumped up and dashed outside, sprinting across the road.

He could barely breathe as a sense of horror began to grow in his gut, if Prince Casper emerged from that building then the mission would be aborted. Hearing the sound of the revving Rolls Royce engine as it coasted down the exit ramp, Tony wanted to pretend to be looking in the window of the adjacent shop window; but he simply could not pull his eyes away from that exit for fear of missing the occupants.

Time seemed to be frozen, and the world moving impossibly slowly as the vehicle emerged into the night; Tony's eyes fell on the driver and Manfred stared right back, the old man seemed to have a smirk on his face. Without even realising Tony stepped off the curb, and as the car veered to avoid him, he got a good long look in the back of the car; No Casper, just a young woman.

"I can't…!" Brianne cried anxiously; her face painted with fear she trembled uncontrollably. "I can't go..! They'll kill us!

"If you stay, you die!" Holly growled. "I haven't got time for this bullshit! Now move or so help me god I will drag you through that door!"

Mentally and physically exhausted Brianne collapsed to her knees. "I don't want to die!" she sobbed.

"Look, I'm sorry that you ended up in this awful situation but crying and collapsing on the floor isn't helping!" Suddenly Brianne looked so young, almost childlike as she sat there sobbing. "Ok, just wait here!" Holly relented. "And I'll go see if the coast is clear," Then she gently took hold of her hand. "I'll be back in a minute, I promise!"

Brianne nodded and wiped tears from her grubby and wet-stained cheeks.

After listening for any signs of the guards, Holly slid the door open just enough to squeeze through the gap. Stepping out, and feeling exposed she pressed her back against the wall and slowly began edging along the passage. The quiet and still atmosphere roused her confidence and she dared to step out of the shadows, the moment she did so, the sudden echo of a distant voice slammed her back into the wall; hugging the shadows she froze, hardly daring to breathe for fear of being heard. An adrenaline overdose fired up her senses and sent them spiralling into overdrive, her whole body tingled as fight or flight took over and prepared her for violence.

The DeadBeats

The one voice, even though it was Russian had the tone of someone speaking on the telephone. Fear began to wane as the voice grew silent and after listening for a while she reluctantly set off once more.

The guard, consumed with a tatty old car magazine and oblivious to the imminent danger, sat with his back to her, at a desk situated at the far end of the passageway. Boredom saw him humming a tune and occasionally throwing in a verse or a line from the song.

With the adrenaline surge now under control she silently edged forward, focusing on the back of the guard's head each step seemed like a mile and each second an eternity.

He tilted his head as he craned to see the half-naked girl sprawled over the bonnet of a Ferrari on page seven. Holly paused- daring not to breathe she took another step and moved closer.

Even seated he looked like a big man and she doubted she could beat him in a straight fight; she would need help, and help looked like it was about to come in the form of a rusty old shovel which was leaning against the wall.

Silently sidling over to the shovel, she gently teased it away from the wall and then grasping the shank firmly in both hands she turned, and as she walked toward her target she raised it high above her head. Once in position, she stood on her tiptoes and summoning all

of her might crashed the shovel down squarely on his head.

The guard slumped forward unconscious, without uttering a sound

before falling sideways out of his chair. Holly winced as his head

smashed onto the stone floor.

"The first one was on me, dude! The second one was all you!" she

said, and removing his pistol from its holster she chambered a round

and Snatched up the large bunch of keys laying on the table.

Sprinting beyond the guard to the first door she hurriedly unlocked

it and stepped inside.

A young woman huddled in the corner clutching her knees rocked

gently back and forth. "Hello..!" Holly said softly. "My name is

Holly; I've come to take you home!"

The girl ceased rocking and slowly looked up at her would-be

rescuer.

Holly gasped at the sight of her face; her left eye was blackened and

bloody, her left cheek swollen, bruised and blood-stained and her lips

were split and covered in bloody scabs- worse still, the flimsy red shirt which she was struggling to cover herself with, looked like it had been torn from her shoulders more than once.

The girl simply uttered one word. "Home!"

Holly nodded. "Home- but we have to get out first!" reaching out she offered the girl her hand and when she took it, hauled her to her feet. Then she handed her the keys. "Get all the other girls out, while you're doing that I'll go back for Brianne!"

"Jesus h Christ!" Cowboy baulked through gritted teeth. "Steady, with the crown jewels dude!"

The technician barely raised an eyebrow as he yanked on the Velcro fastener some more. "Sorry, but if this Hardwing isn't super tight Maverick and Goose could go into a flat spin!"

"Oh, I like what you did there! The old Top Gun reference!"

"Well sir, there's no points for crashing and burning in this film!"

"Shut up and listen up!" Harker bellowed over the heads of the swarming technicians and the sounds of the C130 as it warmed up outside the hanger door. "Let's go over this thing one more time! Mitch, you will jump first, sixty seconds later cowboy, you will follow him. Use the GPS on your wrist to navigate, a pre-planned route has been programmed in for you! Once you're over the border stay under the radar until you're right on top of the castle, at which point you go vertical to one thousand feet; disengage the Hardwing and deploy your chutes... Once you land Mitch, you will have one minute to stow your parachute and get the hell out of Cowboy's way... Are there any questions?" Ignoring both men he answered the question himself. "No? Well let's do this and be home for breakfast-Gentlemen, it's been mostly a pleasure, I would ask you to try not to die, Uncle Sam spent a lot of money on your training and getting you to where you are now! if you would like to board the aircraft we'll get underway!"

The two men shuffled along under the huge weight they were wearing and had to be physically helped and pushed up the ramp and onto the aircraft where they were clipped into an overhead rack to take the weight until they arrived at the drop zone.

"Would it upset anyone, if I said that I needed the John!"

"Shut up Cowboy! If you got business to do I suggest you do it in your pants. Ok, guys!" Harker said. "Comms check!"

The DeadBeats

"Sabre one loud and clear!" Mitch shouted above the roar of the engines.

"Roger that!" Harker replied. "The other teams are in position- Watch out for friendly faces when you get down there!"

Mitch frowned. "What's that supposed to mean? What friendly faces?"

"Well! We have friendly assets already inside the castle- in fact, I'd go as far as to say SHE has probably already started the party without you!"

"She?" Cowboy asked incredulously. "Are you talking about who I think you're talking about!"

Harker simply grinned and raised his eyebrows.

"She's alive? I'm pretty sure we all watched her die!" cowboy cried barely believing his own words. "If I wasn't wearing this Transformers cosplay getup... Why Sir, I think I might hug you!"

"You son of a bitch! You let us think she was dead? You let us grieve for our friend!" Mitch said and shook his head in disbelief. "Hell, Cowboy here near on took your head off with that dammed chair!"

"Calm down, I didn't know myself until a little while ago when her tracker suddenly started transmitting signs of life. Since then, she's begun moving and from what we've seen of her heart rate and blood pressure I'd say she's currently on mission!"

"On mission? You're telling me she's running around that castle on her own? Get this bird in the air right now!"

"I should have known she wasn't dead!" Cowboy cried.

"Why's that?"

"Because sir! The Devil's scared of her and I doubt she'd ever make it into heaven! - Sir before I jump..!" Cowboy held out his hand. "I'd just like to take this opportunity to say from the bottom of my heart... You're a real asshole Sir, but you're our asshole! So that kinda makes you a special kinda asshole!"

"Thanks, you oversized butt plug- I think that's the nicest thing anyone has ever said to me!" Harker said and shook his hand.

Once the aircraft had taxied to the end of the runway, the engines began to rev, screaming to be unleashed from its earthly constraints. Lurching forward, the aircraft began hurtling down the tarmac and then rotated near vertical into the sky.

"All call signs this is Sunray; Sabre two respond over!"

"Sunray this is Sabre two, nice of you to join us over!" Scott said and shot Martello an excited look.

"Send sitrep over!"

"We're in a holding pattern at the start point over!"

"Roger that! Sabre one is ten minutes out, I say again ten minutes from your location, wait out!"

"I guess it's time to set the explosives!" Scott said. "Cover me!" Then, breaking out into the open he moved up the slope toward the east door.

Slinging his weapon, Scott removed the fist-sized and malleable C4 explosives from a pouch on the front of his rig; shaping the conglomerate he pushed it firmly into the lock and then attached a remote-controlled detonator. Happy with his work he returned to his laying up position behind a large boulder.

Clapping his cold hands to try and put some feeling back into them Martello glanced up at the sky. "Looks like a storm is coming!"

"Yeah, let's hope it doesn't hit before we go in, Just another few minutes and I get to go kill that son of a bitch! He's gonna pay for what he's done!"

"Sixty seconds!" Harker said over the intercom, and as he finished speaking the Pilot switched on the night lights of the aircraft bathing the interior in a dull red glow.

Suddenly, the loadmaster ducked around and in front of Mitch smiling broadly and offering him the thumbs-up sign, he responded likewise. "What's the chance of an upgrade to first class?" He asked, and then lowered his face mask, wriggling it side to side to ensure a comfortable and tight fit.

"This is first class! You should see what it's like in economy!"

With surging adrenaline and butterflies beginning to flutter wildly in his stomach Mitch began to steady his breathing and prepare himself for the task ahead.

"This is gonna be one hell of a ride!" Cowboy cried over the intercom.

397

The DeadBeats

Mitch wasn't quite so enthusiastic and knew anything could go wrong at any time. "In all honesty, there are other places I'd rather be right now!" He cried over his shoulder and then braced himself as the aircraft suddenly juddered signalling the ramp mechanism operating and lowering of the tailgate. Cold air charged in unchecked smashing into their bodies buffeting them around in the fuselage like rag dolls.

"Thirty seconds!"

Suddenly the loadmaster reappeared and unclipped Mitch from the overhead tether. "Walk forward!" He cried. "Walk forward!"

He shuffled forward until he could see the twinkling of street lights and the faint outlines of houses in a tiny village far below. Suddenly the interior lights turned green.

"Go...Go!" The Loadmaster bellowed in his ear and pointed to the open sky.

Taking two steps Mitch launched himself into the night sky, and as he began to plummet he adopted the flight position and gave the tiny jet engines a burst to stabilise his flight and go level with the ground.

Gradually descending in altitude to three hundred feet he gave the boosters a four-second burst accelerating toward the far horizon.

Flanked by Austrian mountains on each side and barely skimming some of the taller evergreens, he used the control unit in his right hand to change direction and the one in his left to fire the small rocket packs.

"Sabre One, you are twenty meters above the ceiling, we require you to descend immediately over!"

"Roger that, descending now!" Mitch said and slightly adjusted his wing trim, causing a sudden and gut-churning descent. "How far to the border over?"

"Sabre one, seven hundred and fifty meters over!"

"Roger that, stand by!"

Skimming through a thin veil of low-laying clouds, Mitch immerged with the castle clearly visible in the far distance.

"Sabre one prepare to go vertical!"

"Roger that, going vertical in three two one... now, wait out!" Mitch said and fired the rockets instantly sending him soaring skyward, above the castle. The altimeter raced to two thousand feet and Mitch released the wing sending himself into immediate freefall.

The DeadBeats

"All stations, this is Sunray; The clock is now ticking… Good luck; Out!"

Plummeting groundward within fingertip distance of the cliff face Mitch checked his altimeter and at six hundred meters pulled the rip cord deploying his chute. As soon as the chute was fully deployed he released his rucksack which fell twenty meters below him suspended on a nylon rope.

The Rucksack hit the ledge first and three seconds later Mitch joined it. Rushing to pull his chute in, he bundled it up in a ball and the grabbing his rucksack moved to the cliff face. He'd barely got out of the way before Cowboy's rucksack hit the ledge followed almost instantly by the big Texan.

"Holy shit dude!" He cried as he wound his chute in. "That was insane, at one point there, I touched the top of one of those big old trees… I can't believe they pay me to do this! Hell, I'd do this for free!"

Stowing their chutes and harnesses under some loose rocks on the ledge they opened their rucksacks and carefully took out ropes and climbing gear. Working in silence they attached anchors to the cliff face and then clipped on their carabiners, after tossing the remaining rope over the edge they watched as the ends landed on the very top battlement.

"You ready?"

"Ready as I'll ever be!" Cowboy said as he threaded the rope through the belay and friction device. "Let's do this!"

After giving their ropes a tug, they leaned back and began abseiling down the rockface in short jumping bounds; as their confidence grew the bounds became bigger and soon they were standing on the castle's battlement.

Disengaging from the ropes, they cocked their weapons, jumped down off the short castellated wall and made for a heavy-looking oak door.

Trying the handle, the door opened. "Well, looky here!" Cowboy said. "They must have been expecting us!"

"Sunray this is Sabre one now at the start position over!"

"Roger that! Hello all callsigns this is Sunray one standby... Good luck Gentlemen! You have a GO! Sabre two acknowledge over!"

"Sabre two roger out!"

The second he heard the word 'Go' Scott pressed the button on the remote control, and watched as the C4 exploded punching a hole through the door and destroying the lock. Breaking cover both men sprinted to the opening

Flicking down the AN/PSQ night vision attachment Scott reached the door first and booting it open covered the interior as Martello pushed through into the building.

"Room clear!"

"Roger that!" Scott replied and followed him in.

With no shouting, noise or orders being barked from above it seemed no one had heard the explosion.

Moving quickly beyond His partner Scott made for a spiral staircase and then giving cover allowed Martello to leapfrog his position.

"Stairs clear, moving up now!" Martello said into his throat mic and then, taking the steps two at a time rushed to the top and halted when he saw an exit door.

Quietly positioning himself against the wall beside the door, Scott took hold of the handle and slowly turned; the door instantly gave on its rusty old hinges and creaked open slightly.

Peering through the gap between the door and the doorframe he counted five mercenaries, one sat on a bunk cleaning his weapon and the other four were sitting around a table playing cards; with no way around, they would have to go through.

Silently signalling to Martello how many targets were on the other side he then began to count down from three.

On one, they both stepped into the chamber. The mercenaries all stopped what they were doing and stared at the strangers, unsure who they were or what they were doing.

"Hi, guys!" Scott said and grinned. "Wow, if you could see the looks on your faces right now."

A sudden thud of realisation and panic slammed into them; The table tipped over in an explosion of movement, scattering playing cards and beer bottles, chairs and bodies flew in all directions as they dove for their weapons or tried to reach cover.

With the silenced MP5s wedged into the shoulder Scott and Martello fired double taps into each of the mercenaries, and when the smoke cleared all lay dead on the floor.

"Sunray, Sabre two room clear!"

"Roger that Sabre two, be aware we have a friendly face on the ground!"

"Roger that!" Scott said and turning to Martello shrugged. "What was that all about?"

"I think they want us to check our targets before we shoot!"

"Why they wanna go and spoil all my fun?"

"Manfred..!" Casper shouted anxiously. "Manfred! Where are you? What..? What was that noise?" Slowly standing up from his computer, he pushed the chair back out of the way. "Manfred, I need you! Come at once!" All of a sudden there was an emptiness about the castle, a stillness in the air and somehow he suddenly felt very alone. Nervously approaching the door, he popped his head out and looked both ways in the corridor. "Manfred... Manfred! Dammit, man! Where are you? Guard!" And then louder. "Guard- I need a guard!"

The sound of heavy boots running on stone preceded the arrival of someone Casper didn't recognise. "Sir!" The man said and stood to attention.

"Err, I was looking for Manfred!" He said tentatively trying his best to sound unafraid and authoritative. "Have you seen him?"

"Yes sir, he's taken the new maid down to town?

"New maid? What..? What new maid?"

"The new maid sir!"

"We don't have a new maid!" Casper said, as his patience began to wear.

The two men stared at each other. "What was that noise? I heard a noise?"

The guard shrugged. "We didn't hear anything downstairs sir!"

"Have the remaining girls taken to the arena! It's time for the final game!" He said and then added. "There's something wrong! Have the men take a look around!"

"At once Sir!" The guard said, turned and ran back in the direction from which he had come.

The DeadBeats

Casper hesitated; he couldn't shrug off the feeling something was quite wrong. There was no new maid, and if Manfred had taken the gondola with a female in tow then who was she and why had Manfred felt the need to accompany her. Casper looked at his watch, the old butler should have been in the kitchens now preparing his hot chocolate. The feeling of unease grew and Casper suddenly found himself in the drawing room staring at the safe.

"No!" He whispered, not daring to believe what was swirling around in his brain. "No Manfred..! You wouldn't..! Would you?" Rushing to the safe, he entered the combination and threw open the door. Sinking to his knees he stared at the empty spot where the crown jewels had once sat. "Manfred, what have you done?"

Chapter 22

"Sabre one, moving in wait out!" Allowing Cowboy to quietly open the door, Mitch stepped inside and immediately found himself at the top of an old stone spiral staircase, with nothing else to do he proceeded rapidly down the steps.

The nearer he moved to the bottom the surer he became that he could hear whispering, and as he peered around the final curve a figure dashed past in the gloom beyond the open door. Levelling his weapon, he crept to the door and knelt, signalling Cowboy to hold his position.

Suddenly another figure loomed out from along the corridor and attempted to run past the opening, reacting to the movement Mitch shot his hand out, grabbing the person and dragging them back into the darkness of the stairs. The figure made to scream but her sound only met his grasping hand.

"Quiet!" Mitch insisted. "Be quiet! Who are you?" Then nodded to Cowboy to cover them.

"Brianne..!" She whispered fearfully.

"Just the girl we're looking for!" Cowboy said and stood up. "We've come to get you out of here!"

"There's more of us, we're trying to get to the Gondola!"

"Do you know a girl called Holly? Is she with you?"

"Yes, she's just down the corridor, but there are guards everywhere-we can't get past them."

"Cowboy!" Mitch said.

Without replying or needing any more instruction, Cowboy stepped out of the stairwell and began jogging along the corridor, ignoring the several girls crouching beside various bits of furniture. Then he stopped dead in his tracks. "I watched you die!" He said. "You were dead! And now I'm standing here and you're all alive and stuff; I gotta say it's kinda disappointing! Thought the band was finally gonna get a half-decent drummer."

Holly turned, hardly daring to believe her own ears. "Cowboy! You came!" She cried and threw her arms around his neck. "You came-Where's Mitch and the others?"

"Don't worry cupcake, everyone came to your party… You got a weapon?"

Still grinning, she held up the Kalashnikov she'd taken from the guard. "There's a lot of them in there, and it seems to be the only way through!"

"Jeez woman, If you fire that thing, you'll wake up every mercenary and Russian soldier between here and Moscow."

"Hollybobs!" Mitch said and put his hand on her shoulder. "Nice to see you're still with us."

"Mitch, you guys are a sight for sore eyes!"

"Sunray this is Sabre one," Mitch said. "Callsign Sabre four says hello."

"Roger that Sabre one!"

"Sabre four?" Scott said. "Who the hell is Sabre four?"

Martello grinned. "I think someone just came back from the dead!"

Feeling the dark cloud lift from his soul Scott slumped against the wall. "What the hell, we saw her die!"

"Come on, let's get this thing finished and get the hell out of this dump."

"I hear you brother, I hear you!"

"You ready?"

Scott nodded, opening the door he tossed in a flashbang; and awaited the detonation.

"Holly, gather all the girls together and wait for my signal!" Mitch said and received a nod in response before she disappeared back along the corridor. "You ready Cowboy?"

"Ready as I'll ever be!"

Opening the door he threw in a flashbang, only to hear two detonations one immediately after the other. Weapons up in the ready position they rushed in firing quickly into the multiple targets. Bodies tumbled to the floor, already dazed and confused mercenaries slumped dead in chairs or died on their bunks. As the firing petered out and the smoke cleared Mitch lowered his weapon and peered over the top only to see Scott and Martello doing the same thing on the other side of the room.

"Sunray, Sabre one, Room clear! We have the package and are heading for the exit over!"

"Roger that, hello Sabre three this is Sunray, you have a go!"

Tony responded immediately. "Sabre three, roger wait out!" Starting the engine of the old school bus, he drove the two hundred meters down the street to the Gondola station entrance and pulled over. Outside, the streets had long since fallen quiet, and now belonged to the whims of the low cloud and falling snow.

Climbing to his carbon fibre feet he pulled out his silenced nine millimetre and sent a round into the breach. After carefully checking the streets once more he exited the bus and walked with purpose up the ramp into the station.

The guard, busy eating biscuits and drinking coffee as he watched something on a computer screen was oblivious to the approaching danger. Tapping on the glass window with his pistol, Tony pointed to the locked door and then aimed his weapon at the man's chest.

The guard responded by dropping the biscuit in his coffee and tentatively raising his hands over his head; Once more Tony pointed at the door.

"Open the door!" Tony mouthed in his best German.

The man nodded in terror and being careful to keep his hands on show climbed out of the chair and unlocked the door. Keeping his pistol trained on the guard he backed him up to the rear wall and considered just shooting him. But there was something pathetic about this short, middle-aged and slightly overweight man; he looked more like a local employee than a highly trained mercenary.

"Are you married?"

The man nodded and wiggled the finger containing his wedding band.

"Do you have children?"

"Three!" He gasped. "Please don't kill me!"

Tony nodded. "Ok..! Ok you can live!" He conceded and without warning pistol-whipped him across the side of the head, knocking him to the ground. "Don't worry you'll see your kids again." After giving the Gondola controls a once over he sat down. "Sunray, this is Sabre three we have the gondola control over!" Tony said and noticed the coffee machine, he then smiled when saw the half-full

packet of biscuits.

"Roger that, wait out!"

Scott held Holly tight, her head barely reached the bottom of his

chest. "I wouldn't have believed it if I hadn't seen you with my own

eyes!" He said.

"Guys, let's do this whole hugging thing later, we need to get out of

here before they realise we've killed some of their friends…!" His

words came a second too late as machine gun fire ripped across the

room. "Take cover!" He shouted over the girls screaming and then

fired a return burst at the door; the attacker fell forward and stumbled

dead down the steps. "Ok, they know we're here; Holly keep the girls

moving; Scott, Martello watch our six and we'll take the lead!"

Charging forward Cowboy tossed a flashbang into the room and

followed it up by firing two bursts from his MP5. The moment the

explosive device went off both Mitch and Cowboy moved rapidly

through the door firing at anything that moved. Suddenly stumbling

Mitch steadied himself against the wall, as bullets pinged and ricocheted all around off the stone walls.

"Keep moving!" He cried breathlessly. "You're nearly there! The Gondola is through that door! Come on… Move it!"

"Room clear!" Cowboy cried. "Let's get everyone in here right now!"

"Let's go..! Let's move it!" Scott cried. "They're moving in force to the rear!" He then threw a smoke grenade and fired off a long burst to halt the advance. "Martello move it I'll cover you!"

The Agent dashed to the door and then turned to cover Scott who was already sprinting towards him.

"Go! Move!" He cried and as he followed Martello through the door he slammed it behind him and slid the bolts closed.

"Is everyone here?" Mitch cried.

"Yes!" Holly said. "We're all here!"

"Ok everyone in the gondola; Come on move it, they'll be through that door any second!" Mitch gasped breathlessly and then suddenly slumped to one knee.

"What's up, Mitch?" Cowboy said but feared he already knew the answer.

"I'm hit..!"

"Shit! Sabre three, Sabre one let's get this Gondola moving!" Cowboy said and then picking Mitch up dragged him into the carriage.

"Sabre three, it ain't working man, there's something wrong up there, it's not responding."

"Jesus Christ!" Cowboy barked and passed Mitch over to Scott, then he jumped out of the Gondola and ran to the control panel. "It's taken fire; I don't know if it going to work." Near panic, he pressed buttons and moved levers until the gondola jerked forwards. Running back to the Gondola he skidded to a halt. "Guys it's screwed, the only way to make this thing move is if one of us stays up here!"

Mitch untangled himself from Scott's grip and took a step forward. "I'll do it, I'm pretty much finished anyway!"

"You dumb shit!" Cowboy said. "It's just an itty-bitty little slug! You ain't going to die! This is on me... I've got to be the one to stay!"

"No!" Mitch barked. "And that's an order, now get your ass on the gondola!"

"Sorry brother!" Cowboy said and pushed Mitch back into the vice-like grip of Scott's arms. "This team needs you more than it needs me; the group needs you more than it needs me!"

"There's got to be another way?"

"There's no other way-" He paused and turned toward the door where the hammering was growing louder and louder. "It's been a real blast guys; take care!"

"Cowboy!" Holly cried and attempted to join him only to also be held back by Scott. "No..!" She shrieked as she struggled to break free. "Let me go!"

"Cupcake! I watched you die once! I can't do that again!" He said and slammed the door closed. "I'll see you all later!" Then sprinting back to the control panel, he pressed what was left of the smashed button and watched the cable car disappear from view. With one hand firmly pressed on the button he levelled his MP5 off on the door with the other, which was now shaking violently under the concussive impact of whatever was hitting it from the other side.

Allowing the weapon to drop to his side on its sling, Cowboy used his now free hand to extract a fragmentation grenade from his pouch; pulling the pin he held the grenade and the moment the door flew off its hinges he tossed the grenade through the gap. The explosion tore

apart all those in its range, the shockwave ripped through the corridor

and into the control room tossing Cowboy hard against the wall,

where he crumpled groaning to the floor.

Winded, and slightly concussed he forced himself to his knees and

then to his feet. The ringing in his ears scrambled his mind and sent

searing bolts of pain through his head, fighting the dizziness and

knowing he had only given himself a few seconds before they

regrouped and attacked, he stumbled to the window to see how far

the carriage had travelled, and he cursed when he saw it was only

three-quarters of the way down and immediately ran back to press

the button once more.

The remnants of the mercenaries had now regrouped and Cowboy

could hear their leaders' shouting instructions as they made their

assault on his position. Machine gun fire began tearing into the room

signalling their advance, seeking cover Cowboy knelt behind the

control counter, he figured it would afford him some protection but it

wouldn't last. As he pondered dashing to the window, the question in his mind was answered as the return gondola arrived; they were down and now he was released to do the one thing he was good at.

Fitting a fresh magazine to his weapon he stood and headed toward the gunfire; tossing another grenade, he stood behind the doorframe until it exploded and then quickly moved into the corridor firing two rounds at each target as it presented. The grenade had done its job all too well and Soon the targets and return gunfire petered out and became groans and cries for help.

Standing in the smoke and breathing heavily Cowboy checked himself for wounds but found none. "Where are you, Casper?" He shouted breathlessly. "My little Prince of darkness! Come out, come out wherever you are!" Suddenly a bleeding and bruised mercenary stepped clumsily out of a doorway, the man stared blankly at Cowboy and then slowly sank to his knees and tumbled over dead. "You better get out here you little pussy! Because I am not leaving this dump until I've shot you in the face!"

"I can see flashes up there!" Holly cried as she wiped condensation off the glass and gazed back up at the castle. "We've gotta go back! He's all alone goddamit!"

"Holly!" Mitch said weakly. "The mission was to save these girls- He knew what he was doing- There was no other way!"

"You should have let me stay!"

Looking into her eyes he suddenly understood. "I'm sorry... I'd change places with him in a second if I could!"

She nodded and wiped tears from her eyes. "I know you would... Now stop talking and save your energy; I can't lose you too!"

As the carriage lurched to a halt, Tony threw open the door. "Ok guys, let's get a wriggle on! Down the ramp and straight on the bus..." Sensing the atmosphere he ticked off the faces in his mind. "Cowboy... Where's Cowboy?" He cried.

Scott shook his head. "The dude stayed behind... He saved us all!"

"What the hell? We can't leave him, since when do we leave Marines behind?"

Cradling Mitch, Holly looked up. "We have to go, Mitch is kinda shot up... It's not good, and besides you know what Cowboys like-

He'll probably kill everyone up there, then go sleep with their wives!"

"So, we just leave him?"

"It's what we all signed on for," Mitch said and coughed as a trickle of blood rolled out of his mouth. "We have to get these girls out of here."

"Jesus Mitch..!" Tony said as he saw the blood and realised how bad he was. "Ok... Let's go then!"

Taking Mitch between them, Scott and Martello carried him down the ramp and laid him down on the back seat of the bus.

"Let's get the hell out of here!" Scott cried.

Gunning the engine, the vehicle lurched forward violently hurling the passengers around in their seats, and throwing Mitch on the floor. "Sorry guys!" Tony cried. "My bad!"

Rushing to Mitch's side she realised to her horror that he was now unconscious. "Scott!" She cried out and then felt for a pulse.

"What's up?" The big man said as he stepped over one of the girls who had fallen out of her seat.

"He's got a pulse but it's weak!"

"Ok, that's down to the heavy blood loss, he's probably suffering from traumatic shock too," Scott said. "Just leave him on the floor and try to keep him warm!"

"Hold on Mitch!" She said. "Just hold on!"

Without warning, the back window exploded in a hail of gunfire; as the bus lurched across the road Tony fought the steering wheel trying to control the vehicle. "Shooters on our six!" He cried out.

"Really how can you tell?" Martello barked and running to the rear of the bus returned fire on the following jeep. "Oh shit!" He cried. "We got a jeep and at least six motorcycles!"

A single motorcycle charged past the Jeep and the rider fired bursts of machine gun fire, which missed its target, hitting road signs and shattering shop windows.

"Guys!" Tony shouted. "Hold on tight!" Allowing the bike to close up he suddenly and violently braked; man, and machine slammed into four tonnes of school bus and exploded in a fireball, lifting the back end of the bus off the ground.

With the pursuers now bearing down and the passenger firing wildly, Tony hit the accelerator and moved clunkily up through the gears. "Will someone please shoot that Jeep!"

"Sunray this is Sabre three we have one man injured and one man still on location!"

"Roger that Sabre three!"

"We are being pursued and under heavy fire!"

"Roger that, the extraction site is hot and awaiting your arrival!"

Making her way over to Scott, Holly grabbed him by his harness to steady herself. "Ask them about Cowboy!"

"Sunray this is Sabre three can you give us a sitrep on Sabre one over?"

"Roger that, One member of Sabre one is alive and currently moving toward the east of the castle!"

"He's alive and on the move!" Scott said.

"If he's alive there's always a chance he'll find a way out!"

"Yeah, all he needs is a chance!"

Now completely in the zone, Cowboy moved with purpose and speed, there was only one other way out of the castle, and his one meeting with Casper told him the man was a snivelling coward and would run for his dear life.

The sounds of distant gunfire, and panicked shouting gave him a sense of comfort, the surviving mercenaries were clearly in disarray and far too busy firing at phantoms to give him any trouble.

Now in what was clearly the living quarters of the castle Cowboy arrived at an open door, the interior was brightly lit and very modern looking compared to everywhere else; with many computers and video recording equipment it was an amateurish attempt at some kind of recording studio. With all the equipment still switched on and running, the room had the air of somewhere recently deserted.

"Sabre one this is Sunray send sitrep over!"

"Sabre one, I'm still on location and attempting to locate the prime target over!"

"Roger that Sabre one, you are required to exfiltrate immediately over!"

"Roger that!" He said and cursed under his breath.

The DeadBeats

The east gate was still two floors down, setting off at a jog he took the first stairs he found and descended quickly. Feeling a blast of icy cold air hit him in the face told him he was near; what was left of the door was strewn across the floor only the hinges and lock remained in place.

The snow was falling harder now but Cowboy's attention was quickly drawn to a figure skiing at speed down the side of the mountain; that could only be one person and he wasn't too far away. Frantically searching the immediate area, he soon found an old wooden storage container, throwing it open he smiled at his own good luck and pulled out an old and well-worn snowboard. Sprinting back to the door he rapidly strapped into the board and launched himself out into the night, and immediately began plummeting down the impossibly steep snow field. Staying on the severest slopes he began to reel his prey in, the fact he wasn't yet aware he was being chased seemed to help. The figure was now in the very bottom of the valley and had turned south, he seemed to know where he was going and Cowboy was happy to stay high and maintain his speed.

Suddenly the target turned east again and headed for a dense row of evergreen trees, figuring he was now on a lower piste Cowboy kicked up the speed, dropped into the valley and shot through the trees.

Casper, unaware he was being stalked seemed to have slowed and had his skis in the snow plough position to control his speed. Now only fifty meters behind Cowboy let off a burst with his MP5 and watch as Casper tumbled over in the snow, unclipped his skis and began running.

Cowboy released another burst tearing up the snow by his feet.

Halted by a steep snow-covered drop off Casper turned and put his hands shakily above his head. "Don't kill me!" He cried. "I surrender! I surrender! I'm sorry, I didn't mean to hurt those girls! I made them famous!"

"There's no backsies in this game you asshole!" Cowboy growled. "You wanted your fifteen minutes of fame! Well, you can have it!" Just as he began to squeeze the trigger the ground beneath Casper's feet began to crack and fracture, causing the Prince's eyes to widen in terror, suddenly the ground seemed to swallow him up as the whole area gave way crashing down in a thunderous tidal wave of snow, rocks and trees. The rupture picked up speed and mass as it smashed its way down what turned out to be a steep and boulder-strewn cliff face, destroying everything in its path. Sliding to the drop-off Cowboy surveyed the carnage, and once he had satisfied himself that no one could have possibly survived he headed to the lights of the nearest village.

Stealing the Skidoo from a house was easy, catching up with the others was going to be near on impossible. "Sunray this is Sabre One! The primary suspect is deceased! Send directions over!"

"Roger, the team is currently four miles due west of your location…We'll adjust directions as you travel over."

"Roger, out!"

Figuring if he could traverse the landscape as the crow flies he might just catch them up. Revving the powerful seven hundred and fifty CC engine he made for a wooded area atop a re-entrant along the valley. Gaining altitude fast he weaved in and out of the trees eventually finding an old track which followed the ridgeline and then curved around into the next valley which is where he hoped he would see his friends.

Carefully riding out onto more open landscape he increased his speed, and then far below in the valley he spotted the red tail lights of a bus on the road; there was also a Jeep and at least four motorcycles chasing aggressively, and they were catching fast.

"Sabre One you are five hundred meters out!"

Not bothering to answer, he ploughed on down the slope until he was parallel but well ahead of the coach and then stopped. Raising the MP5 he fired a burst into an overhanging snow bank; at first, nothing happened so he fired again. This time, the snow bank let go of its tentative grip on the rockface and collapsed; the avalanche began tearing down the slope, as it collected speed so it picked up snow, rocks and trees. Crashing into the road barriers and telephone posts collapsed,

Charging flat out Tony grimaced as the vehicle jumped red lights, swerving around cars and side-swiping others. "Have we lost them yet?" He cried.

"What do you think?" Scott replied and fired off a burst from his weapon.

Suddenly movement on his right-hand side caused Tony to take a second, but longer look; the ground itself seemed to be moving as a thunderous rumble of noise shuddered through the vehicle. "Avalanche..!" He screamed. "Hold on!" The forward edge of the wall of snow, ice and rocks hit like a dead weight, side-swiping the bus. Wrestling with the steering wheel Tony accelerated and regained control then charged flat out for safety, outrunning the tidal wave of destruction.

The pursuing Jeep fared less well and took the full brunt of the impact, mangled beyond recognition and swallowed by the sea of ice, it vanished from sight.

Scott hollered with delight. "That's right assholes, you shoot at us and we avalanche your asses!"

"Just the bikes now guys!"

"Sabre two, this is Sabre one hold your guns, I'm coming up on your six!"

Scott frowned hardly daring to believe his ears. "Roger that Sabre one! Be advised we are currently taking fire!"

"Roger that, on my way!" Swooping down parallel to the road, he spotted a snow bank and prayed it was solid; twisting the accelerator he gunned the engine giving it full revs, hitting the ramp the skidoo

went airborne, cleared a fence and as it did Cowboy fired a burst

down onto the nearest Motorbike, which skidded onto its side and

crashed into a farmer's gate.

Landing heavily, the vehicle bounced violently on the compacted

snow; he was now at the Skidoo's limit as he charged up behind the

next bike and rammed it, sending the rider over the handlebars and

into a snow drift.

With only one to go Cowboy moved into position behind and fired a

burst at the rear wheel which exploded, causing the bike to veer off

and crash into a tree. Moving up beside the bus he gave a thumbs up

and then fell in behind.

The border guards had the barrier up and waved them through with

barely any reaction. "Sunray this is Sabre two, we are incoming! We

have a medical emergency over!" Scott said.

"Roger that Sabre two, we have a trauma team aboard."

Turning off the main road Tony immediately saw the red flares and

slowed as he drove toward the Chinook Helicopter. As he came to a

halt Marines ran toward the bus and threw out a security cordon while the passengers were unceremoniously disembarked and herded

aboard the helicopter.

"Get the medics over here right now!" Holly cried as she cradled

Mitch's head. "Hold on Mitch, don't you go dying on me now! Don't

forget we got a concert tonight in Berlin, and I ain't missing that just

because you decided to die!"

As the Medics swarmed the bus Cowboy boarded and pulled Holly

to her feet, dragging her through the melee of doctors and corpsmen.

"Come on Holly, let these men do their jobs!"

"You lived!" She said as tears rolled down her cheeks. "How the

hell did you make it out of there?"

"They pissed me off! They shouldn't have done that!" He said and

grinned. "I took care of that asshole Casper too! He won't hurt any

more girls!"

"Really..?"

"Yeah! You could say I put him on ice!"

Once Mitch was stabilised and strapped into a stretcher, the medics

carefully loaded him onto the chinook and the aircraft lifted off rising

quickly through the heavy snow and headed back to Ramstein.

Prologue

The noise, a deafening cacophonous and thundering din reverberated around the Mercedes Benz Arena in Berlin. A swaying grind of human flesh on human flesh moved to a beat as they excitedly awaited their first sighting of the band. Overcome young girls wearing face paint wept inconsolably and others screamed as they waved pictures of their favourite band member. Without warning the noise levels erupted off the scale as the band ran waving onto the stage.

Taking her place at the drums Holly waved back and the crowd erupted, Cowboy placed the strap of his guitar over his shoulders and swung the guitar around until it was in a comfortable position; he then smiled and pointed at some random young girl in the front row who began screaming with excitement. Tony stood waving at the crowd and then sat down and readied himself; Scott loomed large at the front of the stage and clapped back at the seething mass.

People in the front began to notice Mitch's absence and started chanting his name, the chant spread throughout the whole arena until the din was deafening.

Scott held up his hand to quieten the thundering mass. "Ladies and Gentlemen it's so good to be here in this amazing arena here in Berlin." The crowd roared their appreciation. "And I'd like to thank the wonderful and amazing Strawberry Island for inviting us to their concert, but I got some news for you people. Yesterday Mitch injured himself playing football so we can't do that song you all know us for, So tonight we're gonna perform our new song, it's called 'Johnny can't dance' and it's for all you lonely men out there- Ladies and Gentlemen I give you Mitch Calvert...!"

And the crowd erupted...